# NOT FORGOTTEN

GEORGE LEE MILLER

FRIO PRESS LLC

Hardcover ISBN: 978-1-7341564-2-3
Paperback ISBN: 978-1-7341564-0-9
E-book ISBN: 978-1-7341564-1-6

Cover design by Lance Buckley
Interior design by Lisa Gilliam

Published by Frio Press LLC FRIO 2019

*For my dad and my brother and all those who stood the watch.*

# PROLOGUE

HE WORE A FRINGED BUCKSKIN jacket that was a size too large and a coonskin cap that fell loosely over his right eye, and insisted his parents call him Davy Crockett, King of the Wild Frontier. In one pint-sized hand, he carried a replica flintlock pistol with an orange plastic muzzle-cap. In his other, he held a genuine, rubber Jim Bowie knife. It was fifteen minutes to eight on the fifth of July, and the temperature was already eighty-five degrees and climbing rapidly. By noon it would be ninety with matching humidity. He had been up since the crack of dawn, keeping watch out the hotel windows and waiting impatiently for his mother and father to wake up. Now, finally on patrol along the San Antonio River Walk, he breathed the stagnant air that smelled like stale beer and damp tree bark and covered the man-made canal between the buildings like Grandma's quilt on a warm day.

He imagined himself at the battle of 1836 just the way it was depicted in the diorama at the Alamo gift shop where his father had purchased his replica gear. The tiny men thrust bayonets and fired at point-blank range, reminding him of an ant bed he'd once uncovered with his plastic shovel. When school started next fall, he knew he would be the envy of all his classmates in his hometown of Stuttgart.

Davy was on the alert for any enemies of Texas when he saw a man with a scruffy salt-and-pepper beard sitting with his back against one of the ancient cypress trees. He pointed his Jim Bowie knife and cocked his flintlock pistol, posing like the figurines in the diorama.

The man exhaled a lungful of cigarette smoke and gave him a toothless smile. "Easy, Davy," the man drawled. "I's friendly. You huntin' Santa Annie?" The man wore an Army cap and camo jacket despite the heat and carried a cardboard sign with a hand-scrawled message that read *Iraq Veteran, please help*.

Davy stopped in his tracks. At just under three feet tall, he came face-to-face with the seated man and stared with unblinking curiosity. He struggled to understand his accent. The missing teeth gave his speech a slight lisp. Like all of the kids his age growing up in Germany, he was fluent in English, but this was his first trip to Texas and some of the locals were difficult to understand.

"I's pretty sure I seen him under that bridge," the man lisped, and cocked his whiskers toward the nearby stone footbridge.

"*Danke*," Davy said. He slipped into his native tongue when he got excited. He gazed at the bridge beyond the patio of a Mexican restaurant. The meaning behind the accent slowly sank in. The man had called him *Davy*. He stood rail-straight and brushed the tail of his coonskin cap over his shoulder.

Someone had recognized him. He was Davy Crockett. He watched his mother give the man an American dollar.

The man nodded. "God bless you," he said.

Davy peered in the direction the man had indicated. The majestic cypress trees and tall buildings created deep shadows in the early morning, making it hard for him to see under the bridge. He took an intrepid step forward. His mother held firm.

"This place is open." She motioned with her head toward the restaurant. "We're stopping for breakfast."

"*Nein, Mutter, es ist Santa Anna*," Davy said, trying to pull free.

"Santa Anna is just a story," his mother reassured him. "Tell him, Gunther," she addressed her husband. "Why did you buy him that gun?" She appealed to her husband, irritated at being up so early in the sizzling July heat.

"It's part of history—" Davy's father began to explain.

His wife cut him off for the hundredth time. "You're glorifying it for him. He thinks the gun's real," she said, searching for a table near one of the large outdoor fans.

Davy followed his mother to a metal chair beneath a faded green canvas umbrella and near a fan that was taller than he was. The waitress put down her broom and came with a smile, wearing a white Mexican peasant dress with a red-lace apron that flapped in the breeze created by the big fan. She gave the three of them each a tall glass of ice water and a basket of tortilla chips and waited patiently while his father read the laminated menu out loud over staccato mariachi music coming from the restaurant speakers.

Davy announced that he wanted cornflakes, then turned his attention back to the shadows under the bridge. When he adjusted his chair, he could see between the red, white, and blue banners on the handrailing. He placed his flintlock near his fork. He could feel danger in the air. To him it was as real as the crispy tortilla chips and spicy red salsa resting on the table. His skin tingled with excitement. If Santa Anna was under the bridge, as the man said, he would be ready. Two pigeons suddenly landed beneath his mother's chair.

"*Scheiße!*" she exclaimed, startled.

Davy ignored her. His father shooed the birds away. Then Davy saw something moving slowly out of the shadows, floating in the murky water, and drifting into a pool of sunlight. The bend in the narrow water channel forced the large object directly toward him.

He grabbed his flintlock and tore through the Fourth of July banner.

"*Schau, Mutter*! Look!" he shouted. "Santa Anna!" He raced to the water's edge.

"Not now." She sighed, pressing the cold glass to her hot forehead.

"Bam, bam!" Davy shouted, aiming at the object in the water, the toy pistol making rapid metal clicking sounds. He saw what looked like a hand and forearm extended above the surface of the water as if buoyed by an unseen rope.

The object bumped against the limestone steps. Now Davy saw what it was. A woman. Facedown. Dark shoulder-length hair tangled about her head. Small American flags decorated her blue tank top. A black skirt floated above her waist exposing yellow-lace panties, and her submerged legs appeared waxy green.

Davy dropped his replica flintlock.

"*Mutter*!" he cried, and his mother was beside him, wrapping him in her arms and forcing his terrified face into her breast.

"*Es tut mir Leid, Mutter*," Davy trembled. *I'm sorry*, he thought, believing he had killed the woman with his replica flintlock.

"*Es ist nicht deine Schuld*," his mother said, transfixed by the woman in the water.

"It's not your fault, Philip," his father repeated, using his real name. "It's only a toy gun."

A crowd quickly gathered. A young woman wearing an orange sports bra and lime-green jogging shorts took charge. "You call 911," she commanded the waitress. She grabbed the woman's foot and pulled her closer to shore.

"Gunther, *hilf irh*!" Davy's mother shouted.

Before her husband could reach the water's edge, the toothless veteran pulled the woman's head up by her tangled hair. The restaurant speakers were playing "Guantanamera." The woman's face was frozen into a puffy smile. The crowd gasped and took a step back when they saw the skin around her eyes was swollen and a shade darker than her olive skin, as if she wore a masquerade mask.

"She's dead," the veteran pronounced, as if he were the authority. His words transformed the mood of the crowd from horror to morbid curiosity. The woman with the orange sports bra began to video the scene with her cell phone.

"We're going," Davy's mother announced. She grabbed her son's toy pistol and tossed it in the garbage bin. She shot a pointed look at her husband as if the toy flintlock he bought for their son were to blame for ruining their vacation.

"*Wer war sie, Mutter*?" Davy asked, staring over his mother's shoulder at the body in the water. He was still shaking but beginning to breathe normally.

His mother hugged him tightly and took the stone steps up to the street level. "We don't know who she was."

"Why did she die?" he asked. He calmed down when the dead woman was out of sight.

She studied the street signs trying to formulate an answer to satisfy her son. She couldn't think of anything. "How about some ice cream?"

# CHAPTER ONE

I PRESSED THE DOWN BUTTON ON the limo's automatic window to let my client's dense cloud of leather-and-spice cologne escape. The fresh San Antonio air, though sticky-humid and tinged with exhaust fumes, cleared my head. It was five minutes to nine on a Friday night and the temperature hovered near eighty-five degrees, typical first of September weather in South Texas. I was getting a fat paycheck to provide security for Javier Sosa, a businessman from Mexico City in town to attend a last-ditch fundraising effort for Marcus Antonio Lopez's gubernatorial campaign, and grateful to be working. I hadn't had a paying assignment since the end of July, putting a serious strain on my pursuit of the American Dream. My credit cards were maxed out, and my mortgage payment was past due. Everything I owned was invested in my new Fischer Private Investigations and Security business. Since payment came after the work was done, everything I had was riding on me keeping Sosa safe and sound.

The job was to get Sosa from the airport to the convention center, and after the reception, back to his hotel. He said his personal security team would be in place by then and would take it from there for the rest of his trip. So far, the only problem had been the traffic jam on Highway 281 caused by two local colleges battling it out in the Alamodome for their football season opener. I wished I could say I had a dozen jobs like this lined up, but my new business calendar was empty for the next several weeks.

I did have one other prospect, but I didn't think it would amount to much. A woman, who wouldn't give her name, had called my cell phone before seven that morning. She said she was on her way to work but asked if she could come to my office the next morning to meet me in person. My usual answer was no when a prospective client wouldn't share their basic information over the phone, but I couldn't afford to turn her down. I was running out of money, and my girlfriend was urging me to go back to law school. If business didn't pick up soon, I might have to consider her suggestion or a new line of work.

The woman caller sounded like she was in her late forties or early fifties with a strong Spanish accent, which could be attributed to sixty percent of the local population. That she had a job and it got her out of the house before seven a.m. was a good sign. It meant she could pay for my services. I was quickly learning that one downside of working as a private investigator was that people would come to you in dire straits, asking for miracles involving weeks or months of hard work while forgetting to put up any money. Which didn't pay the mortgage.

"Thank you, Mr. Fischer, for accepting employment with minimum notification," Sosa said. He compensated for his thick Spanish accent by overenunciating his words. "Forgive me for noticing your, uh… your scars."

"No problem," I said. "And call me Nick." When I had picked him up at the airport, he stared for an extra moment at the star-shaped scars that formed a constellation across my brow, curtesy of an IED that shattered the windshield of my Humvee on my final deployment. They were an advantage in a fight. My opponent knew I wasn't worried about ruining my good looks, but I tried to smile at strangers; otherwise, they would get nervous and start looking for an exit.

As we inched south on the freeway, I caught Sosa glancing at the 750-foot Tower of the Americas built for the 1968 World's Fair. It dominated the flat but colorful Alamo City skyline and towered directly above our destination like an air traffic control tower on stilts. The closer we got, the more nervous and chattier Mr. Sosa became.

"Do you know anything about the oil business?" Sosa asked. He didn't fit the Texas-oilman stereotype. He had narrow shoulders made square by a padded tux coat and wore zip-up, high-heeled, patent-leather boots to compensate for his five-foot-nothing stature. "It's a volatile industry," he said, and waited for me to ask why. I didn't bite. I hated idle chitchat mainly because I wasn't good at it.

"My job's to protect you," I told him. "I don't care about your business or your politics."

"I like your philosophy. It fits your reputation." He tapped a Marlboro cigarette against the armrest and thoughtfully lit it up with a silver-plated lighter. "What's your opinion of Mr. Lopez?"

I rolled the window down a little more and let the smoke escape. Marcus Lopez's face was plastered on billboards all over town. We'd passed four on the way in from the airport. He was an ambitious local attorney whose campaign slogan was "Taking care of Texans." The polls put him in the lead, but rumor had it he was running out of money and desperately searching for a new source of revenue. I had met Lopez before because my girlfriend, Sylvia Flores, was trying to make partner in his law firm. I couldn't imagine him taking care of anything other than his ego. Sylvia thought he was the greatest thing since wireless earbuds, so I kept my opinion to myself.

"He's a lawyer and a politician," I said. "That's two strikes against him."

Sosa chuckled. "You and I are in agreement, my friend, but both are necessary to do business."

"Fair enough," I said.

He checked the proximity of the Tower again to gauge our time of arrival. I didn't mind the accent or even the zipper boots, but something about Javier Sosa reminded me of the kind of used-car salesman who would sell his grandmother a car with no engine. My research showed his main business was with PEMEX—the state-owned Mexican petroleum company. Whatever deal he had with Marcus Lopez was probably not strictly legal.

"Do you think he is a man of his word?" Sosa leaned forward, anticipating an answer as if my notion of Marcus Lopez would make or break his trip. The question was more complicated than it should be. I didn't care for politics or lawyers, although I had spent two years in law school. It was Sylvia that kept me from completely thrashing Marcus's character. Since she chose me and we had been together three years, I couldn't really question her judgment of character.

"Like I said, he's a lawyer and a politician, but since society needs both, Marcus Lopez is probably as good as any."

"Thank you, Mr. Fischer." Sosa leaned back in his seat and lit another Marlboro. He let the smoke trickle through his nose, then offered me the red-and-white package.

"No, thanks." I'd never picked up the habit. I smoked a cigar on special occasions, but lately those were few and far between, and Sylvia couldn't stand the smell. I preferred smokeless tobacco when I was younger but gave it up when I went to work for myself. The only professionals I knew that still dipped snuff at work were baseball players and rodeo cowboys.

Sosa tossed the package on the seat. "I'll leave those here," he said, referring to the cigarettes. "Americans don't respect the Marlboro Man anymore."

I thought about telling him the tobacco company had highjacked the iconic cowboy image and that several of the models for the Marlboro Man had died of lung cancer, but I knew Sosa wouldn't understand the irony or care.

"Not much respect for anything," I said. He nodded like we'd shared an inside joke.

When the driver finally made it to the East Commerce Street exit near the convention center, I made a show of checking my weapon. Sosa watched me work the butter-smooth action on my Para-Ordnance P14-45 pistol. It was an awesome weapon with the two qualities necessary to win a gunfight—a large caliber and a high-capacity magazine. He seemed curious but not upset, which was a good sign. If I needed to draw a weapon, I liked to know that my client wasn't going to turn into a three-year-old with a bee sting.

I rated every job on a risk level of one to ten. A risk-level-one job was taking Sylvia on a date and fending off the riffraff making catcalls. A ten was the equivalent of storming a safe house in Fallujah, something I'd done in my previous life and counted myself lucky to have survived. This job rated a five. I took all my normal precautions, plus I carried a .38 Smith & Wesson hammerless revolver on my ankle—my weapon of last resort. I had checked it when I left the house and didn't take it out in the limo. I wanted Sosa to be impressed, but not overconfident. I carried the .38 for personal protection. I was pretty sure he hadn't told me all the reasons he wanted my services.

Sosa watched me slip the Para-Ordnance back into my leather shoulder holster. The closer we got to the convention center, the more nervous he got. He had told me in the Skype interview that he was most concerned about protesters. I told him the local cops would take care of that, but he had been insistent on hiring me and I couldn't afford to turn down a paycheck. I had a feeling there was someone else he was concerned about.

The driver made a U-turn on Alamo Street and pulled into a bumper-to-bumper line of limos waiting to drop off other friends of the candidate. Close to fifty people stood behind a police barricade near the entrance. A dozen carried hand-painted signs and chanted a sing-song refrain that drifted through the open window.

"No more fracking… no more fracking!" They didn't seem dangerous and reminded me of my small-town high school pep rallies.

I had done my homework on the vocal environmental group after my interview with Sosa. They called themselves Citizens for a Clean County. None of the local members had police records, but they were funded by a national organization with a reputation for chaining themselves to courthouse doors and blocking refinery entrances and pipeline construction sites.

"Looks like the SAPD has your opposition group safely under control, Mr. Sosa. No need to worry," I assured him. He was watching the crowd intently. He lit another cigarette and inhaled a cloud of Marlboro courage. The limo inched to a stop at the front door of the convention center. There was a small group of reporters gathered on the sidewalk.

"Sit tight," I said, and waited for Sosa to exhale a lungful of smoke out the window. If the good citizens group was watching, I was sure the smoke would be another black mark against him. I dished out last minute instructions: "I'll assess the danger then open your door. Stay close and follow me to the entrance." Sosa snubbed out his cigarette on the door handle. "Are you ready?" I asked.

"*Sí, vamonos,*" he said. The sweat trickling down his forehead was caused by more than just the heat. Someone or something out there scared him and put me on alert.

The reporters snapped photos as I opened the door and seemed disappointed that it was me. I unbuttoned the top button on my tux when I felt the wool material stretch a little too tight around the butt of my .45. It had been nine months since I'd put on the monkey suit that Sylvia had picked out for me, and I could tell I needed to get back in the gym before I broke it out again, or better yet, left it in the closet along with the other style upgrades Sylvia had picked out for me. I preferred jeans and boots.

The paparazzi displayed their usual rudeness, jostling each other for the best picture angle, hoping for a real celebrity. I checked their hands. They all held mics or cameras, not the kinds of weapons I was paid to protect Sosa from. I scoured the street and the line of attendees waiting at the security checkpoint. It was a black-tie affair, and there was a red carpet laid out like the entrance to a movie premiere. Candidate Lopez hadn't spared any expense. I half expected to see Ryan Seacrest on the sidewalk with a microphone, poised to ask me what I thought of the latest Twitter gossip.

I counted six uniformed policemen on duty. They looked bored and ready for happy hour. I recognized one of the cops, and we exchanged nods, paying our respects. I had worked my way through college in Austin as a reserve deputy with the Travis County sheriff's department.

When I decided the coast was clear, I opened Sosa's door. He took his time getting out and made a show of smiling for the cameras. He definitely had his mojo back.

A young female reporter in a loose silk blouse and wavy TV-hair thrust her microphone forward and shouted: "Do you support candidate Lopez's clean county initiative?"

Sosa was ready for her. "Yes, that's why I'm here." He waved at the protesters.

"Stay close and follow me," I urged him. If we were going to be ambushed, standing in a circle of reporters lit up by camera lights would be a likely place.

Ms. Silk Blouse shouted another question. "Where do you stand on the proposed fracking ban in Bexar county?" She forced her voice down a note in an effort to sound more serious. I was already taking a step to cut her off when Sosa stopped me with a squeeze to my elbow. He wasn't too spooked to push a little PR.

"The practice of fracking is a perfectly safe and effective drilling technique that is of great benefit to the State of Texas and my country. But I'm here to support Mr. Lopez's candidacy for governor. He understands the strong cultural connections between Mexico and Texas, and he will work hard to strengthen our business relationship. Texas and Mexico can and should always work together." When he finished his little speech, he let go of my elbow. I took that as a sign to move forward. I maneuvered Sosa around Silk Blouse and her cameraman and hustled toward the security gate.

# CHAPTER TWO

THE GRAND HALL OF THE convention center was decorated with red, white, and blue political banners and a movie-screen-sized photo of Marcus Lopez's smiling face. He had just turned forty, but his dark hair was free of gray and stylishly disheveled, and his light-brown skin was without a wrinkle—courtesy of the frequent Botox and salon treatments his personal secretary scheduled. Sylvia loved to share the office gossip. I was seven years younger, but if you compared our mug shots, nobody would believe it. In addition to my star-shaped scars, my bent nose was a constant reminder that riding saddle broncs was a lot tougher than it looked.

On a platform near the bar, a local band played a distinctive San Antonio groove—an eclectic mixture of old jazz standards influenced my mariachi and ranchera music. The locals called it a *West Side* sound. I liked it when I heard it. Not something you expected to run across in South Texas. The music mixed with clinking glasses and laughter created an atmosphere more like Christmas than Labor Day weekend. All the movers and shakers seemed to think they had a candidate that would really roll up his sleeves and get to work. By that they meant support policies that would help their bottom line and pet projects. On a national scale, Marcus drew fawning accolades because of his calculated support for all the hot-button liberal issues. The national media considered him the tip of the spear in the battle to turn Texas blue. Some business leaders considered him too radical and had accused him of wanting to create a state income tax, but he had the support of urban voters, and the major newspapers in Dallas, Houston, and of course Austin endorsed him. Compared to the other party's candidate, Marcus Lopez was a rock star. With the election only two months away, it seemed inevitable that Governor Lopez would take up residence in Austin.

The hall held close to a thousand of San Antonio's finest, dressed to the nines. There were state and local politicians rubbing elbows with academics and charity foundation presidents all soliciting donations from the business leader with the biggest pocketbook.

The man on the top of the list was Patrick Allison, who I knew by name and reputation. His presence was hard to miss. He stood six-foot-three and wore a gray cowboy hat with his signature rattlesnake-skin hatband. His carefully clipped mustache drooped over his top lip and the corners of his mouth. There were a dozen other men in cowboy hats in the room, but Allison stood out like a sheriff on a dusty western movie set. He was holding court in a corner away from the band. A circle of ten or twelve men huddled around him like they had been granted an audience with John Wayne.

Javier Sosa said he had private business, so I reluctantly gave him a pager and watched him make a beeline for Allison once we were through security. With the heavy guard outside and at the door, I didn't anticipate any problems inside the convention center. I suspected whatever business deal he had going would involve one of the biggest oil men in the state. I spotted two short-hairs with tight suits and earpieces within ten feet of the big man. Obviously,

Patrick's personal security. I was satisfied Sosa was safe for the moment.

While my client hobnobbed with the movers and shakers, I headed to the back of the hall to look for Sylvia. I spied her chatting with a group of socialites. She looked every bit as beautiful as the day I met her at St. Mary's Law School. She held a glass of champagne like she was born with it in her hand. This was her element. She was a daddy's girl who grew up tagging along with her father to all the social events in San Antonio. I watched her touch the ends of her dark shoulder-length hair, which she did when she was excited.

Sylvia knew I would be there, of course, but we had agreed not to make it a date. I was working, and she was there in her official capacity as assistant campaign manager or advisor or whatever she was that week. When Marcus Lopez decided to run for governor, all of the staff who had not yet made partner in his law firm took on unpaid roles in the campaign.

I put my elbow on the bar between two younger guys wearing stylishly tight suits and too much hair product and ordered a tonic with extra lime to keep my senses sharp. Sylvia peeled off from the socialites and walked in my direction. The two young guys followed her movements with slightly open mouths.

"Hello, gorgeous," I said when she was within earshot. I had to speak up because the band was louder at the bar. She stopped beside me and touched my arm, sending a little jolt of electricity through me.

"Why're you here?" It came out louder than she expected. The two young guys at my elbow decided to move on to avoid a confrontation.

"I'm working, remember?"

"I meant at the bar, silly," she said and studied my tonic and lime.

"I'm not drinking, just killing time. You look fabulous."

She took compliments without the slightest hint of self-consciousness. "Where's your client?"

"Sosa's rubbing elbows with the rich and obnoxious. He said he didn't need me until later. Last I saw him he was closing in on Patrick Allison."

"Of course. Marcus's biggest client."

"I thought he supported the other party," I said.

"Oh, *Big Tex* likes parties and being the center of attention. Besides, they've been together forever."

"What do you think of the tux? It still fits." I knew she regarded my wearing the penguin suit as a fashion coup in her battle to transform me into an urban sophisticate.

"I remember picking it out last year. I had to drag you kicking and screaming to Alamo Heights for a fitting." She enjoyed teasing me.

"Hey, the party was great." I opened my mouth and inserted my patent leather shoe. I was still trying to master the subtle art of idle chitchat.

"Until you insulted my new boss."

"He made fun of the Marine Corps." I tried to recover.

"You knew he was talking about gays in the military."

"He said gays would improve the Marines."

"You're homophobic."

"I don't care who joins. My point was that the Marines should invest in weapons, not fight social issues." I remembered the party conversation as another of my bungled attempts at idle chitchat.

She flashed a perfectly polished smile, knowing she had me.

"What can I say? Your boyfriend's a redneck."

"You always use that excuse, but you're too smart for that. You don't even have any redneck friends." She was right, the only real snuff-dipping, flag-waving, honkytonk-cruising redneck I called a friend was Rocky Velosic. He was the quarterback on my high school football team and now the head coach, but I only talked to him once a year at the Fredericksburg Oktoberfest.

"You want me to turn in my redneck card?" I asked.

She laughed. "I'm just pointing out the obvious. You're more like one of those characters from your Texas history books."

"I'm trying to keep the pioneer spirit alive," I said.

She let out a deep breath and shook her head. It was a sign that I had made her point. "Don't you have someone to protect?" she chided.

I took her hand. "Yes, I do."

She held my gaze. For a brief moment we were back in law school, agreeing to disagree on a point of law before diving into the twin bed in her studio apartment. Arguing was like breathing to her, she could do it at the drop of a hat, but she could make love in the same breath.

"You're a card that needs to be dealt with," she whispered, not pulling away. I couldn't get enough. Those moments kept me from dismissing our fragile relationship. We could spend a sweaty hour in the limo and continue afterward as if nothing had happened. We moved closer together, shutting out the clamor around us.

"There you are." Marcus Lopez cut through the crowd, his voice loud and sharp as if he and Sylvia had been playing hide-and-seek.

She instantly slipped on her business armor and turned toward him. Her hand slipped from mine and touched his shoulder. "Marcus, you've met Nick Fischer," she said, as if introducing a business associate, suddenly dismissing the moment we'd shared.

"Yes, I remember Nick. The ex-Marine." He offered his hand. Said ex-Marine like I'd just gotten out of prison. He gave my hand a hard squeeze trying to overcompensate for his lack of muscle tone. Sylvia said he spent a lot of time on his Cannondale mountain bike because he liked the way he looked in his spandex bikewear and matching helmet.

"There are no ex-Marines," I said.

"Did Sylvia put you on the guest list?" He knew I wasn't on the list.

"I was in the neighborhood. Thought I'd stop by and make a donation."

"Really? I thought your money would be on the other party," he said through a smile so stiff it looked spray-painted on his face.

"Nick's not into politics," Sylvia interrupted, pinching my elbow.

"Perhaps he'll change his mind when he sees how much I can do for the people of Texas."

"I'm pretty sure Texans can fend for themselves." I felt Sylvia squeeze my elbow harder, her way of saying, *put a sock in it*. So, I added: "But I wish you all the best," and smiled.

"Nick's actually working tonight for one of your guests. Mr. Sosa."

"Right, you're the security guard." The left side of his mouth curled up when he talked.

"Private investigator," I said. Before he could respond, my pager went off. "Duty calls. Nice talkin' to ya." I flashed Sylvia a smile that Marcus couldn't see.

She rolled her eyes.

I mouthed: "See you later?"

She winked, and I took off to find my client.

# CHAPTER THREE

I QUICKLY SCANNED THE ROOM IN case the page from Sosa required a show of force. He stood with his hand up in a friendly wave toward me from the corner of the auditorium. His smile told me I wouldn't need to run or draw my pistol. He was still standing next to Patrick Allison. The court of admirers around him had thinned to one: a younger blond man who looked to be in his mid-twenties. He was the same height as Allison, and his facial features were almost identical—like twins, only one was frozen at birth and thawed out fifty years later. The two short-hairs with earpieces had backed off to a respectable thirty feet.

When I reached the trio, there were smiles all around. The highest wattage came from Javier Sosa, erasing the nervous dread that hung over him on the trip from the airport. Allison was more reserved but seemed self-satisfied, like he had just given Sosa an early Christmas present. The younger man had a goofy grin and constantly nodded like a puppy just glad to be up this late at night and playing with the adults. He was clean-shaven, and his cheeks had an alcohol flush.

"Nick Fischer, I'd like you to meet Patrick and Danny Allison,"

Sosa said. "I told Mr. Allison about your willingness to take on my job at short notice. He wanted to meet you."

"Howdy," I said. If I was going to be treated like a hired gunslinger, I'd play the part.

"Nice to meet ya, son," Allison said with a raspy, Texas drawl and extended his hand in a move that was friendly and rehearsed at the same time. He had an air of self-confidence that came with money and success. Unlike Marcus Lopez, Allison exuded power and influence rather than craved it. He was used to being in charge and the center of attention. I got the feeling I was supposed to be flattered that I had been summoned for a meeting.

"Call me, Nick." I took his big hand and was surprised at his weak grip and how brittle his bones felt compared to how robust he appeared. He sized me up like he would a quarter horse at Ruidoso Downs.

"This here's my grandson, Danny. He just graduated from Texas Tech." He gestured toward the younger man, as if his recent graduation explained the kid's goofy appearance. Up close, there was no question that the two came from the same gene pool. Danny didn't wear a hat, although I could see the tan line where one had recently been. Probably from golf or tennis. Danny's muscles bulged through his stylishly tight tux jacket. He reminded me of a sports announcer trying to show he was in as good of shape as the athletes on the field.

"Hey, Nick. Glad to meet you, buddy." Danny flashed a boyish grin. He hadn't quite mastered his grandfather's command and control, but he was working on it. He had a hint of a Texas accent, holding the vowels a little longer and adding in a few more syllables than some words called for, as if he was working at being a good ol' boy. He took my hand and squeezed it like a frat-boy challenge and stared at my forehead like he'd never seen scars before.

"You're chiseling out quite a reputation in this town, Nick. I'm glad to finally meet you," Patrick Allison said.

I hadn't expected a compliment and wondered what was really behind the introduction. "Thank you, Mr. Allison. I try not to let my clients down."

"Tell you what. Call me Pat," he said. "I hear you take on the lost causes."

"I always root for the underdog," I said.

Allison smiled and motioned Danny and Sosa into a tighter circle like we were members of a secret society. "Nick here saved a man from death row," he said and paused for effect. "That's right. That apartment fire that killed twenty people on the east side. The local police nailed the wrong man. Blamed it on that ex-football player from Texas. The one who was drafted by the Redskins but never played a down. What was his name?"

"Skeeter Davis," I said. "He lost his arm in a car accident before training camp."

"That's right. Ol' Skeeter. But you tracked down the real killer."

"That's about it," I said. That wasn't it. The investigation had nearly killed me, but I didn't want to get into the details.

"How did you know the police had the wrong man? The DA told me all the evidence pointed to ol' Skeeter," Allison said, like he was a close personal friend of the district attorney.

"The evidence doesn't always point to the truth," I said, trying to sound more practical than philosophical.

Patrick smiled at this. He seemed to have more on his mind than friendly chitchat. "You do believe in following the law, now don't you?" he drawled. He focused his watery eyes on me.

"Unless it convicts an innocent man," I said.

Patrick seemed to like my answer. "Well, there you go. We are in the company of a bon-i-fide hero." Patrick rolled the word off his tongue and touched the brim of his Stetson.

Being enlisted, I'd never been saluted, and the gesture gave me a strange feeling. I studied his face to see if he was serious or making a joke. There was a twinkle in his rheumy eyes, but his expression was hard to read because his mustache covered his lips.

"Mr. Allison is the one who recommended you," Sosa interjected.

"Thank you," I said. He *was* sizing me up. Maybe protecting Sosa was a test for a job working for him. "I do personal security on the side. My main business is private investigations." I produced a new business card. The logo design was simple—two crossed swords below the Marine Corps motto. He glanced at it briefly.

Danny reached over and snagged my card. "Cool. What's semper fi?" Danny smirked, pronouncing it *semper fee*. He had definitely had more than his share of the free drinks.

I smiled. If those words didn't mean anything to him, I had nothing to say.

"He was in the Marine Corps, Danny," Pat said patiently. "Thank you for your service, Nick." Pat seemed slightly embarrassed by his grandson.

"Can't say it was a pleasure, but I was happy to serve." I had a complicated relationship to the military. I loved my brothers and the fight, but like most combat vets, I hated the mind-numbing bureaucracy. Patrick Allison knew a lot more about me than I knew about him, and that made me uncomfortable. I was also getting the feeling that his cowboy demeanor was all an act. I had grown up with authentic western men like my grandfather, and Patrick Allison's cowboy image was just a little too polished.

"See any action?" Danny said, eager for a war story. The kid was an idiot.

"That's what you do in the Marine Corps, Danny," I said.

"Is that where you got the…" He pointed to the scars on my forehead. He definitely had no manners. I smiled and nodded. I had had enough chitchat, and both Allisons were starting to get on my nerves.

I turned to Sosa. "You ready, Mr. Sosa?" I caught him off guard. He seemed to be enjoying my confrontation with the Allison clan.

"Oh, uh… no," he stuttered, glancing around the room. "I still need to conclude my business with Marcus… Mr. Lopez. Excuse me. I'll hit the pager when I'm ready." He made a big show of shaking hands and thanking Patrick Allison for whatever deal they had struck, then he took off through the crowd. I nodded goodbye also.

The old man took my hand and focused his watery green eyes on me. "Are you related to Otto Fischer?" he asked.

"He's my grandfather," I said.

"He's a good man."

"I think so." I didn't mention several unfavorable stories that Grandpa told about the Allison family from the early pioneer days.

"Your father was a good man too. Good sheriff. Did they ever find out who killed him?"

"No," I said. "No, they never did."

He seemed to be waiting for me to say more, hoping for some gossip that he could share with his hunting buddies. My father's unsolved murder was the last thing I wanted to discuss with Patrick Allison.

"How would you feel about working for me?" he asked.

There it was. He was offering me a job. He had orchestrated the whole encounter. I had no reason to turn him down, but something about Patrick Allison put me on guard.

"I'm trying to make it as an independent, but thanks for the offer."

"I'll keep you in mind if I ever need your services," he said. With no one around but the three of us, Patrick Allison seemed to shrink in size and energy level as if he'd been putting on a front for an audience and suddenly stepped backstage. He glanced at Danny and began to cough. He quickly covered his mouth with a white handkerchief he obviously kept close at hand in his suit coat pocket. It was a deep, lung-rattling cough that heavy smokers get. He held Danny's elbow for support.

I wasn't sure whether to walk away or wait for him to finish. He held up his free hand for me to wait as if reading my mind. There was one more thing he wanted to say. I waited, looking around to see if anyone else noticed. No one did, or they pretended not to. The cough shook the old man to his core.

"My grandson could use someone like you around," he finally said, and wiped crimson spit from his chin and carefully trimmed mustache.

I nodded. I didn't know what to say to that. Did he want me to babysit Danny on weekends?

"Come on out to the ranch sometime, and Danny can show you around."

I'd heard about his ranch. It was one of the biggest in the state and had a reputation for exotic trophy animals and extreme privacy.

"Love to," I said. Talking to Allison put me on alert, like I should be on my toes, but I didn't know why. As long as we were being friendly, I decided to ask him why he was there. "Why are you backing Lopez?" I asked. "Isn't he the enemy?"

The old man's eyes narrowed. He studied me for several moments. I held his gaze, feeling a little uncomfortable—like I was waiting for a palm reader to give me some bad news about my future.

"There are a lot of ways to back a candidate," he said. I waited for him to explain, but he was finished. He seemed to have found what he was searching for. "Take care now," he said.

I got the feeling I had been dismissed, so I walked to the front door, thinking the first chance I got, I would ask Grandpa about Patrick Allison.

Danny followed me like a lost puppy. He carried a drink with lime that was probably pure vodka in one hand and an empty cup in the other. His bottom lip bulged with an inch of brown snuff. Away from Patrick, he was indulging his vices.

"Granddad likes you," he said, like he expected me to be flattered. He took a big drink of vodka, making up for lost time. He spit into his empty cup. "I work out at Lucky's gym on the west side. Mixed martial arts. Just amateur. I started in college. Keeps me in shape." The band had quit playing and were packing up their instruments.

"Good for you," I said. "Everyone needs a hobby."

"Ever do any fighting? MMA, I mean? Do they do that in the Corps?" He said "Corps" like it was some kind of frat house where they offered intermural sports. Snuff juice dribbled down his chin.

I knew Lucky's gym and worked out there regularly, but I didn't share that with Danny. I needed to locate Sosa and get the hell out of there. I was getting paid, but I'd rather get a root canal than spend time in a too-tight tux chatting with the privileged class.

Before I could locate Sosa, Danny said: "I'd like to get a piece of that," and made a hole in his fist and pumped it up and down over his middle finger.

I saw the leer in his expression and followed his gaze to Sylvia. She was turned sideways to us about thirty feet way. The stylish cut of her dress accentuated her curves and made me excited and protective at the same time.

Just as I was about to reprimand the kid's behavior, Marcus Lopez stepped up beside Sylvia and put his hand on the small of her back. He whispered something in her ear, which produced a laugh from her. I couldn't tell whether she touched his arm to push his hand away from her ass or if she was flirting with him. I couldn't see the expression on her face. I saw the expression on his. I didn't like it. She turned toward the bar and walked away.

"Too bad," Danny said, sounding truly disappointed. "She's with Marcus."

"She's my girlfriend," I said more to myself than to Danny, still trying to process what I'd just seen.

"You don't want to mess with him. He's Granddad's lawyer." Danny said it like he meant it, like he was talking about bad, bad Leroy Brown. His flushed cheeks lost some color, and he drew his lips tight. I'd heard Marcus was cutthroat in the courtroom, but Danny seemed to be talking about something more than judiciary tactics.

"What're you talking about?"

"Just sayin', you want him on your side."

Before I could press him on the issue, Sosa shouted at Marcus, "*Esto no está terminado.*" Whatever business deal Sosa wanted with Marcus hadn't gone well.

Sosa made a chopping movement with his right hand and stomped toward the door. His zip-up bootheels clicked on the marble tiles. He waved at me to follow. He had lost the happy animated look he wore when he was with Allison.

"Gotta go, Danny. Nice talking with you." I put two long strides between us.

"Lucky's gym, killer. I'm there on Mondays when you're ready to mix it up," Danny shouted.

I waved without looking back. I had the nagging feeling that I would run into him again.

# CHAPTER FOUR

THE SEPTEMBER NIGHT OUTSIDE THE convention center seemed even warmer than when I left it two hours ago. I always wondered how the first four generations of Fischers had survived without air conditioning in the Texas heat. I found the limo driver on the sidewalk chewing the fat with a group of his colleagues. I asked him to pull up to the curb and went back inside to collect Sosa. His hotel wasn't far, and with any luck, I would be home by midnight. I was eager to finish the job so I could focus my attention on Sylvia. I was trying to decide whether to ask her about the encounter with Marcus or let it go. I wasn't much good at letting things go.

Danny's reaction to Marcus bothered me. I had always thought of Sylvia's boss as a pompous ass but never a dangerous man. Underneath the drunk frat-boy bravado, genuine fear crossed Danny's face when Marcus entered the picture. Obviously, he was well connected to the Allison family, and Marcus had a particular hold over Danny.

Sosa was ready to go and not in a talkative mood, which suited me just fine. The citizens for the environment had gotten bored and left right after the media had their sound bite for the ten o'clock news. The SAPD presence had dwindled down to two uniformed officers.

Once Sosa was carefully belted into the back seat, I told the driver to take Commerce Street to St. Mary's before making the U-turn to Market Street and driving back to the Westin hotel on the River Walk. I always followed all the safety protocols whether it was a level one job or a level ten. Bad guys keyed on patterns and obvious moves. Using a random route or changing plans midstream often meant the difference between life and death. One thing being in combat taught me was to be present. I was trying to adapt my combat training to the business of private investigations. The action part was a direct translation, but I needed work on my people skills.

I checked the street behind us to make sure we weren't being followed, then had the driver take another loop around the block. His downturned lips told me he didn't like it, but as screwy as the night had been, I wanted to be sure. Sosa was on his second Marlboro and hadn't said a word since leaving the party. I didn't want to pry into his business, but I was curious about Marcus Lopez.

"Your business deal didn't work out?" I asked, trying to sound offhanded.

"It's complicated. The deal was to provide pipe and equipment for Allison's leases in Edwards County. Marcus Lopez wanted to renegotiate." He forced smoke through his nostrils.

"What would Marcus Lopez have to do with it?"

"Marcus and Patrick are partners," he said.

The limo stopped at his hotel. I didn't have time to push him for more information. The street entrance to the hotel was quiet for a Friday night. There was one minivan with a family of four waiting for the valet attendant. They stood on the sidewalk dressed alike in shorts and Hawaiian shirts, looking dazed from a long airplane ride. The main foot traffic was on the river side of the building. This time of night the River Walk was always jammed with tourists and active-duty military personnel on weekend passes from one of several nearby bases.

The bellhop approached the door, but I beat him to it. I wasn't taking any chances. I wanted to be sure I escorted Mr. Sosa safely to his room and into the hands of his regular security team and the mistress he said would be waiting.

The driver popped the trunk and handed the bellhop a single black leather suitcase and a matching carry-on bag. Mr. Sosa traveled stylish and light. The bellhop took the luggage and hustled toward the hotel entrance.

"*Gracias*, Mr. Fischer. You have fulfilled your obligation," Sosa said when I let him out of the back seat. He offered me a wad of Ben Franklins and shook my hand.

"You paid for the full service," I told him. "That means door to door."

"Please, I can take it from here," he said. "I will wire money to—"

A blast of compressed air cut him off in midsentence, punctuated by a hollow *thunk*. Blood sprayed my face and flooded Sosa's shirt. He spun to the ground with a loud groan.

I pulled my .45 and covered Sosa with my body. From the amount of blood, I knew the shot came from a heavy caliber rifle. The minimal sound signaled a serious suppressor that masked the shooter's location and told me he was a professional.

The air blast came again. The bullet took a bite out of the retaining wall, showering us with small chunks of concrete. From the angle, I guessed the shooter was in the parking garage across the street.

"Run!" I yelled at the family in Hawaiian shirts.

They took off for the street corner. I pulled Sosa toward the curb and opened the front door of the limo. The driver had wedged himself under the dashboard, shaking like a leaf.

"Focus," I told him. His wide eyes tilted up. I kept my voice even and calm. "Sosa's hit. I need you to drive him to the emergency room."

"Shit, no. C-call an ambulance," he stuttered.

"He'll be dead before they get here." Another shot hit the roof of the limo and sounded like a hammer hitting sheet metal.

"They's still shootin' at us," he stammered with an accent I'd not heard him use when he picked us up. He squeezed further under the dashboard.

"Get up and drive," I ordered. I set my pistol on the sidewalk and lifted Sosa into the front seat. The bullet had hit him in the left shoulder. His shirt and coat were soaked crimson-red, and blood flowed out of him like water from a broken pipe. He still had a pulse, but his short, shallow breathing told me that he wouldn't last long. I'd seen it happen more times than I cared to remember.

"You wanna be here when the shooter crosses the street?" I reached over Sosa and slapped the driver's head. "Get the fuck up."

"He-he's comin' here?" The driver scrambled behind the wheel.

I didn't know what the shooter's next move was, but I needed to get Sosa out of harm's way and to the emergency room before I dealt with it. I didn't want to lose a client.

"One second," I commanded while I stripped off my tux jacket and wrapped it as tightly as I could around the leak in Sosa's chest. "Put pressure on this," I instructed the driver. He reluctantly put his hand out. I pushed it down hard over the coat. "Pressure," I repeated, "or he won't make it. Do you know where you're going?"

He nodded and accelerated away from the curb before I could slam the door shut.

Another whoosh of air. The sidewalk exploded near my feet. I dove behind the next parked car. Whoever was behind the rifle was taking his time and placing his shots—a professional using a rifle with serious noise suppression technology.

A city bus lumbered toward me. I waited until it was almost directly in front of the hotel, then dashed across the street. Another shot hit the street bricks. This time I saw a flicker of light that must have been the muzzle flash. It came from the top floor of the parking garage and looked more like the flash of a cigarette lighter than a muzzle blast from a high-powered rifle.

I squeezed off three quick rounds in the shooter's direction. His ultra-quiet weapon hadn't brought an SAPD response, but I knew the booming explosions from my .45 definitely would. I sprinted to the garage's car exit. Sirens approached from more than one direction.

Tires squealed, and a vehicle descended from the parking garage's upper level. I paused behind the automated ticket booth. If the shooter came this way, he was a dead man. The engine noise receded. I heard a final squeal, then acceleration. The vehicle was headed to the Commerce Street exit on the opposite side of the building.

I jumped the parking barrier and sprinted across the ground floor, hoping to have a shot or at least catch a glimpse of the shooter's license plate.

Instead, I ran headlong into four howling SAPD squad cars with flashing emergency lights. A spotlight hit me in the face, and a burly beat cop drew his service weapon and trained it on my chest.

"Down on the ground!" he ordered.

# CHAPTER FIVE

"YOU'RE TELLING ME MR. SOSA was threatened by the Citizens for a Clean County, so he hired you to protect him?" Detective Milo Peterson, aka Tomahawk, thumbed through his notes, making a show of sounding skeptical. He had a wedge-shaped nose and a thin face topped by an unruly patch of bleached-blond hair that showed signs of gray in the roots. The skin around his eyes was pulled tight like he'd had some work done, and his forearm muscles were cut like he spent nights at the gym. From my awkward position, handcuffed in the back seat of a royal-blue Crown Vic, his silhouette looked like a tomahawk, the kind of authentic replica they sold in the Alamo gift shop. That distinctive look and a nasty reputation had earned him the nickname. We knew each other, but he was playing dumb. He was part of that law enforcement crowd who seemed to resent ex-military, and he had a particular axe to grind with me.

"You catch on quick, Detective," I said. It didn't make sense to me either, but Peterson seemed more interested in giving me a hard time than doing any detective work. There was something Sosa hadn't told me before I took the job. To find out what it was, I would have to wait until he woke up in the hospital. If he woke up. Another missed payday, and a step backward for my business venture.

I'd been sitting for over an hour—the first thirty minutes in the squad car waiting for Peterson and his partner to arrive, then the last thirty minutes while the detective made notes and asked stupid questions. Meanwhile, the shooter was long gone.

Peterson turned to his partner, Detective Diana Ochoa. She had dark skin and too much makeup. From the lines on her face, I guessed she was either in her early thirties, or late twenties and very worried about something. From the way she hung on Peterson's every inane question, I put her fresh out of whatever detective training they provided. She carried a few extra pounds, mainly in her chest, but she looked like she could handle herself.

"Detective Ochoa, doesn't your grandmother belong to the Citizens for a Clean County?"

She caught his sarcastic tone and played along. "Yeah, that's right. She does, Detective Peterson."

"How old is she?" he asked.

"She's eighty-six tomorrow," she said, barely containing a smile.

"Well, wish Granny a happy birthday. Would you say she's a violent person?" Detective Peterson was proud of his sense of humor.

"Homicidal. She once slapped my *primo* for drinking milk out of the carton." She couldn't hold it any longer. Both laughed out loud.

"You two practicing that routine for a YouTube video? Ask Granny if she knows where the CCC gets its funding." The cuffs were getting tight, it was after midnight, and I'd had enough of these two clowns. "If your uniform unit hadn't threatened to kill me, I'd have had the shooter's car and this case would be over by now."

Detective Peterson dropped the smile and tried to sound tough. "A civilian skipping down the street wearing a bloody shirt and waving a .45 is a threat. My officers are trained to react to shots fired. You're lucky I wasn't there. I'd have put you down."

"All right," I said, trying to sound conciliatory. "I get it, they were just doing their job. You're just doing yours."

"Look, Fischer. I know who you are and your reputation," Peterson said.

"Thanks. Now, I'd like to check on my client." I thought I was finally getting through to him.

"That wasn't a compliment," he said. Obviously, he wanted to get something off his chest.

Both detectives stared at me over the dark-blue vinyl seat. It wasn't the kind of stare that's followed by a French kiss and a warm hug. Peterson was part of the team that had taken down Skeeter Davis for setting fire to an apartment building that killed twenty people. The case that Allison brought up and the one that made me the St. Jude of private detectives, according to Skeeter's mother.

"You found one killer and put that big, one-armed jig back on the streets." Peterson couldn't stand it. He had to bring it up. I didn't know which pissed him off more, the fact that Skeeter was innocent or the fact that he was a very large black man. When he leaned further over the seat, I couldn't help imagining feathers dangling from his ears.

"Skeeter didn't do it," I said.

"Maybe, maybe not. He was there. He wasn't innocent."

"He didn't start the fire. He didn't kill those people. You nailed the wrong guy."

"You know how many cases we have to clear every month?" Ochoa jumped into the fray. Her new partner had obviously briefed her on his side of the story, probably as a cautionary tale to a new recruit. "You solved one little case and you're a hero?"

"You're pissed 'cause I don't work on volume?"

She wasn't going to see it my way no matter how much I argued, because she had to work with Tomahawk. I pitied her.

"Let's talk about recent history," I said. "An hour ago, my client was shot in downtown San Antonio by a sniper using a high-powered rifle that sounded more like an air gun. Doesn't that make you the least bit anxious to find a suspect?"

"We found one," he said, still staring at me.

I met his gaze. "Unless you're gonna charge me with the attempted murder of my own client, turn me loose. Mr. Sosa needs armed protection in the hospital, and the real shooter isn't going to turn himself in."

"Your job ended when Sosa took a bullet," Peterson snapped. "I don't care if you're a private dick. This case is ours. Stay the fuck out of it. And stay close to home. The DA may still want to press charges. Detective Ochoa will be in touch."

"For what?"

"Incompetence for one." He exposed his small sharp teeth, but he wasn't smiling. He looked more like a guard dog showing his fangs.

I didn't say anything. They weren't going to listen to me, and I didn't want to listen to them any longer than it took to get out of the Crown Vic. I leaned forward in the seat and held my handcuffed hands up. Detective Ochoa reluctantly unlocked them.

"My weapons?" I said.

Peterson examined the Para-Ordnance .45 before he handed it over with the S&W .38. "Didn't Remington buy Para-Ordnance?" he asked as if he thought my weapon was somehow out of date. It was true they weren't making that model anymore, but I still trusted it.

"It gets the job done," I said. "You forget something?" Both weapons were unloaded.

"I don't remember them being loaded. You should be more careful. Don't forget what I said. Keep your nose out of this case."

I stepped out of the car and strapped my empty pistols back in place. Tomahawk sneered through his open window. I should have kept my mouth shut, but I couldn't resist.

"Think of it this way, Detective. We're on the same team. I only take the cases y'all can't solve."

Ochoa shouted something, but Peterson rolled the window up and drove away.

## CHAPTER SIX

I HIKED EAST ON MARKET STREET looking for a cab. The River Walk bars were open for another hour. The tourist children were in their hotel rooms playing video games, and the adults were doing shots of tequila. I wished I was holding something with lime and salt or a cold beer to wash away the bad taste in my mouth and mitigate the smell of Sosa's blood on my shirt. Despite Tomahawk's warning, I couldn't stay away from the Sosa case. I'd promised door to door service. He had never made it to his door. It wasn't just the paycheck; my reputation was on the line.

When I didn't see a cab, I hit the Uber app on my cell phone and waited for the driver by the life-sized bronze sculpture of the famous cattleman Charles Goodnight that stood guard alongside Quanah Parker, the last Comanche war chief, in front of the Briscoe Western Art Museum. Both figures were so realistic that they seemed to come alive in the dim light of the streetlamp. Goodnight's cowboy hat was pulled low on his stoic face, reminding me of Patrick Allison's determined expression when he had been searching my soul. There was no other way to describe it. I wondered why he had focused on me. Men like Patrick Allison always had an agenda. Maybe it was my suspicious nature, but I couldn't shake the feeling that the events in the convention center were connected to Sosa's shooting. Had Detective Peterson been interested in doing his job, he would have asked about Sosa's contacts at the fundraiser. Sosa had told me that much and that the oil business was volatile. I didn't think the real source of his concern was the CCC.

The Uber driver didn't bat an eye when he saw my bloodstained tux shirt. "Some party?"

I wondered what kind of late-night fares he normally pulled in. "The usual," I said, just to keep him guessing. I figured he'd have a good story to tell the other drivers at Starbucks after the bars closed. He dropped me off at the airport, where I'd left my pickup, then I swung by the hospital to check on Javier Sosa.

He was out of surgery but still in critical condition. No chance to ask him any questions. I talked to the head of hospital security and told her what had happened. She said Detective Peterson had briefed her and left two uniforms on the ICU floor. I hadn't expected that. Tomahawk was doing his job. I also talked to Sosa's head of security, the man who should have been waiting outside the hotel. His English was limited, but he seemed confident that his team could protect his boss in the hospital. He couldn't explain why he wasn't outside the hotel.

On the drive home, I tried to sort out what had happened. Some details about the shooting seemed out of place. The location was good. The street was quiet. The parking garage provided cover and easy access with multiple exits. Sosa had a regular security team that was going to take over for the rest of his Texas trip. That meant higher security and less opportunity after he left my service. The timing was perfect. The part that bugged me was that the shooter had stayed in position after his initial shot. He would have seen Sosa was hit and assumed it was a kill. The distance wasn't that great. The buildings were close together. If his target was Sosa, why did he keep shooting at me? The thought caused the hair to stand up on the back of my neck. The shooter used a high-powered rifle that was Hollywood quiet—that impossibly quiet whisper that can only be reproduced in the movies. My first thought was that the weapon had to be a military-grade system, but I'd served three tours of duty and had never heard anything that silent. The constant ringing in my ears was proof of that.

I tried to come up with a list of people who wanted me pushing up daisies. I had made a few enemies in my short career as a private eye, but none were the kind to hire a sniper. If the gangster involved in Skeeter's case wanted me dead, his thugs would have already come after me. Their style was to roll up next to you on the street corner and open fire with a Glock 19 pistol—the gangster weapon of choice. The scumbag that burned down the apartment building and framed Skeeter was in prison, and his thug friends were too busy cooking and selling more meth to care about me. I crossed him off the list.

Before that, a number of wives had hired me to catch their husbands with their pants down, but I figured the husbands were too embarrassed or too busy remodeling the kitchen to come after me. The two women I'd caught in compromising positions were happily suing the husbands that hired me. I couldn't see them spending any money to have me killed.

The only other work I'd done was for an insurance company, documenting fraud. The guy was getting four grand a month for a claim against a trucking company that he and his high-profile lawyer said put him in a wheelchair. I found him playing golf at the north side country club. The guy was doing time, and his lawyer was counter-suing. I crossed them off the list too. I didn't think I'd been in business long enough to be on anyone's hit list.

I turned right on St. Mary's Street in front of the neighborhood Mennonite church. A busload of recent immigrants was unloading in the parking lot, fresh from one of the detention centers in Dilley or Karnes City. The Mennonites always had their doors open.

I lived south of downtown on the border of one of the older neighborhoods of San Antonio called King William, named after Kaiser Wilhelm I of Prussia. So many Germans moved to that area along the San Antonio River in the late 1800s, it became known as Sauerkraut Bend. They built majestic Victorian and Greek Revival homes and enjoyed fishing in the nearby river. Like all neighborhoods, it had gone through a period of decline, but now many of the old homes had been renovated, giving the neighborhood a gentrified feel. When I bought the house, I was hoping to cash in on that feeling by buying a fixer-upper on the edge of the main district. I was also trying to impress Sylvia by being a homeowner. When I got around to the fix and repair part, it might work.

The street was lined with similar houses in different stages of renovation. Some had been turned into rental properties, others were falling down. Mine wasn't the worst.

I pulled into my driveway and checked for lights in my neighbor's window. Her name was Rose Gustafson, and she was a retired university biology professor who was born in the neighborhood in 1939. I tried to always check up on her when I got home late. In return, she liked to remind me what day the city collected trash.

I came in through the front door and let Sam, my four-year-old chocolate Lab, examine the holes in my ruined tuxedo and sniff Sosa's dried blood. He was named after Sam Houston, a hero of the Texas Revolution. He occasionally took himself too seriously, and I wasn't entirely sure whether it was because of his namesake or his breed.

Once Sam decided the holes in my clothes weren't from another dog, he waited by the back door for me to change into my running shorts. He didn't seem to care that it was pushing two a.m. or that I had been shot at and interrogated. We ran every night when I got home. It wasn't his fault I was late. You can't argue with a Labrador retriever.

We jogged to the San Antonio River trail south of the popular tourist loop. It was well lit and paved for most of the fifteen or so miles extending south to the four lesser known Spanish missions. A welcome breeze ruffled the mesquite tree leaves and Johnson grass lining the trail. A rare summer shower had dumped an inch of rain the week before and turned everything green and added to the humidity. Streetlamps illuminated patches of wild sunflowers that the moisture had revived.

We skipped our usual route and ran north for twenty-five minutes. Although I couldn't come up with anyone who wanted me dead, experience taught me to err on the side of caution. We passed the old US Arsenal that now housed the headquarters of a local grocery chain, and the backsides of a dozen historic buildings. Farther north, the buildings got newer and closer to the channel. One of the few remaining older structures was the landmark VFW. The building was a white Victorian house nestled in an ever-expanding condo jungle. The trail had a European vibe without the graffiti. When I was released from the hospital in Germany after my last deployment, I took a week to travel the countryside. Every building and outdoor fixture was covered with graffiti that the locals seemed to ignore. The tagging that did show up in the tourist sections of San Antonio was quickly washed off and painted over.

The north part of the trail reeked of urban renewal, which translated into housing I couldn't afford. We took the steps to the street level and came face-to-face with Sylvia's engaging smile adorning a bus stop ad for her father's furniture store. He called himself the Furniture King and had made a fortune selling overpriced household furnishings using his daughter's alluring features. Her life from birth through college was catalogued on benches all over the city. I was thinking about her encounter with Marcus at the convention center. I should have gotten over being jealous, but it was hard when every man in town could admire her picture at the bus stop. I decided to let it go. Why provoke her into a fight when the encounter probably meant nothing? I was turning over a new leaf.

We stopped at the base of a newer complex. The ground floor units all had private patios surrounded by six-foot wooden fences that faced the river. Sam sniffed out the last gate in a row of twelve then proudly looked back at me.

I looked at my watch. It was two thirty a.m. I probably should have called her earlier, but I had a lot on my mind. Sam pawed at the gate impatiently. I tested the handle. "It's locked," I told him. He didn't seem to think it was a problem. "Fine," I said. He was right. We both wanted to see her. I lifted myself over the gate and onto Sylvia's small patio.

I let Sam in, and he went straight for the bowl of water and food. She didn't forget, and neither did he. The sliding glass door was open, and I let myself into a dark living room and left Sam to finish his late-night snack.

Sylvia met me in the dark and wrapped her warm arms around my sweat-soaked T-shirt. "Are you all right?" she asked. I could hear the concern in her voice.

"Just a little out of breath from the run."

She pushed me away and put her hands on her hips. Her white robe fell open to her waist. "Don't play games," she said.

"How did you find out?"

"The police questioned Marcus." She pulled her robe closed and secured it with the belt.

I grabbed a beer and flopped down on the couch. Sylvia threw me a hand towel from the kitchen and flipped on the lamp. I explained the evening's events while she stood examining me for holes in my skin or my story.

"Someone shot at you, and you go for a jog? No tears? No shouting? You make a sarcastic joke and move on," she said.

"What do you want me to do?"

"I don't know. Yell at the wall? Shed a tear? Something to show you're human."

"Yell at the wall?"

"You know what I mean. I'm glad they stopped you before you could chase down an armed suspect in the dark." Her robe fell open again. She wasn't wearing anything underneath.

This time I couldn't resist. I reached inside the robe and pulled her closer to me. "You forget my background, counselor. My specialty is chasing down armed suspects in the dark."

"You were wearing a tuxedo, which is probably ruined, and not a helmet and body armor. Do you have to pretend you're a badass all the time?" She moved closer to me and let me explore under her robe.

"Who's pretending?" I asked.

"Can you *ever* be serious?"

"I'm compensating for my lack of emotion," I said, suppressing a smirk.

"This is a good example of why you should go back to law school."

"Because I lack emotions?"

"Stop!" she said, exasperated.

"Sosa was a lawyer. Look what it got him," I said, pulling her robe further open.

"You know what I mean." She took my hands, halting my exploration. "You should have quit after Skeeter's case. Now this? You can't pretend it's safe being a private investigator."

"Driving a car in the city isn't safe either, but it's necessary."

"Nick, please. Stop the private eye thing. Let the police solve crimes. No more getting shot at. You don't have anything to prove."

"The police don't always get the job done." I finished my beer.

"So now you're the Caped Crusader?"

"Every city needs one," I said.

She usually laughed at my jokes. She wasn't smiling. "You're not in a comic book. Your client's in a real hospital."

"And that's why I can't quit."

"Stop. Please? Go back to school." She let her robe slip from her shoulders. It wasn't the first time she had given me a not-so-subtle hint that the future of our relationship hinged on whether I continued as a private investigator or went back to law school. Her huge brown eyes and glistening bare skin were hard to argue against.

"It's late. We can argue then have make-up sex or have make-up sex and argue tomorrow." I buried my head between her round breasts. She put both arms around my neck. "I'm ready to show some emotion," I said.

"What am I gonna do with you?" She laughed.

"I've an idea." I lifted her by her narrow waist and carried her down the hall. Sexual chemistry had never been our problem.

We were both naked before we landed on her king-sized bed.

# CHAPTER SEVEN

SAM AND I CROSSED THE river on the Navarro Bridge and jogged south toward Market Street. I was hoping detective Peterson's team would be finished so I could take a look at the crime scene without bullets flying over my head or him asking stupid questions. Once CSI was finished, there was no law against taking a look.

I left Sylvia sleeping and mumbling something about being careful. For her, being careful meant staying home. For me, it meant finding out what the hell was going on. Being warned off the case didn't stop me from wanting to know who took a shot at Javier Sosa. I didn't believe that the tree huggers would hire a hit man to take out Sosa. There may be a list of enemies that wanted him dead in Mexico, but why risk killing him in Texas? The murder rates in Mexico were five times higher. No one would bat an eye if he got shot south of the border. Downtown San Antonio was different.

A freight train blew its whistle and clacked along the downtown tracks. No one seemed to be listening. Even the white-winged doves had turned in for the night. This section of river had been inhabited for centuries by native tribes, then the Spanish, and finally new European immigrants. I wondered if one group was more civilized than the other or if the advance of civilization was just an illusion. Sure, people used Uber instead of wagons and had air conditioning, but they were still killing each other.

My encounter with Detective Peterson didn't leave me with much confidence he could solve the case on his own. His partner, Ochoa, seemed a bit more intelligent, but she was a rookie investigator and would have to follow Peterson's lead. I didn't make a habit of interfering with police investigations, but this was personal. Someone had taken out my client and stuck around to fire a few shots at me. It was in my best interest to find out who did it.

Sam and I entered the parking garage across the street from Sosa's hotel. The crime investigation team was gone and had left behind a few broken strips of yellow caution tape. We slipped past the ticket booth and walked up to the fourth floor. Sam sniffed a crumpled orange-and-white Whataburger bag for signs of food. I picked it up and tossed it in the trash, doing my civic duty.

I checked the angle and found a perfect view of the hotel entrance across the street. Crouching down, I put my hands in position on the concrete ledge as if I were holding a rifle. The shooter pulled the trigger from that spot. He had chosen well for the first shot, but he had not anticipated the cover created by the limo and the other cars on the street. As soon as Sosa went down, he would have been out of sight for the follow-up shot that hit the steps over our heads. The street was deserted now and so was the entrance to the hotel. No cars parked on the street. I visualized the height of a parked limo and saw where the second bullet had hit.

I moved farther down, recreating the sequence of events. Once Sosa left in the limo, I guessed the shooter changed position to gain a better angle. I found another place that offered a clear view of the sidewalk on the opposite side of the street.

Sam watched me with interest, then started to sniff the parking spots. He wasn't a trained police dog, but he had that Labrador knack for always wanting to be helpful. If I looked for something, he would look too. If I was angry, he would bark. If I was happy, he would lick my hand. The parking garage seemed to be swept clean. Sam wasn't so sure. He kept looking. Either Detective Peterson's team had done a thorough search or, more likely, there had been nothing to find. The shooter was a professional.

Sam whined, and I turned to see him scratching at something stuck between the curb and a concrete tire barrier. I reached down to scratch his ears. When he didn't give up, I took a closer look. Stuck in the crack was a spent rifle casing. It was directly behind where I guessed the last shot would have come from. At that point in the attack, I was running across the street. The shooter wouldn't have had time to look for the missing brass. He must have ejected the spent round, which took an unlucky bounce, and jumped into his car while I ran to the garage entrance. Maybe he hadn't counted on my return fire bringing a quick police response.

I took a picture of the location with my cell phone, then snapped a few extra photos of the parking garage. Sam posed next to his find. The police had been here, searched the place, and cleared the crime scene. I was doing my civic duty. I found a spent popsicle stick and used it to lift the casing from its hiding place. It was a Winchester .308. Whoever used this had picked a lethal round. I was sure the shooter used a suppressor. If he hadn't, the explosion from the .308 round would have echoed off the walls of the Alamo and caused panic in the tourists along the River Walk. It didn't explain why it was Hollywood quiet. There were no clues on the brass. I got out a poop baggie I carried to clean up after Sam—a yellow plastic baggie with the image of a dog doing his business. I couldn't wait to see the look on Detective Peterson's face when I showed it to him.

"Good work, Sam," I said.

He tilted his head, disappointed that I didn't offer him more of a reward. I slipped the bag in my pocket and looked at my watch. It was four fifteen. Sam and I walked down to the ground floor and took a route home that crossed the Alamo Plaza. The lights were still shining on the adobe bricks of the old mission, a constant reminder that sometimes you had to fight even though the odds were not in your favor.

We paused briefly at the cenotaph to pay our respects. The massive marble monument depicted the names and faces of the men who died in the Battle of the Alamo. It was known as *The Spirit of Sacrifice* and was dedicated in 1936 on the one hundredth anniversary of the fight that took place across the street. Full-sized statues of Davy Crockett and William Travis stared down at us.

I read part of the inscription chiseled in stone: *Erected in memory of the heroes who sacrificed their lives... They chose never to surrender nor retreat.* I remembered my brothers-in-arms who hadn't made it back from Afghanistan. There was no monument honoring the sacrifice they made, but their names were etched in my memory and their faces haunted my dreams.

Sam took a dump. Luckily, I had an extra yellow poop bag. I'm sure he didn't mean any disrespect.

# CHAPTER EIGHT

A VERY INSISTENT KNOCKING INTERRUPTED MY plans to sleep till noon. The remnants of a familiar nightmare stuck to my skin like sweat from the South Texas heat. In the dream, I was trapped in a Humvee while my platoon took on an enemy ambush. An IED had crushed the dashboard against my thighs and blown out the windshield. When the firefight was over, I was the only one left alive. The dream always left me feeling guilty and helpless. Not a good way to start the day.

Sam sensed my distress and licked my face.

"Easy, buddy. I'm okay. I'm awake," I told him as I moved to an upright position. The knocking continued.

The digital clock read seven thirty a.m. I didn't want to deal with anyone displaying those knocking skills after only three hours of sleep. I rolled over and tried to wait them out. Maybe whoever it was would go away. Sam wasn't having any of it. Sometimes I wished I were a cat lover like my next-door neighbor. Cats didn't care about your friends or enemies and weren't concerned about visitors. A Lab needed to be a part of everything. Sam tore the pillow out of my hand, then pounced on my chest. It was going to be a long day. I found my shorts and a T-shirt and made my way downstairs.

Sam barked a few times and went to the window to alert the visitor that I was awake and on my final approach. I peered through the peephole to determine the threat level of the caller. I kept a Mossberg 12-gauge pump-action shotgun leaning against the doorframe for anyone not spreading good cheer.

The visitor was an earnest and determined-looking woman. She was late forties or early fifties judging by the hint of gray around her forehead and the lines around her eyes that were partially covered by makeup. Her attire was modest—a white blouse over a denim skirt that extended to just above her knees. She wore sturdy tennis shoes that had covered their share of dirty pavement, and around her neck was a large silver cross.

Sam barked again. He was focused on the yard, where a younger version of the woman bounced a tennis ball on the sidewalk. The girl looked to be about eleven or twelve—in the preteen stage where she dabbled with makeup and hair products but wasn't afraid to play with a ball or a dog. Sam spotted this trait instantly.

I left the shotgun on the peg and opened the door. Sam ripped through my legs and into the yard. My visitor turned to watch him plant himself in front of the girl and her tennis ball.

"Is he friendly?" the woman asked, taking a defensive step toward the young girl.

"He's never met a young person he didn't like," I assured her.

The girl knew what he wanted and flicked the ball into the pecan leaves mixed with overgrown grass. Sam had the ball in his mouth before it took a second bounce. No matter how this encounter went, Sam had found a friend.

Relieved, the woman turned back to me and extended her hand. "Mr. Fischer?" She had the strong grip of someone who worked with her hands.

"Yes?" I said.

"My name is Araceli Luna. Lola Davis suggested I contact you. It's about my daughter, Mr. Fischer. She was murdered. I want you to find out who did it."

Out of habit, I quickly scanned up and down the street for anything unusual—occupied vehicles or people loitering at the bus stop on the corner. I didn't see anything out of place, only the usual rising steam from the dew on the grass and the steady hum of cicadas. Rose Gustafson waved at me from her front flowerbed. She wore white rubber shrimp boots and a pair of leather gloves. Her gray hair was braided and coiled on top of her head like an aging Viking princess. The pile of brush by her gate was a sign she'd been working since dawn, taking advantage of the relative cool.

"Would you like to come inside?" I offered.

She glanced at the young girl still playing ball with Sam and said something in rapid-fire Spanish. The girl presented herself to me and extended her hand.

"This is my youngest daughter," she said.

"My name is Leticia Luna, Mr. Fischer," the girl said. She suddenly noticed my scars and stared.

"Leticia!" her mother scolded. "I'm sorry," she said to me.

"It's okay." I knelt in front of Leticia and smiled. "I was hurt overseas by a roadside bomb. Glass cut my face. I was in the military."

"Are you okay?" she asked.

"It's all healed," I said. That seemed to satisfy her curiosity. It was healed, on the outside. The rest I was still working on. Sam barked, irritated that I had interrupted his play.

"May I play with your dog?" she asked.

"He wouldn't have it any other way," I said. "His name is Sam."

I left Sam and Leticia in the yard, led Araceli Luna into the living room, and excused myself while I started the coffee maker and wiped dust from two mismatched mugs. I wanted to be fully awake when Mrs. Luna gave me the details. It wasn't every day someone dropped by before seven to offer me a murder case.

While the coffee maker did its thing, I took the opportunity to study Mrs. Luna. She paced my living room nervously while examining my collection of family photos. She seemed anxious to tell her story. It was a good sign that she was on the level. I got at least two calls a week from someone who wanted me to harass a business associate for screwing them over or a disgruntled worker wanting to stick it to their ex-boss.

She said Skeeter's mother had recommended me. That meant her being here was set in motion yesterday or even the day before. She stopped in front of the pictures of my father. There was one of him in his highway patrol uniform and one of him with his cowboy hat and sheriff's badge. There was an older picture of him in a Marine uniform, and a triangular mahogany display case with his burial flag.

"Was this your father?" she called to me. People had a hard time believing we were related.

"Yeah," I said, filling two mugs with coffee.

I motioned Mrs. Luna into one of two matching overstuffed leather chairs. I placed the mugs on a small carved coffee table from Mexico that I'd inherited from Great-Grandpa. The only other furniture in the room was a floor-to-ceiling bookcase stuffed with my eclectic collection of Texas history, case law, and my complete collection of Tony Hillerman mysteries.

"I'm sorry for your loss," I said.

Her hands trembled. "Thank you, Mr. Fischer. It's been over two months. The pain never goes away. They told me to forget, but I see her face every day." She gestured toward the flag on the mantel. "You know what it's like to lose someone close."

"I was sixteen when he died, but I do understand," I said. "What did Lola Davis tell you about me?"

"That you were the one to call if there was no one else to turn to."

"Why do you feel that way?"

"The police have done nothing. They said it was an accident. She was found in the San Antonio River. On the River Walk. It was the day after the Fourth of July. They said she was drunk. My daughter never drank."

She took a deep breath. Her hands stopped shaking. She took a sip from the coffee cup. I let her collect herself in silence. It dawned on me who her daughter was. The story had made the national news because she was found by a little boy wearing a coonskin cap. As usual, there was no follow-up story. The novelty had worn off. The little boy was the hook for the national news, and he had gone back to Germany with his souvenirs and a story to tell. The dead woman was forgotten. No one cared about her except her mother.

"Did Mrs. Davis tell you that I do private investigation for a living?" I didn't want to come off as an asshole, but I couldn't afford to run a charity. I had a mortgage on my fixer-upper and was trying to build a business.

"Oh, yes, of course," she insisted.

"I get five thousand to cover my expenses and another five if I get results. That does not include thirty dollars an hour plus mileage. You don't have to worry. I keep meticulous records, and I'll send you an invoice at the end of each week. This kind of investigation could take some time."

She reached in her purse and took out a new bank envelope. "I pay now?" she asked, offering me the envelope. "There's five thousand."

I checked the envelope and found a stack of hundred-dollar bills. Lola must have mentioned an amount. This bundle was probably at least a month's paycheck. I wondered how far in advance she had planned this meeting and who else she had told about it.

"I can get the rest when you find the truth."

I had no doubt she would get more money and that all of it would come from sweat and hard work.

"Thank you, Mrs. Luna," I said, and handed the envelope back to her.

"It's not enough?" She looked surprised and hurt.

Five thousand dollars would come in handy, but I didn't take money unless I knew I could make a difference. The PI business was built on reputation and referrals. I had decided from the beginning to pick and choose my cases carefully.

"The money's fine." I waited for her to take in a deep breath. "First, I need to know what happened. I won't take your money unless I think I can help you."

She took a sip of coffee.

I stood up. "Give me a moment." I walked back to the kitchen for a coffee refill. "Would you like anything else to drink?" I called to her.

"No, gracias," she said.

I stopped by the front window on my way back into the living room to check on Sam and her daughter. Sam was crouched at her heel. Leticia pointed into the yard. Sam would keep her occupied as long as she was willing to throw the ball. I studied the street again. A black Ford Super Duty pickup drove slowly past my yard. The heavy dew was gone, replaced by heat waves off the pavement. White-winged doves joined the cicadas, adding their slightly mournful notes to the clash of neighborhood noise. Rose was still working on her pyracantha and keeping a sharp eye on the neighborhood.

I broke out a new spiral notebook and a Bic pen and took a seat behind my desk. "Why don't you start at the beginning?"

Araceli Luna recited her story while I took occasional notes of times and places. There wasn't anything unusual, except for the fact that Marissa was the first in her family to go to college and she had gotten a scholarship to Texas Tech. She seemed like a typical young woman with big ambitions for the future. Mrs. Luna showed me the newspaper clipping. There was a photo of a man with a scruffy salt-and-pepper beard standing by the River Walk. He had a toothless smile and wore an Army cap and camo jacket. The article described him as being on site when Marissa was found.

The police had found no evidence of a struggle or foul play. An autopsy revealed Marissa had alcohol in her system. A friend said she left a dance club alone around midnight and was never seen alive again. I wrote down the friend's name. I also made a note of the night club near the River Walk. Without any evidence to the contrary, the medical examiner ruled it an accidental death by drowning. Case closed. I took a closer look at the autopsy report.

"Is this all the police gave you?" I asked.

Mrs. Luna nodded. The ME usually listed additional findings at the end of the report. What she gave me had nothing.

"My Marissa never drank, Mr. Fischer. That's how I know the police are wrong." She said this last part with particular conviction.

"She was a young woman out partying with her friends. You said she liked to dance. Are you sure she never drank? Not even a little? She was over twenty-one. It wasn't illegal."

"She was very health conscious. She was studying to be a nurse. One more year and she would have graduated from Texas Tech. She always took care of herself."

"Did she have any enemies? Maybe her friends were jealous?"

"Absolutely not, Mr. Fischer. Everyone loved her."

I tapped on my notebook. "This is a cold case, Mrs. Luna. Chances are I won't be able to find anything."

Disappointment tugged at the corner of her lips. "But Mrs. Davis said you helped her son," she insisted.

"Sometimes, there's nothing anyone can do. It's hard to take, but accidents do happen. There's no one to blame. It's better to forget the tragedy and remember the joy they brought to you." It was the hard truth that most people couldn't accept. I didn't want to give Mrs. Luna any false hope. Despite what Skeeter's mother told her, my chances of finding her daughter's killer were very slim at best.

Mrs. Luna folded her hands in her lap. Her look told me I couldn't budge her with a front-end loader unless I agreed to take her case.

"Have you discussed your case with anyone else besides Mrs. Davis?" I asked.

"No," she said abruptly. "Absolutely not." Her quick response suggested otherwise, but I would deal with that later.

I tapped on my notebook. "I know this is painful, but I will need to do some checking and make a few phone calls before I will commit to your case."

"Mrs. Davis said you were skeptical of everything."

"I don't take money unless I know I can help. If I do take your case, I will get to the truth. Are you willing to accept that?" I always asked this last question before a case. Some people who came to me only wanted me to find their version of the truth.

"Please, find out who killed my daughter."

"If I can help, I'll let you know."

She leaped from the chair and grabbed both my arms. "Thank you. Thank you. I knew you would help. Mrs. Davis was right. You are an angel," she gushed.

"I'm far from an angel," I said, extracting myself from her grasp. "Give me twenty-four hours. I'll make some phone calls and do a little digging."

"Yes, of course. I understand," she said. From the smile on her face, all she heard me say was that I would take the case. "I knew today would be a special day."

"Why is that?" I asked.

"Today is Marissa's birthday. She would have been twenty-three."

I walked her to the door and saw Sam on his back getting his belly rubbed. He had made a new friend. He didn't bother to look at me. Shameless.

"One more question. Who was the officer in charge of the investigation?"

"Detective Peterson," she said.

# CHAPTER NINE

IT WAS CLOSE TO TEN o'clock Saturday morning when I left Sam in his backyard pool, cooling off from his play-date with Marissa's younger sister and sulking because he held me responsible for cutting it short. I had done my preliminary research by checking the public records available for Marissa Luna. She didn't leave much of a paper trail in her short life. I found a Facebook tribute and a few pictures on Instagram, along with her police report courtesy of the Texas Public Information Act. For the nitty-gritty details, I would call Skeeter. That was his specialty. When he wasn't working for me, he installed security systems for big businesses around San Antonio and Austin and did background checks for an insurance company. He worked for me to pay off the three months and countless hours I'd spent finding the thug who set him up. I had thrown the dice when I took on his case free of charge hoping my success would spin into positive publicity and more referrals to boost my fledgling business. If I took the Luna case, it might finally pay off.

I drove my pickup to the SAPD headquarters on Santa Rosa Avenue hoping to catch Detective Peterson. Any other detective I would have called in advance to set up a meeting, but I knew

Peterson would tell me to piss up a rope before answering any questions about the Luna case.

I was going to use the casing Sam found to work a trade for information. The pressure on Peterson to show results or turn over the investigation to the FBI would be immense. Javier Sosa was a Mexican citizen. Mexico didn't seem to mind if their citizens were assassinated in their own country, but they took exception to attempts on US soil.

Knowing Peterson was a prick, I would have to handle the negotiations as delicately as possible. Not one of my stronger points. That was why I waited fifteen minutes for a bag of taquitos at the Las Tapatias drive-through when I usually made my own breakfast. I was going to offer San Antonio's finest a peace offering.

I parked in the parking garage and wondered if Peterson would validate my ticket. The building looked like a prison with its white limestone blocks and small windows. The public art on display out front consisted of what looked like leftover metal beams painted white and standing on end like unstable teepee poles in a gale force wind. Nothing says "public safety" like a precarious stack of thirty-foot-tall metal poles.

I recognized the sergeant working the front desk. His name was Hugo Vera, an old-timer who had retired once but came back to work part-time because he said his wife got tired of seeing him around the house all day long. He had also known my father and had a vacation home in Fredericksburg, where I'd met him when I was a kid.

"How's the PI business?" he asked.

"Maybe I should have opened a barbecue joint. At least I'd know where my next meal was coming from."

"Hang in there. It takes a while to get established." It was always nice to hear a bit of encouragement. "What brings you down here, Nick?" Vera asked.

"I need to talk to Detective Peterson," I said.

When he heard the detective's name, his grizzled face looked like he'd bit a lemon. "I would advise against it. Tomahawk's been here all night talking to the Feds about your late-night shootout."

"Is he ever in a good mood?" I asked.

Vera grinned. "He was happier when he worked SWAT."

"Peterson was on the SWAT team?" I asked. "When was that?" I couldn't picture the guy having any tactical skills.

"Fifteen years ago," he said. "Before your time."

"Why'd he switch to homicide?"

"He was asked to leave. Too many bodies were piling up. Nothing official, but he had a reputation for shooting first."

"This can't wait," I said.

He shrugged. "Don't say I didn't warn you, kid," he said and buzzed me through to the upstairs offices.

I found Peterson in his cubicle looking like he'd spent the night there. He wore the same shirt, minus the tie, and there was a stack of paper cups from the coffee machine threatening to stage a rebellion against the file folders on his desk.

I perched three large coffees and a white bag of taquitos in the mix. He looked at me like I had just stepped out of a stale *Saturday Night Live* skit.

"Who let you in here?" he asked.

I ignored the question. "There's eggs and chorizo, eggs and barbacoa, or eggs and brisket. Help yourself." I took the lid off one of the coffees and took a sip like we did this every day. There was a desk next to his sporting a picture of Ochoa and a five- or six-year-old boy with an angelic smile and hair that was colored dark purple. "Where's Ochoa?" I asked.

"Busy. What the fuck're you doin' here?"

"Nice to see you again, too, Detective. How's the Sosa investigation going?"

"You're still the number one suspect."

"So, you got nothin'?"

"It's my case. I told you to stay the fuck away from it."

"It's all yours. I'm here about the Luna case. Apparent drowning victim. Marissa Luna. Found in the river by Davy Crockett."

"Come on, Fischer. I was up all night babysitting the forensics team. I spent two hours briefing the FBI, and an hour getting chewed out by the captain for not giving them enough information." He peeled away the foil wrapper on the taquito and took a big bite. "Thanks for breakfast," he said around a mouthful of egg and brisket. "Now, get the fuck out."

I took out Sam's poop bag and dangled it in the air.

Peterson took one look and spit out his mouthful of breakfast. "This some kind of a joke?"

"Relax, it's evidence from the parking garage. I was in the area walking my dog and couldn't resist taking a look."

"You interfered with a crime scene?"

"I waited till your guys were gone. This is something they missed."

"A stool sample from the shooter?"

"Maybe I scared the shit out of him," I said. It was easy to forget people skills talking to this guy.

"Take a hike, Fischer." He stood and pointed at the cubicle opening.

I didn't move. "Relax, it's not shit. I was fresh out of evidence bags. It's a .308 shell casing."

"How do I know that came from the scene?"

"I thought you'd say that." I took out my cell phone and showed him the pictures of Sam and the parking garage. "Actually, Sam found it. Don't worry, I didn't touch it. If I did, my prints are on file anyway."

"Let's have it." He held his hand out for the baggie.

I held it just out of his reach. "How about we trade?"

"You know that's withholding evidence."

"Oh, you're gonna get it. I just thought you'd like to have it first. I could take it downstairs and ask Sergeant Vera to run it through the system. He could run it for fingerprints and ballistics and take the credit. You could keep the poop bag."

Peterson sat back down and took another bite of taquito, then washed it down with a swallow of coffee. He was thinking. I expected him to come up with another reason not to share any information with me. I took a step toward the door to prove I was willing to take the evidence downstairs.

"All right," he blurted out, before I could take another step. "What d'you wanna know?"

"The autopsy for one," I said. "Why did you leave out the additional findings?"

He took another swallow of coffee. "Because they showed elevated HCG."

"She was pregnant?"

He wiped his mouth with a paper napkin. His facial expression didn't change. I waited for more explanation. None came.

"You didn't want her mother to know, or you didn't think it was important?"

"Look, the girl was careless. You follow? Her kind usually are. It was a judgment call."

"Her kind?"

"You some kind of bleeding heart?"

"She was a college student in Lubbock," I said.

"Doesn't change where she came from." The guy was waving red flags in my face.

"You don't think the father is a suspect? Isn't it odd he didn't come forward?"

"A suspect in what? There's no foul play. We can't prove the father knew about the baby."

"You have fetal DNA. You could ask him," I said.

"The girl had two boyfriends since high school that we could find. They were Facebook friends, whatever that means. They both volunteered DNA. Both came up negative. Like I said, she was careless. The bottom line here is the girl went out dancing, got wasted, and fell in the river. It's tragic. It's random. It happens. You can tell Mrs. Luna the same thing I told her—her daughter's death was an accident. I thought you were a Boy Scout. I didn't figure you were the kind to take a woman's money and yank her chain." He stood up, ending our conversation.

"A Boy Scout?" I asked. No one had ever called me that.

"Yeah, you act like you're working on a merit badge—helping out the underprivileged."

"Who said I was working for Mrs. Luna?"

"She calls me once a week. I figured somebody might have slipped her your number."

"I'm just curious by nature. I ran across the pint-sized Davy Crockett picture."

He gave me a strange look and waited for me to tell him more. I stayed quiet. I didn't owe him an explanation. His ears turned red. It was time to go.

"Go find some skirt-chaser to photograph. You're good at that."

I smiled. "Thanks. Good advice. I'll call your wife." I slipped out the hall door before he could respond. I'd heard all I needed to hear. Halfway down the hall, I realized I'd forgotten to ask him to validate my parking ticket.

Before I could turn around, I ran into Detective Ochoa. She had an armload of files and an up-all-night look on her face. Seeing me didn't cheer her up.

"Busy night?" I said, trying to be nice and hoping to win her over to my side.

"You have no idea," she said.

"I left a coffee and a taquito on your desk, if your partner didn't take them."

"You talked to him?" She sounded exasperated.

"Tried to get some information on another case."

“Thanks a lot,” she said with a big dose of sarcasm. “He’s already pissed because he’s missing church.” She actually seemed nice when her partner wasn’t around.

“Church? It’s Saturday,” I said.

“On the seventh day He rested,” she said. “He’s Seventh-day Adventist.”

“Doesn’t strike me as the religious type,” I said.

She shrugged. “Just do us both a favor and stay away from Peterson.”

# CHAPTER TEN

By the time I hit the parking garage, the rubber soles on my Justin boots were sticking to the superheated asphalt. A haze had settled over the city that was a mixture of heat rising off the pavement and a cloud of dust the local meteorologist claimed blew in from North Africa. My eyes and nose started dripping before I could climb into my eight-year-old F-150 and crank the air conditioning. For the last ten thousand miles it had only worked at one speed. I was glad that speed was high. While I waited for the air vents to dry the moisture on my face and shirt, I searched the glovebox for an antihistamine. I found the empty package and remembered I'd taken the last one during a recent wave of cedar pollen. I wouldn't get far without them.

I thought about Marissa Luna. The picture Peterson painted was of a party girl who had one too many and did a swan dive into the river, quite different than what her mother described. His story about withholding the news of Marissa being pregnant because he was being sensitive didn't hold water. He didn't strike me as the altruistic type. On the other hand, he wouldn't have anything to gain by covering up a murder unless he was involved, and that didn't seem likely. He worked homicide and cleared murder cases for a living. He'd made mistakes before, as I proved in Skeeter's case, but that was partly the DA's fault. Peterson seemed like the kind of guy that if he sniffed foul play, he would have kept the case open. According to Sergeant Vera, he was transferred to homicide for being too gung ho, not lazy. I couldn't really hold that against him. There was nothing in his report that screamed murder. There was no evidence of assault or rape, and there were no witnesses. If Marissa Luna was murdered, the killer had covered his tracks. Picking up the cold trail wasn't going to be easy.

I turned north on Market Street and admired the red sandstone exterior of the courthouse complex. It looked like something you'd see in Arizona, and much better designed than the SAPD building. I was going to track down the place where the police report said Marissa Luna had fallen in the river. I didn't expect to find anything at a two-month-old crime scene, but Peterson's revelation about Marissa being pregnant had left me wondering what else he might have overlooked or withheld. It was a place to start.

I found a rare open downtown parking spot, locked my pickup, and took the steps down to the River Walk. I walked across the Commerce Street footbridge and found myself staring at the huge bald cypress tree named for Ben Milam, a veteran of the War of 1812 and the Texas Revolution. He had survived war, encounters with Comanches, and prison in Mexico, only to be shot in the head by a Mexican sniper while he stopped at this tree to relieve himself. That extra pint of beer made him one of the first casualties of the battle for the Alamo three months later. The tree was only a little over three hundred yards from where a sniper put a bullet in my client and Marissa Luna had taken her last breath.

I got the strange feeling that I was being watched. The shooting put me on edge. It was the same feeling I used to get on patrol in Afghanistan. The extra shots fired in my direction still bothered me. Maybe the killer was simply covering his escape, but the fact that he was still out there didn't make me feel any safer. A dust-filled wind rustled the cypress limbs and sent me into a sneezing fit. I needed to find the nearest pharmacy.

The place described in the police report was underneath the Travis Street bridge where the river ran through a canyon of buildings and parking garages. I had passed the spot a dozen times since that night in July when she entered the water. Below a tile mural of the Alamo, I found an Our Lady of Guadalupe candle, along with a bundle of plastic roses and a white cross held upright in a Folgers coffee can filled with rocks. It was a shrine to honor her death. For the Catholic Hispanics it was known as a *descansos*, a common sight along the highways in South Texas.

A young woman wearing black yoga pants knelt in front of the candle. I stopped a respectable distance away and watched while she finished her prayer and crossed herself. She used a paper clip to attach a five-by-seven photo of Marissa to the coffee can, then stood and walked to the flagstones lining the river. She pulled what looked like a bracelet from her wrist, held it to her lips, then tossed it in the river.

"Tragic," I said loud enough for the young woman to hear.

She glanced over her shoulder, startled. Her eyes were wet with tears.

"Sorry to scare you. Was that a present for Marissa?" I pointed to the place in the river where whatever she'd thrown had sunk.

"Did you know her?" she asked, wiping her face with her fingertips. Her eyes lingered on my forehead scars. I remembered to smile.

"Unfortunately, no," I said, "but I know her mother."

Her eyes darted across the river to an older couple walking a toy poodle. She seemed nervous.

"I'm Nick Fischer," I said, smiling a little bigger.

"It's her birthday. First time we..." She paused to take a deep breath, still looking at the spot where she had tossed the bracelet. "First time we haven't been together." She turned her focus to me. "Beth Renfro," she said.

I recognized the name. She was the friend Marissa was with that night. I offered my hand. She didn't take it. I realized I was still holding the paper towel I was using to wipe my runny nose.

"Were you good friends with Marissa?" I asked.

"Yeah. We went to high school together. We kinda lost track when she went to college, but she always came home in the summer."

"Do you know what happened to her?"

"She drowned in the river," she said without hesitation, like she'd rehearsed the line.

"How do you know?"

"I was with her that night. We were drinking and dancing. It was a party night."

"Her mother said she didn't drink," I said.

Beth looked taken aback, like she wasn't expecting to be questioned. "Are you a cop?" She acted like she wanted to walk away.

"Just a friend of the family," I said, stifling another sneeze.

"There's a lot of things her mother didn't know."

"Like she was pregnant?" I asked. Beth hesitated, weighing her options for a response. When she didn't say anything, I added: "Did she have a boyfriend?"

"Not that I know of. She didn't talk about it. But, again, she'd been gone. Other than Facebook, we didn't really keep in touch."

"Did she dance with anybody in particular?"

"No." Her answers came quickly.

"Did she leave with anybody?"

"I told the police everything. No one saw her leave."

"What time did you notice she was gone?"

"Around midnight, I guess. We wanted to leave before the bars closed. When I looked around for Marissa, she was gone. The detective said they found her shoe here. It had a broken heel. She always liked high heels." She chewed on her bottom lip. She wasn't going to tell me anything more about Marissa.

"Thanks for your help."

She immediately turned and walked away. I blew my nose and watched Beth's ponytail dance from side to side as she broke into a jog.

I wondered why she had lied. I also wondered what present she had tossed into the river on Marissa's birthday. I stood for a long moment contemplating the place where I'd seen the object drop into the murky water. This time of year, with the late summer drought, the water was less than two feet deep, yet it was still too dirty to see the rocky, moss-covered bottom. In the winter the river was diverted so that certain portions could be drained for cleaning.

A man with a salt-and-pepper beard shuffled out of the shadows. He knelt on the flagstone edge of the River Walk and stared into the murky water. I thought he looked vaguely familiar, then I remembered the picture of the man in the newspaper clipping Mrs. Luna had shown me. He wore the same Army cap and camo jacket. I hadn't noticed him before; he must have been standing behind the bridge support waiting for Beth to leave.

Suddenly, the man stepped into the water and waded to the center of the river. The water came up to his knees. I knew what he was looking for. I watched him fish with both hands in the water. In a few moments he came up with a bracelet and smiled, exposing missing teeth.

"Hey!" I yelled at him. "Leave that alone."

He turned toward the opposite bank and sloshed toward the flagstones.

I jumped in the lukewarm water and splashed across toward him. "That's not yours," I said.

"The lady throwed it away," he mumbled when I caught up to him. "It's mine now."

I could see it was gold and consisted of three bands connected by a lopsided heart shape. I dug in my wallet for a twenty-dollar bill and held it out to the man. "Here," I said. "I'll trade you."

The man quickly snatched the money and handed over the bracelet. I climbed out of the river and examined it more closely. On the inside of the heart the initials M. L. were engraved.

The man climbed out of the water and hurried off, holding the twenty above his head.

"Hey," I called.

The man kept walking. He seemed afraid I would change my mind and take the money back. I took out another twenty and waved it in his direction.

"Wanna make another twenty," I said. That got his attention. The man swiftly made an about-face and waited for me to catch up. "Were you on the River Walk the day after the Fourth of July?" I asked him.

He scratched his salt-and-pepper whiskers with a wet hand. "Maybe," he said.

"There was a dead girl found in the water. Were you there?"

His eyes lit up. "Davy Crockett," he said.

"That's right. A kid dressed in a coonskin cap found her."

"No, it was Davy Crockett. I seen him. He shot her dead."

"Shot her? I thought she was already dead."

The man held out his hand for the twenty I was holding. I handed it over.

"He shot her with his flintlock," he shouted for emphasis.

"A toy gun?" I asked.

He flashed a toothless grin. "She looked like a raccoon."

I looked at him, waiting for him to explain. When he turned to go, I asked: "Why did she look like a raccoon?"

"Both eyes was black," he said. "She wearin' a mask."

I watched him shuffle away and wondered what he would spend his money on first. I also wondered why the autopsy I read hadn't mentioned the fracture to the base of Marissa's skull which would have accounted for two black eyes.

# CHAPTER ELEVEN

There was a ticket tucked under my washer blade when I got back to my pickup. Turns out the space was only free until eleven thirty a.m. I checked my watch. Eleven thirty-seven. The meter maid must have been waiting on the corner. Luckily, it was only the class C twenty-five-dollar variety. I tossed the ticket with the others in my glovebox. I would need that five grand Mrs. Luna had offered me just to keep parking in the city of San Antonio.

I cranked up the a/c and waited for my sneezing fit to subside. Then I took Commerce Street west and headed for Marcus Lopez's law office. My plan was to catch Sylvia on her lunch break and share the news that I was on a murder case. It was too soon to say it was murder, but I wasn't satisfied with Peterson's conclusion, and Marissa's friend was less than convincing.

Why would someone want Marissa Luna dead? The obvious answer seemed to have something to do with her being pregnant. The bracelet, if it was hers, might have come from the father. But would he give her an expensive bracelet and then kill her? Maybe it was a peace offering that she couldn't accept? How did it end up with Marissa's friend? Obviously, she didn't share it with the police. The question was, Why, and was she involved?

Traffic was heavy, and I waited through two lights on South San Saba Street watching a group of teenagers on electric scooters zip around pedestrians in Milam Park. When the light finally turned green, a woman in a white Range Rover cut me off making a U-turn. I honked, and she gave me the middle finger. The heat put everybody on edge.

I found a grocery store a few blocks from Sylvia's office building and made a quick stop to grab a little token of my affection and a package of antihistamine. She always said she didn't want me to spend money on flowers, but she never seemed to mind when I did. I bought the only bouquet of yellow tulips I could find. They weren't the freshest I'd ever seen, but yellow tulips were Sylvia's favorite and they came with a red vase. I found my miracle drug and got in line behind a guy who just remembered something else his wife wanted him to pick up. He wondered if I minded waiting while he went to look for it.

"Why should I mind?" I asked him, sneezing into my hand. "Shopping for half-dead tulips is the highlight of my day. Why not make it last?"

He gave me a nervous laugh and shuffled toward the canned goods aisle. He seemed to think I was joking. While Sylvia's tulips wilted a little more, and my nose ran a little harder, I remembered one of my dad's favorite Johnny Cash songs about a guy in Folsom Prison who killed a man in Reno just to watch him die. I wondered if he'd made up the lyrics while standing in a grocery store checkout line.

Marcus Lopez's law office was a four-story neo-Spanish colonial-style building, complete with a faux bell tower and a Spanish-tile courtyard featuring a koi pond in the center. Its west side location was surrounded by a vacant lot, abandoned businesses, and a car body shop. Behind the building stretched neglected tract houses with dirt front lawns enclosed in hurricane fencing. Marcus had grown up in one of those houses and had acquired most of a city block that he was preparing to demolish and turn into apartments provided he got approval from the city. Sylvia said he chose the location to remind him of his roots, but I knew he did it to show off to his old west side neighbors.

I parked behind the building and waited a few minutes for the wonder drug to take effect. When my sinuses started to clear, I found my way to the rear entrance. Every blank space was covered with election posters featuring Marcus Lopez's smiling face. I skipped the occupied elevator and took the stairs to the third floor, where Sylvia had her office.

Staring at the dozens of political signs plastered with Marcus's smug face reminded me of the storm cloud building over my love life. If he was elected, Sylvia would probably go to Austin to serve in his new cabinet. I understood. It was a career move. If she went, I would have to move to Austin with her or settle for seeing her only on weekends. Austin was only sixty miles north, but I was trying to build my own business in San Antonio. Her argument was that I could be a private eye anywhere, which wasn't necessarily true. I did have a contact in Lubbock from the Marine Corps and a few friends in Austin from my time as a deputy, but I liked San Antonio. Austin was fun if you were into hipster bands and liked watching the University of Texas play football along with a hundred thousand of your closest friends, but it was one of those college towns that went wild in the 1960s and never really grew up. The city slogan was *Keep Austin Weird.*

San Antonio had history. That was the other reason I'd moved here. Besides having enough people to support my new private investigations business, Texas history began at the Alamo. I understood the sacrifice now that my enlistment was over. When I looked at the Alamo building at night with its adobe bricks bathed in white light, I liked to think the heart of the state still beat and that its soul was still authentic. Maybe I was being naïve and the spirit had left long before my time, but I wasn't ready to give up hope on Texas or my relationship with Sylvia.

I caught a glimpse of my profile in the hallway mirror. I was operating on three hours' sleep. My post five o'clock shadow made me look like a Hollywood producer, but the new black T-shirt I wore was damp with sweat. The scars on my forehead had turned purple in the heat, and my nose and eyes were red from breathing African dust. How could she resist my charm and a bouquet of wilted tulips?

Luckily, her overprotective secretary was away from her desk, so I let myself in. Sylvia had a fine eye for decorating. Her office had rustic wood paneling accented with brightly colored paintings depicting blue bonnets, buttercups, and a variety of native Texas wildflowers. There was also a three-panel photo of her favorite yellow tulips. She looked up from her polished oak desk when I entered. I held up the flowers.

"I came to take you to lunch," I said, trying to sound cheerful. I set the flowers on her desk.

"I bet you picked those yourself," she teased, examining the less-than-stellar arrangement.

"I guess tulips are out of season."

"And you got all dressed up," she said, focusing on my dirty jeans still damp from wading the river.

"I can explain," I said. "I've been up since seven thirty, and my allergies are doing battle with the elements."

"The dust, isn't it? You should take an antihistamine," she said, flipping open a file on her desk. "I can't go to lunch," she said. "I've got a meeting in ten minutes. You should've called."

"I'm on a case," I said. No time to beat around the bush. I might as well come clean.

"What case?" she asked. I could hear the disappointment in her voice.

"If I'm gonna go back to school, I'll need money. My GI bill dried up," I told her, thinking on my feet. It was the best I could come up with. She thought about that for a moment. For once, I'd come up with an excuse she might actually buy.

"You have a paying customer?" she asked. "Please tell me it's not one of your lost causes." Her faith in me was overwhelming.

"She offered to pay my full retainer up front."

"Offered? You didn't take the money?"

"I told her I would look into it first and see if I could help her."

Sylvia shrugged. "What's the matter with you? You talked to her, didn't you?"

"Yeah," I said. I knew where she was going with this. It was a new tactic she was using to point out that my business acumen wasn't fully developed.

"And you spent all morning investigating her case?"

"How else am I gonna find out if I can help her?"

"How many times do I have to tell you those are billable hours?" She never used to talk like that when we were in law school. We had both volunteered for St. Mary's Center for Legal and Social Justice. Before I became disillusioned with the idea of becoming a lawyer, we had talked about joining the center full-time after graduation. Only a year of working for Marcus Lopez, and she was talking about billable hours. She checked her watch, reminding me I was on the clock. I thought maybe if I told her the details of the case, she would understand my interest.

"She was the young woman found by the kid dressed up like Davy Crockett. Happened this year on the fifth of July." I let her digest that information.

"I remember that." She stood up from her case file. I saw a flicker of the old Sylvia who enjoyed the challenge of a mystery.

"What can you tell me about this?" I showed her the bracelet.

"It's a bracelet," she deadpanned.

"Brilliant, Doctor Watson."

"It looks exactly like the one you never gave me." She giggled.

"It belonged to the deceased."

"Where did you get it?"

"I fished it out of the river this morning."

"While you were working for free. How do you know it's hers?"

"I ran into a friend of hers who was with her that night. I watched her toss it in the river underneath the bridge where the police said Marissa went into the water."

"Why would she do that?"

"Today was Marissa's birthday."

"You took an offering to the dead?"

"Actually, I saved it from a homeless guy. He saw her toss it in the river and was gonna make off with it. If it turns out not to be important, I'll throw it back. Marissa can wear it in the afterlife." I held up the bracelet so Sylvia could see the engraving. "It has her initials. M. L."

"Could be a coincidence. If I remember right, the police said it was an accident," she said, crossing to the large window that looked west over the vacant lots toward the distant rolling hills covered with cedar trees and new luxury homes that Sylvia couldn't wait to move into. "You read the article. She was drunk and fell in the river."

"She didn't drink."

"What did the friend say?"

"She lied about that too."

"How do you know?"

"I know when someone's lying. Besides, she was a nursing student with big plans for the future."

"Why would her friend lie? You think she's a suspect?" She tapped her teeth with a Cross fountain pen.

"Maybe they were in love with the same man," I said. "Marissa was pregnant."

Sylvia stopped tapping and turned to me. "Where's the boyfriend?" I saw a spark of excitement.

"Exactly. No one knows anything about him. She didn't tell her mom or, apparently, her best friend."

"What did the police say?" she asked.

"Peterson was the detective involved. He didn't even tell the mother. Said it didn't change anything. He checked out two old boyfriends, but neither matched the fetal DNA."

She turned from the window, her brown eyes focused, one hand on her shapely hip and the other holding her Cross pen pointed at me. "You think it was the boyfriend. And you think the bracelet will help you track him down." She paced a few steps back and forth in front of the window like she used to do while we were studying for tests together in law school. "She told the boyfriend about the baby. He buys her a bracelet and tells her to have an abortion. She says no because she's a strict Catholic, or at least her mother is, and he throws her in the river."

"That's what I was thinking," I said.

"If the bracelet's hers, of course." She tapped the pen on her white teeth. "Or," she continued, "she couldn't tell her Catholic mother or go through with an abortion. So she took her own life."

We looked at each other for a moment not speaking. I didn't know which was more tragic, Marissa being murdered by her boyfriend or the thought of her taking her own life because she thought she had no other options.

Sylvia whispered in my ear: "Don't take the case. The firm will hire you. We need investigators. The work is safe, and you'd have time to go back to school."

I wrapped my arms around her, enjoying the warmth of her body and the faint scent of her expensive perfume. She melted against me. I wanted to lock the door and make love to her for the rest of the afternoon.

"You don't have to worry about money." She ran her fingertips across my forehead and into my short-cropped hair.

I needed her. Wanted her. But I couldn't keep my mouth shut.

"You know I could never work for Marcus Lopez." The spell was broken.

She let go and walked back to her desk. "It wouldn't kill you to accept help from somebody. You act like it's a sin or something. Do you think Marcus got where he is without help? You don't always have to do everything on your own." It was the first time she'd compared me to her boss.

I followed her behind her desk, took her hand, hoping to recapture the moment before I left. I leaned in for a final kiss but was interrupted by a cold knock on the door.

Marcus strolled in with a smile on his face. He saw me holding Sylvia, and his smile quickly faded. He stood in the open door like he owned the place, which, of course, he did, but when he surveyed the room, he seemed to claim everything: the carpet, the walls, the double-pane windows, and Sylvia.

"Mr. Anker is in the conference room, Sylvia." He said it like he expected her to jump, which she did.

"I'm ready," she said, and quickly unfolded herself from my arms and picked up the file and a legal pad. She seemed too eager. I knew she wanted to impress this guy to make partner, but jumping when someone gave the command was not the Sylvia I knew.

Marcus's smile returned when Sylvia stepped toward him. It reminded me of the look he gave her at the convention center. "Mr. Fischer. I heard about your trouble last night. Too bad about Javier Sosa. Do the police have any leads?"

"Nothing that I know of. I'm sure they'll know more when they can talk to Sosa."

"You didn't hear? Javier died this morning."

I stared at him not quite understanding. I had talked to the intensive care nurse only a few hours ago. She had told me that his chances of recovery were good. I said nothing.

"Unfortunate," Marcus said. "And, I assume, not very good for your new business." Marcus's lighthearted smile vanished. Something harder and much colder took its place.

"You don't know what the hell you're talking about," I said.

"Nick, he didn't mean anything," Sylvia said.

My eyes were locked on Marcus. He didn't offer an apology. He didn't flinch or blink. I remembered what Danny Allison had said about him being dangerous. That's not why I let it go. I let it go because Sylvia aimed her big brown eyes at me.

"I was just leaving," I said. I kissed her on the cheek and headed for the door.

# CHAPTER TWELVE

Skeeter Davis lived with his mother in a newer, middle-class housing development in far-south San Antonio near Mission San Juan Capistrano. Ask a dozen tourists, and even a few locals, and they couldn't tell you that there were four other missions like the Alamo built by the Spanish during the 1700s, all within a twenty-mile radius of what is now downtown. Ask me as a teen, and I couldn't have cared less. I knew about the history because Grandpa never stopped talking about it, but it wasn't until I mustered out of the Marine Corps that I started paying attention. Studying history was part of my two-part rehabilitation—a recipe Grandpa cooked up that was equal parts work and study. He said history taught you that you're not the only poor son of a bitch suffering in the world, and work kept your mind off the problems that you did have. It was an ongoing process.

I called Skeeter and told him to meet me at Isabella's Mexican restaurant across the street from the mission. Since Sylvia had turned down my lunch offer, I was hungry and craving enchiladas. This was a business meeting. Skeeter was my only employee, we had two cases to solve, and I needed his expertise. Marcus Lopez was right—Sosa's death would hurt my reputation. San Antonio had a million and a half people, but it was a small town when it came to private investigators and security. This was worse than a bad Yelp review. It was the kind of thing that might have me searching for a more stable job unless I found the shooter.

Isabella's was painted bright orange and decorated with Christmas lights—the kind of place that reminded me how close San Antonio was to the Mexican border. I found a rusty chair on the concrete patio close to a large outdoor fan. The antihistamine had kicked in, and I was already feeling better despite the still-hazy sky. An older woman wearing a Spurs basketball T-shirt and jeans handed me a glass of ice water and a basket of tortilla chips. I recognized her as the owner and head chef, Isabella.

"*Buenas tardes*, Mr. Nick," she said.

"No help today?" I asked. She had twin teenaged daughters who usually worked the tables and an older son who helped cook.

"The twins went to college," she said, exasperated. "I don't know what I'm gonna do without them."

"You must be very proud," I said.

"I am, but I can't find help. No one wants to work anymore."

I ordered a Shiner Bock and a plate of beef enchiladas from the lunch-special menu on the chalkboard and a hamburger for Skeeter with iced tea. He had quit drinking after his accident, and he didn't like Mexican food. It was after one, but the place was doing big business on Saturday. Tejano music filled the parking lot. A group of young men in muddy boots and blue overalls fresh off an outdoor job were getting their weekend started with cold Corona longnecks.

I was on my second beer and still waiting for my food when I spotted Skeeter crossing the parking lot. The young workers turned to gawk when he stepped on the patio and made his way toward my table. He wasn't the kind of guy who could travel incognito. He stood six-foot-seven and weighed in at three hundred pounds, and his left arm from the elbow down was made of metal. He cut an imposing figure that sometimes worked to his advantage and sometimes, like when he was on trial for murder, worked against him. People had no trouble believing Skeeter could kill another man. He hadn't always been an introverted computer wizard. Before the auto accident that took his arm, he had completed a stellar career on the gridiron for the University of Texas and had just been drafted by the Washington Redskins. One night of wild partying put him on a different career track.

He pulled up a chair and placed his small black backpack on the table. It held his assortment of electronic gizmos that accompanied him everywhere. Sweat dripped down his forehead and soaked his T-shirt. The workers turned to each other, eyes wide, holding their hands out to indicate Skeeter's size and the prosthesis that extended from his elbow to a double metal hook for a hand.

"You always make a grand entrance," I said, smiling.

"You think they're watchin' me 'cause I'm extra-large, but they're really wondering if I'm stupid enough to sit next to a dude who looks like a psycho-killer."

"Psycho-killer?" I laughed.

"I swear, sometimes you look like you're ready to slice someone's ear off."

"Fair enough. Lot on my mind. Busy twenty-four hours," I said.

"You were in the neighborhood, you should have come to the house." He drank most of his tea in one gulp.

"You know what happens when your mother sees me. I didn't have time to spend the next three hours eating and listening to her." I didn't mind visiting his mother when I had a few hours to kill. Ever since I'd tracked down the guy who framed Skeeter for murder, I was the honored guest in the Davis household. Whenever I showed up, Skeeter's mother would drop whatever she was doing and start cooking. She usually started with something deep-fried, then moved on to cake and cookies. By the time she finished, most of Skeeter's extended family was seated around the small kitchen table listening to his mother tell his story again. She was the kind of woman I couldn't say no to, whether she was asking me to investigate her son's case or offering me another slice of my favorite German chocolate cake.

Skeeter drained the last of his iced tea. I took a moment to scan the parking lot. A black Ford Super Duty pickup had pulled in when I arrived and backed into the far corner of the lot near the street. It was still in the same position with the engine running. The windows were too dark to see into the cab, but no one had gotten out.

"You seem a little jumpy."

"Just being careful. Our client Javier Sosa took a bullet last night."

"Why didn't you call me?" he asked, alarmed.

"There was nothing you could have done. This morning, Sosa died," I said.

"Any suspects?"

"Yeah. Me. Detective Peterson's on the case. He and his partner are chasing their tails around and the FBI is sniffing their butts. He warned me to stay away."

"What're we gonna do?"

"What do you think? See what you can find out about Sosa's business relationship with Marcus and Patrick Allison," I said.

"You think they took a shot at Sosa?"

"I think both are capable. I wanna know which one had more to gain."

Isabella brought our food. While we ate, I brought Skeeter up to date on what I'd gotten from Detective Peterson about Marissa Luna. It didn't take much to convince him that Peterson had bungled the investigation. He had an even lower opinion of the good detective than I did, having been on the receiving end of his crime-fighting work. I also told him about finding the bracelet and the peculiar answers Marissa's friend gave me. When I finished the story and my enchiladas, I pushed my plate away and held up the bracelet.

"Now, put that massive brain of yours to work and tell me how we can use this to get to the boyfriend."

He plucked the bracelet from me using his double hook like a tweezer. "It's a Robert Byrd. The bands are gold. I'm going to say over three grand. Maybe four." He pulled an Apple iPad Pro from his backpack and touched the screen. Moments later he brought up the jeweler's catalog. "It's called a Mother's Love bangle." He whistled through his teeth while staring at the screen. "You say her friend threw this in the river?"

"That's right. She kissed it and tossed in."

"The gold version retails for thirty-six hundred. I've heard of burying treasure with the dead. Was Marissa a Mayan princess?"

"I doubt it. Can you trace who sold it?"

He held the heart design in the air. "Try talking to the Byrd factory store in Kerrville. They might have a record of the engraving. The Kerrville store is open today till six," he said, looking at the iPad screen.

I checked my watch. It was close to two. I had plenty of time to visit Grandpa before closing.

"Sylvia okay with this?" he asked. "She must have been pretty upset. You gettin' shot at and all."

"Your job's electronics, big guy." I raised my voice. As soon as I did, I knew I was being overly sensitive. Sylvia had always been a delicate issue between us. He would never say it out loud, but I knew he didn't like her.

Skeeter raised his plate-sized hand in a sign of surrender. "Enough said," he told me.

Isabella arrived and handed me the check. I gave her a twenty-dollar bill, which covered two lunch specials and a five-dollar tip. That and the homemade tortillas were why I kept coming back.

Skeeter followed me out to my pickup, put his giant hand on my shoulder. "The real reason I asked about Sylvia is I'm worried about you. You're going after two killers. A rich guy who killed his pregnant girlfriend and a professional shooter with a long-range rifle. You always told me never to go into a dangerous situation thinking about something or someone else, 'cause you're likely to get hurt."

We stood for a moment gazing at the brownish sky punctuated with the ever-present puffy cumulus clouds generated by moisture from the Gulf of Mexico. He was right. I was letting my personal life interfere with business.

"Duly noted," I said. "I'll check in with you tomorrow. By the way, how does your mother know Araceli Luna?"

"She don't. Mrs. Luna just showed up at the house a couple of days ago and started asking questions. You know how my mom is."

# CHAPTER THIRTEEN

Araceli Luna lived in the working-class neighborhood on the west side. I found her house behind a dirt yard that was surrounded by a chain-link fence. An angry Chihuahua guarded the porch. Before I could knock, Mrs. Luna opened the front door and got her attack Chihuahua under control.

"Mr. Fischer, come in," she said.

I hadn't called ahead, but she seemed to be waiting by the door for my arrival. I followed her inside and found myself in a shrine to her late daughter. Pictures of Marissa covered the walls of her tiny front room. Baby pictures started at the door and went counterclockwise around the room depicting every stage of growth through college in a patchwork collage. Sadly, the growth stopped at college. Those final smiling pictures showed a Marissa full of life and expectations.

Mrs. Luna offered me lemonade, which I gratefully accepted. Then she left me in the shrine room while she disappeared down a hallway. I knew what it was like to lose someone close and not know how they died. My father was killed when I was sixteen years old. He died serving the community, doing his duty. He had volunteered to put himself in danger and accepted the consequences.

He was the elected sheriff, paid to confront the criminals who killed him.

For Mrs. Luna it was different. Her daughter wasn't a volunteer. Marissa wasn't paid to protect and serve. She was a sweet innocent flower cut down before her life could bloom. Mrs. Luna had lost a daughter and a grandchild, and no one could tell her why. The police had told her it was a tragic accident brought on by too much alcohol. I wanted to find the truth.

I could hear her filling glasses with ice in the kitchen while I examined the photos of Marissa. The window-unit air conditioner provided a constant mechanical hum and made the ancient wooden floors vibrate. The last photo was stamped with the date July 4, the day she died. Marissa wasn't wearing a bracelet. If someone had given her an expensive bracelet, she would have been wearing it. That meant someone had given it to her after the picture was taken.

"I'm sorry. I had to make fresh lemonade. My daughter and her friends drank the pitcher from this morning." Mrs. Luna handed me a sweaty glass.

"When was that picture taken?" I asked, pointing the Fourth of July picture.

She didn't have to think to answer. "At six o'clock. Her friend Beth came to pick her up. She took the picture." Her lip quivered. "Beth had a print made and gave it to me for her birthday."

"You saw Beth today?" I asked.

"This morning."

"Did she say anything about this?" I took out the bracelet and showed it to Mrs. Luna.

She took it and examined it. "Is it real gold?"

"I think so. Look at the engraving," I said, pointing to the letters under the heart shape.

"Where did you get it?" she asked.

"Her friend Beth had it. I saw her today on the River Walk."

"I've never seen it before. Marissa would have shown it to me." She handed me the bracelet, and I sat down on an orange threadbare couch that must have been in style before I was born. Mrs. Luna sat in the matching chair. She folded her hands in her lap and looked at me with anticipation.

"Did you know Marissa was pregnant?" I waited for the full meaning to sink in.

She slowly dissolved into tears. I got up and found a box of tissues and brought them to her. She blew her nose. I waited a full five minutes for her shoulders to stop shaking. She would have made a wonderful grandmother.

"I spoke with detective Peterson. He withheld the information. He said it didn't change the case and he didn't want to… well, to see you like this."

She took a deep breath and blew her nose again. "Thank you for telling me," she said. "Now you see, the case is even more important."

"You had no idea? She never told you?"

She shook her head. "No, she didn't."

"I believe Marissa's death was no accident," I told her. "That doesn't necessarily mean that she was murdered. There is another possibility."

Mrs. Luna understood immediately what I meant. Her nostrils flared. "She didn't take her own life. Not my Marissa. No." She was emphatic. Her resistance to the idea that her daughter would commit suicide was evident, but I needed her to convince me.

"Getting pregnant without a husband and having to face you and your… family creates a lot of pressure," I said.

"She always knew I was here for her no matter what happened. We were very close. She was a happy child. The night she… the night she was murdered, she kissed me goodbye and said, 'Don't wait up, Mama.'"

"But why didn't she tell you about the pregnancy?"

She looked at her hands, trying to justify this to herself. "She came home from Lubbock the last week of June. After a summer class. The first session. It was an English class she said she needed to get out of the way before her senior year. She spent the mornings sleeping. Said she needed the rest..." Her voice trailed off. "Now I know why," she said. "In the evenings, when it was cool, she went running along the River Walk."

Marissa didn't kiss her mother goodbye because she wanted to go commit suicide on the San Antonio River Walk. She wasn't making plans to cut short her senior year. I knew from experience that people didn't subject themselves to exercise when they're too depressed to go on living. When I came home from my final deployment—scarred inside and out—the last thing I wanted to do was go for a jog. In fact, the only time I went out was when I ran out of Jack Daniels. I put on thirty pounds, grew a full beard, and was angry at the world. Moving back in with Grandpa was the only thing that saved me from going off the deep end.

Maybe Marissa had made a decision about the baby that the father didn't go along with. I doubted it was an answer that her Catholic mother would condone. These were all questions detective Peterson didn't ask and didn't have answers to. Marissa had a secret that she took to her grave.

Mrs. Luna took a deep breath. She used a tissue to wipe the tears from her face. She looked at me. Waiting.

"Mrs. Luna, I'll take the case."

The tension left her neck and shoulders. She smiled for the first time since we'd met. "Then you believe me?" she asked, letting out a sigh of relief. "Mrs. Davis was right. You are a saint."

"I can't work miracles, but I will do everything in my power to find out what happened to your daughter."

She got up and lit a Saint Jude candle on the mantel. "Mrs.

Davis's mother called you the Saint Jude of detectives. Saint Jude is the patron saint of lost causes," she said. "I will keep this candle lit and pray for you every day."

"Thank you, Mrs. Luna."

She handed me the envelope full of cash.

I didn't believe in saints, but I took any help I could get. "One last question," I said. "Who gave you Mrs. Davis's name?"

She looked at me and chewed her bottom lip, as if deciding whether to tell me or not. After a few moments she took her Bible from the mantel. Inside there was a newspaper clipping. She handed it to me. I read the familiar headline: Ex-UT Football Player Walks Free.

"Where did you get this?" I asked.

"Someone left it in my mailbox."

# CHAPTER FOURTEEN

THE FACTORY HEADQUARTERS FOR THE Robert Byrd jewelry store was located about sixty-five miles northwest of San Antonio in Kerrville, Texas. I wanted to see if I could track down a buyer for the bracelet. I also wanted to visit Grandpa to pick his brain about Patrick Allison. I'd grown up with stories about the family feud between the Allisons and the Fischers, but Grandpa also kept track of Patrick's recent business because it had an impact on his property. An Allison-controlled company was building a gas pipeline across his land.

I got off the interstate at Welfare, a ghost town settled by German immigrants that reached a peak population of two hundred seventy-five in the 1890s before a boll weevil infestation put an end to local agriculture and wild growth. The countryside was dotted with newer homes and trailer houses occupied by retirees or folks escaping the busy city for one reason or another.

I unrolled the window and let Sam get some fresh air. I had brought him along because he was good company and riding in my pickup was one of his favorite things to do. Number one, of course, was duck hunting. He was bred to be in the water searching for birds. But if he couldn't hunt, he loved hanging his bulky head out the passenger window.

All roads west of San Antonio snaked through the geographical region known as the Texas Hill Country that stretched west from the Balcones Fault, which roughly followed I-35 through Austin and San Antonio. It was a jumbled collection of limestone and granite hills covered with cedar and live oak trees with an occasional flat space for farming. When the first Fischer, along with a boatload of other German immigrants, settled the area in the late 1840s, it was a dangerous frontier between western civilization and native culture dominated by the Kiowa and Comanches. That confrontation lasted longer and was more contentious here than anywhere else in the country and left an indelible impression on the settlers who bore the brunt of the fight and their descedants.

I turned off on the Grape Creek road and noticed that a familiar ranch house that once stood on the corner had been torn down to make way for a new construction. The old homesteads like Grandpa's were getting harder to find unless you knew where to look. The narrow road was paved now, like more and more of the backroads, to accommodate tourists driving sedans while searching for that authentic rural-Texas experience and staying at one of the many new bed and breakfasts. I slowed down behind a herd of brightly colored bicyclists. It was a group of twenty or more all in matching orange-and-black stretch outfits.

There was no room to pass, so I followed the bikers at a crawl until I got to Grandpa's road. It was one of the few left unpaved. In the four miles to his gate, three new houses and a double-wide trailer had been installed since Christmas. The new double-wide already had a pickup on blocks in the yard alongside a plastic, toddler swing set and a stack of used tires. There was a large plywood sign painted yellow and green with the smiling face of a cartoon llama inside the neighbor's pasture advertising a petting zoo.

A neat row of limestone rocks marked the entrance to the ranch. Every winter since I could walk, I had helped Grandpa replace the stones that the weather, animals, or gravity had forced to the ground. I could count on Grandpa to quote his favorite poet while we worked. "Something there is that doesn't love a wall," he'd recite. I agreed. I was one of them. Repairing a rock fence was Grandpa's way of keeping me busy and out of trouble. Work was his answer for everything. It was a pioneer trait that used to be evident on every neat and tidy farm in the county.

When I opened the door, Sam leaped over my lap. He knew that at the end of the hundred-yard driveway was a pond fed by cool spring water. I heard the distinct hum of a Cessna engine. The blue-tipped wings cleared the trees and buzzed close enough to the ground for me to see the slightly crooked smile on Grandpa's face. He was probably laughing because he knew I was going to tell him he was too old to be flying this low. Nothing scared him, and no one was going to tell him how or when to fly. Still, it didn't keep me from reminding him that I'd like to keep him around for another twenty years.

I turned off the a/c and drove with the windows down breathing in the familiar mixture of cedar, fresh-cut hay, and late summer buttercup flowers. The African dust seemed to have stopped at the Balcones Fault line.

Sam ignored me when I circled the pond, his body submerged up to his neck. I drove kicking up a white cloud of caliche dust, passed the tidy limestone-block house and barn built before the Civil War, and crossed the creek before climbing the hill to a level section of land Grandpa used as a runway. I stopped at the small Quonset hut and let the dust settle around me. The field was five hundred yards long and half as wide. Landing and taking off was tricky because of the cedar trees on one end and the abrupt limestone cliff on the other. When the conditions were right, Grandpa only used half of it just to prove he could.

Today, the conditions were right. He swooped over the limestone cliff and touched down like he was practicing carrier landings in the Indian Ocean. He tipped his gray sweat-stained cowboy hat at me when the aircraft coasted to a stop outside the rusty, half-moon building. He didn't wear a rattlesnake-skin hatband or trim his mustache to look like Charles Goodnight. He didn't need to. He climbed down, taking more time than he used to. He still favored the knee he had replaced last year and seemed to be carrying a few extra pounds on his six-foot-two-inch frame, but even though he was over eighty he had no intention of slowing down. He wore a khaki work shirt and Wrangler jeans, the same uniform he'd worn ever since I was old enough to remember. He had a white Cinch shirt with pearl snaps, but it was reserved for church and Oktoberfest.

"Nice landing," I said.

"Saves tires," he said, straight-faced. He was modest to a fault, detested a showoff, and would never consider drawing attention to himself.

We shook hands. His grip was still strong, and his palms were still heavily calloused from years of outdoor work. I could remember only two occasions that he'd ever greeted me with more than a handshake. One was at my dad's funeral when he put his calloused hand on my shoulder. I was sixteen. The other was four years later at Grandma's funeral. He did the same thing. That touch was the most emotion I'd ever seen him display.

"You keepin' your nose clean?" he asked. His voice was raspy from years of smoking cigars and breathing Hill Country dust.

"I stay busy," I said.

"Work is good," he reminded me. He had been reminding me of the virtue of work my whole life. We got in my pickup and headed to the house.

"One of these days, I'm gonna peel you off a mountaintop and there won't be enough left to bury. The neighbor will call me after he sees a puff of smoke," I said.

"The neighbor wouldn't bother. That's why I'm up in the air—chasing his damned llamas from my hay. He called the game warden on me last week for shootin' at one of his miniature horses."

"Why'd you do that?" I asked.

"To scare it from my field. He opened a petting zoo for kids. More traffic up and down my road. They come in my gate asking to take pictures. I've got no time for nonsense. That honyock comes here from Dallas and somehow thinks he's native."

We traveled in silence for five minutes. Neither one of us felt the need to fill in the gaps in conversation. My dad had been the same way. We could go for days without speaking. I never knew that was unusual until Sylvia pointed it out on her first visit to the ranch. She couldn't understand how three people could sit in a room without speaking. Silence drove her crazy.

"Get any rain?" I asked. To a farmer or rancher, speculation about the weather was always a staple of conversation.

"Dry as a bone." He pointed to the dead, ankle-high grass lining the road as proof. "I'll need to buy hay this year, I think."

Sam ran up the road to greet us, his coat covered with mud. I opened the door for him to jump into the back seat. He immediately put his paws on Grandpa's shoulder and began licking him in the face. Labradors had no qualms about showing affection.

"Ah, teach this dog some manners," Grandpa growled. He gave him a playful pat on the head, and Sam happily settled down into the back seat. I noticed Grandpa studying my profile. When I slowed to cross the creek, he asked: "Your fancy girlfriend don't come?"

"Tied up at work," I said. Sylvia was a little too refined for Grandpa's taste, and he never missed a chance to remind me without overdoing it. He was always charming to her when she came with me, but I don't think he ever referred to her by her name. Last Christmas he told me she reminded him of my mother. I thought that was a compliment at first. He waited for me to say more.

When I didn't, he didn't press me on our relationship. He changed the subject.

"I read about that business with the sniper," he said.

I coasted the last fifty yards to the barn. I knew what he meant. He was asking if I was okay, physically and mentally. He didn't have to spell it out. Mentioning the event was enough. He was the main reason I was able to get my shit together when I got out of the Marine Corps. I spent six months trying to drown my guilt in booze. One night after a weeklong bender, I drove out to see him. He listened to me cry in my beer until I fell asleep on the porch. The next morning my keys were gone and my pickup was in the barn. He let me mope around and sober up for about a day and a half, then he put me to work rebuilding fences. It's hard to feel guilty about being the only one of your platoon brothers to come home alive when every muscle in your body aches from digging post holes in the hot sun.

"Fence needs work," he said. I smiled. We both knew what he meant.

"I'm good," I said and parked in the shade of the barn near the deer-high fence surrounding his vegetable garden. "My client met with Patrick Allison the night he was shot. He introduced me to him and his grandson. Allison said he knew you. Offered me a job."

Grandpa's eyes narrowed, and the lines around his mouth deepened into canyons. I listened to a mockingbird run through his repertoire of songs and felt the afternoon heat cast a blanket over the Fischer homestead. Sam licked the side of my face, anxious to take another dip in the spring water. Grandpa finally cleared his throat. Sam and I waited for him to speak.

"You're going to work for Patrick Allison?" he asked, as if I'd just joined a local Al-Qaeda affiliate.

"I didn't take the job. I wanna find out if Patrick could be mixed up with the Sosa shooting."

"He ain't made any friends in this county. Allison is behind a new gas pipeline that's gonna to cut right through my pasture."

I drove to the front gate so Grandpa could point out the swath of property that the proposed pipeline would take.

"They're going to bury a forty-two-inch pipe here and take a hundred feet of easement. And there's nothing anyone can do about it because of eminent domain."

"They're gonna bury the pipe. What difference does it make?"

Grandpa didn't like my attitude. "It's the goddamned principle of the thing," he said.

I changed the subject. "Do you know where Allison's oil lease is in Edwards County?" I asked. I remembered what Sosa had said about Allison and Marcus Lopez being partners.

# CHAPTER FIFTEEN

GRANDPA PULLED A CHURCHILL CIGAR from his shirt pocket, clipped the end, and lit it up. "I wouldn't be surprised if Patrick was up to no good."

I would probably never get the cigar smell out of the upholstery. The price I had to pay for a little information and a visit with Grandpa. He grew up in a time when people didn't care about secondhand smoke. We had driven southwest of Gillespie County toward Mexico and the edge of the Hill Country. The air was dryer and the vegetation limited to cactus and shrubs. Grandpa pointed out a tiny dot on the horizon that he said was an oil derrick. There was nothing wrong with his eyes.

"Take the next gravel road," he said, then tapped his cigar ash into the unused ashtray.

"How'd the Allisons and the Fischers end up on opposite sides," I asked. I had heard the story a dozen times, but I knew Grandpa wouldn't calm down until he told it again, from the beginning.

"In 1848 the Fischers were newcomers from Prussia, and men like Allison didn't trust us. We spoke German and were intellectuals. Some were Catholic. Allison didn't like our politics or religion.

He belonged to a group called The American Party—second and third generation settlers. We were all immigrants, but they got here before us, so they figured they had a prior claim. They used to meet in secret and tried to control elections all over the state. New immigrants were not welcome." He paused to relight his cigar.

"The Civil War added fuel to the fire. The Fischer family and the majority of Gillespie County did not vote to secede from the Union. Our own revolution in the old country had failed to reform the government, and we came here to be free. Allison, and the majority of Texas, saw it differently. They were loyal to the state." He paused to blow a cloud of cigar smoke at a fly that had found its way into the cab.

"What happened during the war?" I asked.

"Allison joined the Confederate Army. He was with that group who chased down the German Unionists trying to make it to Mexico."

"Allison was part of the Battle of the Nueces?" I asked.

Grandpa nodded solemnly. I knew the story of the controversial battle that some called a massacre and some called a war skirmish. The story I read said that both sides were armed and both sides had casualties. The pro-Union Germans traveled south, attempting to escape into Mexico and from there north to join the Unionist forces. A group of Confederate soldiers caught up to them camped out on the bank of the Nueces River. The Germans fought it out and lost. Nineteen of the sixty-plus group were killed and nine wounded. Two of the Confederates were killed and eighteen wounded, including their leader, Lt. C.D. McRae. The massacre part came after the fight when the Confederate soldiers shot the nine wounded they held captive. The tragedy continued when the bodies of the dead were left on the riverbank until after the war when their families gathered their remains and interred them in Comfort, Texas. In 1866 the impressive Treue der Union, a chalk-white, native limestone monument, was dedicated to those who died.

"But our family wasn't with the Unionists," I said.

"The Fischers decided to stay home and defend their land. The Kiowas and the Comanches didn't stop raiding during the war, and the Confederate soldiers harassed all the Germans that held Union sympathies. We planned to join the North if the Union forces invaded Central Texas. Allison took advantage of the turmoil. By the end of the war he had acquired more land and cattle than any bill of sale could account for." He blew another cloud of smoke at the fly and shooed it out the window.

The oil derrick grew in size as we approached. Grandpa cleared his throat and spit out the window. He was coming to the part of the story he liked the best.

"Your great-great-great-granddad, Johann Fischer, caught Allison's son-in-law, Roland McCarthy, with a string of his horses. They were tied to the hitching post in front of Doebbler's Inn all wearing the Fischer brand. Johann waited until Roland came out on the steps and confronted him in front of six witnesses. Roland said he found the horses on Grape Creek. Johann called him a liar. Roland's hand went for his pistol. Johann shot him with his double-barrel shotgun." When he finished, he pointed his cigar at my chest and looked me square in the eyes. "That was last time a Fischer talked to a member of the Allison family."

I pulled to the side of the gravel road. When the dust settled, I opened my window to let the cigar smoke out. "I didn't know I was supposed to be holding a grudge," I said.

"Patrick was made in the mold of his ancestor, just as you are. Just as we all are."

I liked to think people made a choice to act good or evil, but Grandpa believed who you were and how you acted had much more to do with where you came from and how you were raised. I looked at my watch. I still had two hours before the jewelry store closed. I didn't know exactly what I was looking for at Allison's drilling rig, but if I could get anywhere close, I would take a look around.

An oil field water truck pulled through the gate, which explained why it wasn't locked. I followed the truck toward the oil rig.

# CHAPTER SIXTEEN

THE ENTRANCE TO THE DRILLING area was protected by a single guard wearing an orange hard hat and black uniform. He emerged from a portable building, shielding his eyes against the sun and the dust. He waved the water truck through and held his hand up for us to stop. He was a big man in his early thirties with five days' growth of beard. Stacks of drill pipe, machinery, and a dozen metal storage containers were scattered over a muddy ten-acre area, along with two single-wide trailers for the staff and a long row of dirt-encrusted four-wheel-drive pickups.

"What is it you're looking for out here?" Grandpa asked me.

"I don't know exactly. Spare parts from Mexico maybe."

"Usually, it's Texas equipment that ends up down there. That's why the big man in a hard hat is wearing a sidearm," Grandpa commented. I noticed the what looked like a Glock 9mm on the guard's utility belt. He meant business.

"If I can, I'll take a look in one of those metal containers," I said and unrolled my window. Sam stuck his head out, anxious to take a break after the long drive.

"Can I help you, sir?" the guard shouted above the constant roar of the drilling rig. He stood five feet from the door with his hands resting on his wide hips. "What's business vit Allison Oil?" His accent was distinctly German, as if he'd wandered out to South Texas from a Hamburg factory.

Grandpa leaned toward my open window. "*Wo kommen Sie her?*" Grandpa had grown up speaking German, along with most of his generation in Gillespie County. My father had learned it. By the time I came along, there weren't enough kids my age who were interested.

"*Ein Mitdeutscher?*" The guard's eyes lit up like he'd just found a long-lost relative. Seeing a Labrador and an old man seemed to put him at ease.

Grandpa nudged my knee and got out of the pickup. The guard immediately joined him near the bumper. They were shouting at each other in German over the noise. My knowledge of the language was limited to hello and goodbye, and a few German table prayers and hymns we sang in church. After the initial greeting I was lost. Grandpa said something about water, and the guard gestured toward the nearest trailer. The guard glanced in my direction. Grandpa put a hand on his shoulder and shook his head. I gathered he said something about me not going anywhere.

"I'll wait here," I called to them, but they couldn't hear me. I knew Grandpa was happy as a clam getting to speak German. His small group of Texas-German speakers was down to just a handful, and they only got together once a month. All were descendants of the original German settlers.

When they disappeared into the trailer, I let Sam out and we headed for the nearest container. A half dozen other workers in hard hats were busy on the rig itself, but no one within a hundred feet of my pickup. Once I got to the row of containers, I was out of sight. Sam made a beeline for the nearest mudhole, wasting no time cooling himself down in the muddy overflow from a tanker truck. I didn't have time to pull him out. He would need a bath later. I tried the handle on the container and found it open. It was the kind loaded onto to semitrailers and trucked to the site. It was stuffed with motors, gears, couplings, hoses and mechanical parts I'd never seen in action. Working in the oil field was one of the few jobs I hadn't done. I recognized the PEMEX red-and-green logo with the eagle head. Sosa and Patrick Allison were definitely in business together.

"*Halt dich munter*," Grandpa shouted.

I pretended to zip up my fly as I stepped around the front of the container and saw the guard and Grandpa standing by my pickup. The German guard shot me a suspicious look, but Sam immediately rushed to him and rubbed his muddy self on his legs. It was just the distraction I needed to get safely back into my pickup.

"*Halt dich munter*," the guard repeated and let out a belly-shaking laugh. It was a salutation I'd heard Grandpa use all my life. According to him, it meant *keep your chin up*. The native German had probably never heard it before but seemed to understand.

When I got Sam and Grandpa back into the pickup, we took off.

"What'd the square-head have to say?" I asked.

"He's fresh off the boat. Looking for a Texan wife. I told him to try San Antonio."

"Good advice."

"What did you find?" he asked when I'd gotten back to the paved road.

"I found PEMEX equipment. The containers are full of it."

"Hell, the Mexican oil company has gas stations in Texas now," Grandpa said.

"Sosa told me his deal with Allison fell through because of Marcus Lopez."

"That's funny," he said.

"What?"

"The German said he worked for Marcus Lopez. Marcus Lopez took over the drilling operation in the middle of July."

# CHAPTER SEVENTEEN

THE ROBERT BYRD FACTORY STORE was a collection of single-story limestone-block buildings located near the interstate in Kerrville, a medium-sized Hill Country town which supported a university and an annual folk music festival that drew musicians from around the country. I parked under a shade tree near the showroom. The heat from five to six in the afternoon could be lethal in the first week of September, and Sam would have to wait in the pickup. The parking lot was empty as I'd hoped. I was going to have to get creative to find out any info about the bracelet, and I didn't want interference from other customers. I thought I had a good cover story until Sam spotted a flock of semi-domestic ducks swimming in a small man-made pond on the parklike grounds.

I had dropped Grandpa off so he could work on his airplane. Something to do with the hydraulic line. He had given me a warning about Patrick Allison, but I had already been on my guard. The interesting information was that Marcus Lopez had taken over operation of Allison's oil rig in July. I wondered what had prompted the change of ownership.

Sam had enough driving for one day and immediately jumped

out when he saw the pond and the ducks. By the time I got him back in the pickup, it was fifteen minutes till closing time, we were both covered with mud, and the ducks were in the next county.

I walked into the store tracking pond scum and dripping sweat. I pretended to check out the half dozen glass display cases featuring handcrafted silver earrings, necklaces, and bracelets. I wasn't a connoisseur, but Sylvia raved about the designs. I studied a young female clerk who was busy polishing the countertops and making ready for the end of the day. When she didn't look up, I cleared my throat and plunged into my cover story.

"Not too busy today," I said, trying to establish a rapport.

The name on her shirt read Tiff. She glanced at the clock on the wall, trying to decide if I was worth the maximum sales pitch and the commission that came with it or if she should continue her cleaning duties and let me fend for myself. She no doubt had a boyfriend to meet or homework to do.

"I know what you're thinking, Tiff," I said, trying to sound charming. "You think I'm on the hunt for a last-minute gift for my wife or girlfriend. Am I right?"

She stopped cleaning and came over to me. She looked to be in her early twenties, probably a student working her way through the local university. She had rodeo-queen good looks and was dressed casual western, with a thick blond braid reaching the top of her sequined jeans.

"Excuse me," she said. "The rest of the crew..." She paused midsentence. Her eyes lingered on my forehead. I could see that look of fear in her eyes, as if she expected me to pull a pistol and rob the place.

"Don't worry, I'm friendly." I offered what I hoped was a disarming smile. "I'm sorry about the mud," I said, pointing at the splashes on my jeans. "My Labrador found your pond."

Her eyes shifted to my smile. "Mine does that all the time," she said. "Where is he?"

I pointed out the door. Sam had found the driver's seat and was keeping a sharp eye out the window for returning ducks.

"He's adorable," she said. Sam had won her heart and eased her fears.

"I'm in a real jam," I said, and showed her the bracelet. "Do you recognize this?"

"It's ours. A Mother's Love bangle." She walked to a display case and showed me two identical bracelets but made of silver. "Yours is gold. Most of the ones we sell are silver. It's our specialty."

"Could you tell me where it was sold?" I handed it to her so she could take a closer look.

She examined the engraving. "I can tell you this was a special order."

"This is gonna sound crazy. And I'm totally embarrassed. My wife had a baby shower in July. July fifth. Now, the baby's here and everything's fine. But here's the thing… my wife is trying to send thank-you cards to everyone and I… Well, I tossed all the cards."

Tiff looked at me like I'd just fallen off a turnip truck. She was adding the mud and the pickup with the Labrador to my description of dumping the cards and coming up with every dumb cowboy she ever dated. I had gotten the story from Rocky, my redneck high school buddy. It was his explanation for why his wife left him, but I suspected it was only one of many problems she had with his behavior.

Tiff took an involuntary glance at Sam through the glass door. I knew she was almost convinced I was telling the truth.

"If you can't do it, you can't do it. I told my wife it's just a bracelet. She can send out a generic thank-you note to everybody who came and call it good." I acted like I was going to walk out and grabbed the bracelet from the countertop like it was made of plastic.

"That bracelet cost thirty-eight hundred to be exact," she said, sounding slightly hostile. She was a sister-in-arms with my imaginary wife. "Not including the engraving."

"Wow, I never would have guessed."

She raised her left eyebrow like I was a country bumpkin who had a lot to learn. "What were you thinking, throwing out the cards?" She suddenly sounded twenty years older. Her voice shifted from rodeo queen to ranch momma, all apprehension gone.

"I thought I was being helpful. It was a big party. Everything was a mess." I tossed a hundred-dollar bill on the counter. "I'd like to buy her another bracelet too. Something to smooth things over."

She raised her eyebrow again. I'd seen that look before too—the look that said, *you cheap bastard*. I pulled two more hundreds out of my pocket, part of Sosa's final tip. Ranch Momma was making me feel guilty for a social faux pas I'd invented.

"I think that's a good idea," she said, after she saw all three bills were the same denomination. "I can imagine your wife's worried sick about this. I know just what she'd want." She walked toward the front door. "I'll check the sales records from the first week of July," she said. "Let me lock the front door first. The guard will check it at six and come in if it's open." She flipped the deadbolt on the front door, and I followed her into the back office. While she booted up the computer records, I glanced at the photos on the wall. One by the back window caught my eye, a picture of a younger Patrick Allison standing by a man near the same age at some sort of ground-breaking ceremony. The inscription below read, "Boys and Girls Camp Number One."

"Is that Robert Byrd next to Mr. Allison?" I said, pointing to the picture.

She didn't have to look up from the computer records to answer. "Yes," she said. "Mr. Allison and the Byrd family have been partners in a charitable foundation for years."

"Our families have known each other for a long time. Used to be neighbors way back in the day," I told her.

"Really?" she said, not believing a word.

I studied the picture. Allison didn't look like the murderous cutthroat Grandpa described, nor did he act like one when we had met at the fundraiser. But I wasn't naïve enough to believe in appearances. A smile and a charity donation didn't preclude a person from being a cold-blooded killer.

"Here," she said. "On July second we did an engraving on a gold Mother's Love bangle."

"So, you sold it here?"

"No, it was a special order for the La Cantera Parkway store off I-10 in San Antonio."

"Who bought it?"

"You'd have to check with the store."

"Can you call them?"

"I really shouldn't be doing this, you know?"

"Ya gotta help me out. I've been sleeping in the baby's room for three weeks. On top of the nine months before that. I'm goin' crazy, if ya know what I mean."

Tiff's cheeks turned red, and she stifled a smile. "Okay," she said and picked up the phone. She called whoever answered by her first name and explained some of my phony story. Something the clerk said made Tiff laugh. I'm sure it was at my expense. I knew I was letting Rocky and the brotherhood of country boys down, but what the hell. I was on the job.

While Tiff talked, I studied the bracelets in the three-hundred-dollar range by the register. As long as it fit my cover story, I might as well pick out something for Sylvia and see if it would have a better effect than the over-the-hill yellow tulips. I glanced at the engagement rings in the next case. Six months ago, I had been ready to take the plunge. She didn't like my leaving law school, but my private investigations business had started to pick up. Sylvia had taken me to meet her parents, and I had taken her to meet Grandpa. Then the summer slump hit. Now, I was just hoping to save our relationship. Just when I'd made my choice of a silver infinity design, Tiff came out of the back room with a big surprised smile.

"You weren't kidding about knowing Mr. Allison," she said.

I didn't say anything. I hadn't told her a lie, but it was a complicated relationship.

"That bracelet was sold to Danny Allison."

I thought maybe I had heard her wrong. After spending an hour listening to Grandpa talk about the history of the Allison clan, maybe my mind was playing tricks on my hearing.

"Allison?" I asked.

"Yep, Danny Allison. He bought it and had it engraved."

"Thanks for all your help," I said. I stopped myself at the door and remembered the infinity bracelet I picked out for Sylvia. I had almost walked out without paying.

Tiff rang up the sale, and I hurried out to find Sam as anxious to get going as I was.

# CHAPTER EIGHTEEN

PULSING MUSIC VIBRATED THE METAL no parking sign outside the front door to the dance club. I was waiting in line behind a trendy group of partygoers that were dressed like extras in a *Mad Max* movie. I checked the sign to make sure I wasn't at some midnight audition for part four or five or whatever the series was up to these days. It seemed an unlikely venue for a trendy night club. The owners had taken a turn-of-the-century brick structure built by German immigrants, with elaborate white-stone arches over the windows and doors, and added stainless steel and graffiti highlights to give it a modern twist. The security guard wore black leather armbands with metal studs and a matching dog collar. When he checked my ID, I told him I was looking for Mel Gibson. He rolled his eyes.

I had dropped Sam off, changed out of my pond-scum clothes, and decided to visit the place where Marissa was last seen alive. Finding Danny Allison's name was the first solid lead I'd gotten, and I wanted to move on it quickly. If I wanted Detective Peterson to reopen the case, I would need more than just a name and a bracelet.

Inside, the walls of the renovated nineteenth-century building were painted black and overlaid with green and purple glow-in-the-dark graffiti—more of a reflection of modern Germany. There were pieces of chain-link fence lining the dance floor and blocks of concrete used for tables. It had a post-apocalyptic feel. The decorator must have been the same person in charge of the artwork displayed in front of the new public safety building.

When my eyes adjusted to the laser light show, I didn't see anyone doing anything that remotely resembled the dancing I knew. I wasn't a big fan, but my grandma had insisted I learn the two-step and the polka, which required partners to hold each other and attempt to step in time to the music. It required at least a passing knowledge of balance and the rudiments of coordination. The only touching I could see on this dance floor was forced contact because of the limited space. Conversation was out of the question. It was only eleven thirty. The party was just getting started, but the throbbing music and the lights were already giving me a headache.

I searched the ceiling for surveillance cameras, found two on the bar and four on the dance floor, then looked for the manager. A bouncer stood guard near the office. He looked in his late twenties with a serious steroid addiction. Whatever exposed skin I could see was covered with tats like an NBA player. I had one tattoo I'd gotten on my eighteenth birthday. It was a small Chinese character representing family. It was an act of rebellion because Grandpa insisted that I not get a tattoo, so naturally, I had to get one. He didn't say anything when he saw it. He just shook his head. Had he raised hell with me, I probably would have ended up like the bouncer.

I approached Muscle Man and held up my private eye credentials. He didn't smile or talk. Probably a side effect of the 'roids or the excessive body ink. I pointed to the office door behind him. He shook his head. At least he could communicate. I leaned in close to his ear.

"I need to see the manager!" I screamed.

He shrugged as if he couldn't hear me. This guy was in bad shape. He wasn't wearing ear plugs, so I guessed that his hearing was shot to hell. I wondered if his pain receptors were gone as well. I sent my right elbow to his throat to test my theory. He was a couple inches taller than me. The move was a natural uppercut. That got his attention. He dropped to the floor clutching his throat. No one seemed to notice. I stepped over him and through the office door.

Thankfully, the back room was partially soundproof. Only the throbbing continued when I shut the door. A man in his forties looked up from behind a metal desk. His stringy hair was streaked with pink dye and he wore a black T-shirt with a white skull and the name of some music group he thought was important. His earlobes were stretched over black disks the size of silver dollars. I wondered if anyone ever told him that he was appropriating the culture of the Maasai tribe in Africa. He didn't look like he cared.

"You're in the wrong room, asshole," he said. His voice was thin and cracked like he'd spent years talking over that noise outside.

"You the manager?" I asked, moving to the side of the desk.

He shifted in his chair to keep me in front of him. His eyes flicked from my hands to the scars on my forehead. They didn't seem to bother him. He probably thought the marks were self-inflected or a new form of body art. He reached into his desk.

"You don't need that," I said, slamming my hand on the drawer.

"What?" he asked, as if he'd gotten caught with his hand in the cookie jar.

"The pistol," I said and let go of the drawer.

He took out an ink pen to prove me wrong and set it on the desk.

"I'm a private investigator." I held up my credentials.

"So what? This office is restricted. Piss off." He stood and looked at the door, expecting help.

"Your bouncer's recovering. He didn't want me to come in either."

"Are you on something, man?"

"No, but I wouldn't mind a couple of Tylenol. The noise is killing me."

"Where's Gino?"

"If that's your bouncer, he'll be okay in fifteen minutes or so. Don't worry, I'm not here to rob you. I'm on a case. A murder victim. She came in here the night she died. Having been here for five minutes, I'm not ruling out suicide induced by noise and laser lights."

He reached for his cell phone. "I'm calling the cops." He didn't think I was funny.

"Call 'em up. When they get here, I'll show them the weapon in your desk and the bag of coke." I had spotted the bag of white powder on the table behind the desk when I first walked in. I grabbed it and held it up to the light. "Nice stash. Probably helps get you through the night in a place like this."

"Easy with that, asswipe. What'd you want?"

"Tapes, my friend. Surveillance tapes from July fourth. The night Marissa Luna was murdered."

"I don't know nothin'," he sneered.

I grabbed the black disk in his right ear and pulled it toward his desk. I had reached the limit of my people skills. I needed information. "You sure about that?"

"Look, a detective came in and took everything from July second through the fifth. I didn't ask for them back, 'cause I don't care. Why should I? Talk to the cops."

"Wasn't that easier than being a jerk?"

"Fuck you. Let go of my ear, man. Jesus."

I let him go. His hand went to his ear. He was going to need a bigger disk.

"Thanks for your time." I walked out and closed the door.

Gino was standing up and leaning against the bar. The goth barmaid was handing him a shot of something. I headed for the back door before he could see me.

I crossed the street and took the steps down to the River Walk. I took my time and checked my watch to gauge how long it would have taken Marissa to walk from the club to where she entered the river. The crowd was heavy on a Saturday night, but nowhere near what it would have been on the Fourth of July. I noticed a dozen airmen from the local base out on twenty-four-hour passes. Their haircuts were so new I could see the razor marks above their ears. The music was from a live mariachi band and didn't make my teeth rattle. The people were laughing and talking and not taking themselves as seriously as the dance club crowd.

I squeezed past a group of middle-aged men speaking German and dressed alike in jean shorts and new Texas T-shirts. Each sported an elaborate mustache and beard combination that would put General Custer to shame. The only one who spoke English said they were in town to compete in a facial hair contest. He asked if I would take their picture in front of the Republic of Texas steak house. I obliged.

It took me ten minutes of leisurely walking to get to the Ben Milam cypress tree, and another four to the Travis Street bridge. The Our Lady of Guadalupe candle still burned for Marissa beside the bundle of plastic roses. The white cross was still standing upright in the Folgers coffee can. Her picture clipped to the side seemed to be urging me to find her killer.

I studied the parking garage and the buildings rising on both sides of the River Walk, then checked for surveillance cameras under the bridge but didn't see any. It wasn't an obvious place to go. There were condos and a few restaurants to the north along with the VFW bar, but most would have been closed by the time she got there on foot. Marissa could have arranged a meeting here at the bridge. There was easy access to the street, so whoever killed her could escape without notice. Maybe she had taken a walk with Danny. This part of the River Walk was well lit but decidedly less crowded than the loop to the south. It seemed a good place to plan a murder and make it look like an accident.

## CHAPTER NINETEEN

THIRTY MINUTES LATER, I WAS sipping a cold Shiner Bock and waiting for Skeeter at the Esquire Tavern. It was near the dance club but far enough away that I didn't have to feel the music. The crowd was a little older and the setting more laid-back, less concerned about the apocalypse.

Skeeter didn't share my love of the Alamo and didn't care for the River Walk. He called me a tourist for spending time in a place most of the city's one and a half million inhabitants avoided because of the traffic and lack of parking.

I looked around at the other patrons. There was a heavyset man wearing a Hawaiian shirt and cargo shorts sipping an oversized frozen margarita. His female companion wore a matching shirt and a pink straw cowboy hat. Both had white skin burnt to a cherry red from overexposure to the South Texas sun and looked like retirees visiting from Minnesota. Three women in the next booth wore white socks under their Birkenstocks, and tie-dyed shirts. A younger, hipster couple in matching skinny jeans were taking selfies in front of a signed team picture of the Spurs basketball team, the new heroes of Alamo City. Maybe Skeeter was right. Downtown was for tourists.

When he arrived, I signaled him to the booth in the back I'd picked out to avoid being in earshot of the few patrons and the bartender. As usual, everyone in the bar turned to look when he walked in, which reminded me of what he said about my own appearance. I still thought a huge man with a metal hook got more attention than I did.

"How'd you know I wouldn't be out partying?" His voice was a deep rumble and sounded like dynamite exploding inside a mine shaft. He filled his side of the booth like a high school kid in a kindergartner's desk.

"Because you're always working." I watched his belly expand over the edge of the table. "You wanna sit at the bar?"

Skeeter noticed my focus. "I'm all right," he said and chuckled. Another explosion in the mine. "Sylvia know where you're at?"

"I'm supposed to be at the ranch," I said.

"This is what happens. You get wrapped up in a case and you forget everything else. You should have called her."

"Thank you, Oprah. I can handle my own relationships."

"Right. Why can't I be Dr. Phil?" Skeeter pinched a napkin with his prosthesis, wiped his mouth, and pretended to be sensitive.

"Because you're black."

"You're racist." He loved to pull the fake race card just to watch me react.

"That's why I got you off death row. I wanted one more giant black man on the street when I organize my next Klan rally."

Skeeter chuckled, and his shoulders shook. He looked like a volcano before an eruption.

"What'd you find out about Marissa?"

"Everything her mom told you checks out. She was a good student, focused on graduating, and didn't drink. Definitely not a suicide."

"I agree," I said, then explained about Danny Allison's connection to the bracelet.

"Allison? The Allison?" he asked. I nodded. Skeeter sat up straight and glanced around at the faces of the other patrons.

"What is it?" I asked. He seemed more nervous than usual.

"His name keeps popping up around dead people. Sosa and now Marissa."

I let what he said sink in for a moment. There was no reason to think the two murders were connected. They had nothing in particular in common except that I was after both killers. "All right," I said. "One thing at a time. I need help with the security cameras at the dance club."

He dropped the napkin and smiled. The mention of an electronic puzzle flipped a switch in his brain. I explained the situation. Skeeter had an immediate answer. He almost seemed disappointed there wasn't more of a challenge. It turns out he had installed the system two years ago and knew there were backup tapes for all the video on the mainframe. He just needed access to the system.

I finished my beer, then we waited across the street from the dance club in my pickup until closing time. The manager exited through a side door and walked to the parking garage. I took out my lock-picking tools and selected what I thought I would need to access the building.

Skeeter put his hand on my arm. "Why did you even call me?" He nodded toward the tools.

"You said you needed access to the system."

He smiled that smile that someone might flash at Grandma when she needed help with the remote control. "I got this," he said. He opened his laptop with his metal hook and tapped a few keys. "I installed the system, remember? I knew guys like you would be tryin' to break in with tools like that." He pressed one last key and smiled. "Let's go."

Something he'd done unlocked the door and disabled the security alarm. Without the throbbing sound, the laser lights, and the horde of post-apocalyptic dancers, the empty room seemed more like an abandoned warehouse than a trendy night club.

Skeeter led me to a different office where the server and backup tapes were kept. He plugged in his laptop then plopped down in a too-small chair.

While we waited for the tapes to download, I told him what happened in Kerrville.

"She just told you the information, even though that's illegal?"

"You underestimate how charming I can be for a country boy."

"You took Sam, didn't you?"

"He had nothing to do with it," I protested.

"Right." Skeeter pulled his laptop in front of him and tapped a few keys. "What do you know about Danny Allison?"

"He's rich, spoiled, and just graduated from Texas Tech."

"Why'd he buy Marissa an expensive bracelet then kill her?"

"Because he's got money to burn," I said.

"Sometimes these rich kids don't get their money until they come of age." He brought up a database that he shouldn't have had access to and started reading Danny Allison's back story.

"He's a weekend warrior. Amateur MMA fighter. He joined the Tech boxing club his freshman year. Must be pretty good. He won a few tournaments. He played rugby, so he's not a complete loner. His grades were average or a little below counting his freshman year. Someone must have given him a pep talk. He did just enough to graduate on the five-year plan. This is interesting…"

"What?" I was twiddling my thumbs while I watched the gentle giant work.

"His daddy went to Tech and so did his grandpa."

"How did you find all that?"

He smiled. "All here in the university records. Probably part of the trust agreement."

"What's that?"

"His family's filthy rich, but he goes to school in Lubbock. Not exactly the Ivy League. He plays rugby and likes to fight MMA. How many rich kids do you know do that?"

I saw his point. "He's not flashing money around like you might expect with the Allison family fortune behind him. He should be doing the Formula One circuit and flying off to ski the Alps in a private jet. Danny boy spends his weekends getting his ass kicked."

"Actually, he's pretty good, judging by his awards," Skeeter said.

"He's twenty-three. Let's say he doesn't get paid until he's twenty-five, and Grandpa placed certain conditions on the first payment," I said.

"Like graduate from the family alma mater," Skeeter said, nodding.

"And not getting arrested." I was thinking of Danny standing next to his grandpa in the convention center trying to look sober and respectable.

"I'll bet he has to join the family business." Skeeter turned the laptop so I could see a picture of Danny and Patrick in front of an oil derrick somewhere in South Texas wearing hard hats and matching Oxford shirts.

"And don't get some girl pregnant," I said, thinking he was onto something.

"Bingo," Skeeter said and unplugged his laptop. "I got what we need. We gotta go."

"What's the hurry? I thought you installed the system."

"I did. I installed a failsafe in case someone like me did what I'm doing."

"That doesn't sound good," I said.

Skeeter looked at his watch. "We have thirty seconds. The alarm goes off here and at the police station. The building locks down."

"Skeeter," I yelled as we ran for the side door. I could see myself trying to explain this to Detective Peterson and watching him laugh while he shoved me into the back of his Crown Vic.

A half step from the door, an ear-piercing screech shattered the silence. The annoyance level rivaled the pulsing dance music without the bass. I put my hand on the door. Locked. I turned to Skeeter.

"Too late," he said.

"You couldn't get us out before the alarm went off?"

"The download took longer than I thought," he yelled over the noise.

Sirens outside wailed above the sound of the alarm. I didn't want to end up facedown on the parking lot twice in one weekend.

"I don't wanna ever see jail again, man," he shouted. "Get us out of here. I'll buy the pizza."

I motioned for him to follow, and we ran for the emergency fire exit behind the bar. The alarm was already going off, so I didn't think anyone would notice.

The front door burst open.

"Police!"

We ducked behind the bar and scrambled to the door. I reached up and pushed the red handle. A light above the door began to flash. Skeeter followed me through the door to the alley, and I pushed the door closed. Skeeter leaned all his three hundred pounds against it. We waited ten seconds, then fifteen. Skeeter felt the door move against him.

"Here they come," he whispered.

I added my weight to the door. We felt two sharp bumps, as if whoever was checking the door on the inside put his shoulder into it. I heard a muffled voice. In a few moments they would check the outside perimeter. I motioned Skeeter to follow me. We ran down the dark alley to the River Walk and quickly found the stone steps leading to the street level.

# CHAPTER TWENTY

WE WATCHED THE DANCE CLUB surveillance video in fast motion beginning at six o'clock on the evening of July fourth. The stringy-haired manager went through the cash registers, and the muscle-bound bouncer took up his position at the end of the bar. The waitress with the black lipstick wore white. Must have been a phase she was going through or some July fourth social-justice statement I wasn't aware of. She wiped down the shot glasses and loaded ice in the cooler. We watched the comical, frenetic movements of the young people on the dance floor for half an hour with no sign of Marissa or Danny Allison. It was like watching a *National Geographic* documentary on some lost tribe. The ritual dance consisted of an up-down movement combined with arms flailing about. The dress code was a mixture of preppy, urban hip, and jeans and boots, the Texas standby. Most of the participants were college age and younger—the only people with enough stamina to withstand the grinding assault to the senses. It went on for hours, fueled by alcohol and open drug use. I started to wonder if Detective Peterson had reviewed the tapes.

It was three a.m., and we were safely back at my place. After escaping the police response, we had stopped by the twenty-four-hour pizzeria so Skeeter could make good on his promise to buy if I managed to get us out of the dance club without getting arrested. In my experience, we would need food and lots of coffee for the tedious chore of reviewing surveillance tapes.

The good part about it was that there was no sound, and Skeeter manipulated the images so that we could watch eight camera views at once. Two on the bar, four on the dance floor, and one each on the front door and the back entrance. At nine thirty Marissa and her friend Beth entered from the street side and approached the bar.

The two young women placed an order with the barmaid. She wasn't wearing the bracelet, or much jewelry at all. She wore the blue patriotic tank top and the black skirt I recognized from the police report. I watched closely to see if Marissa's mother had overstated her sobriety. The bartender squirted water in a glass with ice and added lemon. Marissa took a thirsty drink. She poured Beth something with carbonation in a copper mug topped with lime.

"That's a Moscow mule," Skeeter said, sounding full of himself.

"Like you would know," I said. "You don't drink."

"I had one last week for a special occasion. Vodka, ginger beer, and a twist of lime. Very refreshing."

"You had a date?"

"Why are you surprised?"

"'Cause you haven't had a date since last October."

"How do you know?"

"I set it up."

"She still calls me."

"That's because you installed her security system. Who was your date with?"

"I took my mom to Applebee's for her birthday," he said. He was a good son.

We watched Marissa and Beth sip their drinks and search the crowd. A guy in a skin-tight silver T-shirt waved his rainbow-colored Mohawk at them like a preening peacock. The girls looked at each other and giggled as the Mohawk pranced in front of them before making his approach. He hopped from one foot to the other and gestured toward the crowded dance floor. Like a bird in the wild, he was committed to the mating ritual. The girls shook their heads. Mohawk persisted. He inserted himself between them and ordered a drink. When he turned, he brushed his hand across Marissa's breast. She grabbed the thumb on his right hand and twisted it up behind his back. Mohawk looked shocked and in pain. He backed away and left the girls alone. I ruled him out as a suspect. Marissa would have kicked his ass.

I was beginning to like Marissa. I wondered where she had learned that move. At the same time, of course, I realized she was dead. Whatever training she had wasn't enough to prevent her death. That told me the killer was persistent and brutal, and made me even more determined to catch him.

The girls continued to watch the crowd and giggle. They looked young and innocent and full of life. I wanted to shout "Go home!" at the screen. But, of course, Skeeter and I could only watch the inevitable. It was like seeing a video of a train wreck before an accident, the passengers were all happy and clueless that death was rushing to meet them.

They left their drinks on the bar and went to the dance floor. Not a good thing to do in a place like this. We watched the drinks for any sign of tampering but only saw the barmaid in the white lipstick sweep them into the sink.

By eleven thirty on the video time stamp, the Fourth of July crowd was double what I had experienced. Just watching it made my ears ring. There was still no sign of Danny Allison. It was four a.m. Sam had lost interest when the pizza ran out and went to sleep in the kitchen.

I put on a pot of coffee. Skeeter and I were taking turns concentrating on the crowd. When there was enough caffeinated liquid accumulated in the pot, I siphoned it off into my mug and took a drink. It contained the double shot of wake-up that I needed.

Finally, at eleven forty-seven, Danny showed up. He wore designer jeans and square-toed cowboy boots. He had on a white Oxford shirt tucked into a western belt. He took a look around as if he'd walked into the wrong party, then waded into the crowd and headed for the bar. He didn't wait for people to move. If they didn't step aside, he gave them a persuasive shove. More than a few didn't seem to like being pushed. One young woman gave him the finger. Danny didn't notice. He never even looked back.

I searched the other cameras but couldn't find Marissa. "Where is she?" I asked Skeeter.

"In the restroom."

"You didn't put a camera in the ladies' room?"

He didn't dignify that with an answer. Even the idea irritated him. He once used his hacking skills to take down a porn site that used public restroom footage.

Danny ordered a drink and leaned against the bar like a cowboy in a Gene Autry movie, fresh off the trail and looking for some action. We spotted Marissa exiting the restroom alone.

"Where's the friend?" I asked.

Skeeter shrugged. Marissa went straight to the bar. She obviously recognized Danny and approached him directly. When he saw her, he pushed away from the bar and reached to hug her. She held up her hands to stop him. Without the sound, it was impossible to judge their conversation, but she wasn't happy, and it looked like Danny was making up an excuse for being late. I recognized the body language because I had done it a few times. It was some version of: *Sorry, honey, there was a lot of traffic,* or *I had to work late.*

Danny reached into his perfectly ironed shirt pocket and brought out his ace in the hole. The bracelet. Four grand worth of *I'm sorry I'm late.* I had Skeeter zoom in, but the lighting was too dim to get a clear picture. I needed her to put it on and hold it up to the light to clearly establish the bracelet as a link between Danny and Marissa.

The angle didn't give a great view of her expression, but even from above it looked like her face registered shock. In the next breath she hit him. Hard. She used a flat right hand and caught him on the lower cheek. In the color video, his skin turned crimson. He grabbed her by the wrist. She hit him with the other hand. Good for her. Too bad she hadn't carried a pistol.

Danny grabbed both her wrists and pushed them down to her sides. The bouncer at the end of the bar did nothing. What a waste of skin. Her friend was nowhere in sight. The whole encounter lasted less than two minutes. Marissa didn't struggle after that, and Danny let her go. She took a step back, said one last thing. Danny held up the bracelet in a gesture of surrender. Marissa took it and walked out.

Danny stayed at the bar and watched her go. She walked out of one camera and into another. Halfway between the bar and the back entrance, she ran into Beth. The two hugged briefly. Marissa wiped her checks with her fingertips, clearly crying. Beth held her hand and seemed to ask pointed questions. Marissa held the bracelet out to Beth. She raised her hands, refusing to take it. Marissa insisted. Beth took the bracelet and put it in her purse. Then Marissa took a step toward the back door. Beth started to follow, but Marissa waved her off.

"Why did she lie to me?" I said. "Beth obviously saw that Marissa was upset."

"Maybe she was too drunk to remember," Skeeter said.

"Maybe someone else got to her."

"You think Danny threatened her?"

I didn't answer. He let the tape roll forward. We watched Danny finish his beer. He didn't seem too upset. At least, he didn't smash his head against the bar or stomp his boots on the floor.

Ten minutes later he set his empty beer on the bar and walked out the street-side entrance.

"Didn't he come in on the other side?" Skeeter asked.

I nodded and sipped my coffee.

"You think that was calculated?" he asked.

I didn't answer.

"He would have known the place had security cameras," Skeeter continued.

I finished my coffee, letting Skeeter blast the air with questions we couldn't answer.

"You gonna solve this case or play dumb?"

I held up my hand. "I'm thinking."

"In that case, I'll just shut the hell up." Skeeter stalked off toward the kitchen.

I picked up my spiral notebook and wrote down the time line from the video. The time of Danny's exit was twelve twenty-eight on the video clock. The time of Marissa's death was listed between one and three a.m. Danny had plenty of time to walk to the Travis Street bridge, but had they set up a meeting? Did he know which way she would walk? He could have followed her progress from bridge to bridge, waiting for a moment when she was alone.

If Detective Peterson had seen this, it wasn't in his report. There was no mention of Danny Allison as a witness or as a suspect. The report didn't mention a fight. The bracelet was only clear to me because I had held it in my hand. Otherwise, it looked like any other bracelet. Peterson had likely not looked at all the tapes. The question was, Why?

Skeeter came back into the room. "What now, Sherlock? Do we grab Danny Allison and haul him down to the police station?"

"No," I said. "Fighting with your date doesn't automatically lead to murder; otherwise our homicide rate would be like Chicago's."

"But you have the bracelet."

"It's not enough." I took my empty coffee mug back to the kitchen. "Check on Sam tomorrow, in case I don't make it back."

"Where you goin'?"

"Lubbock. It's where Danny and Marissa must have hooked up."

"Be careful."

"Something going on in Lubbock I don't know about?"

"Nothing's ever going on in Lubbock. Be careful because Danny's last name is Allison. He's got more money and connections than AT&T." I doubted the Allisons were that rich, but I got his point.

Skeeter took a cab home, and I trudged upstairs. Sam followed me up and jumped on the bed. It was four forty-five. Two nights in a row I was burning the midnight oil. I felt like I was studying for finals, or worse, going out on patrol.

I thought about calling Sylvia, but it was late and the antihistamine had made me drowsy. That was my excuse anyway. I knew I was putting off the inevitable.

# CHAPTER TWENTY-ONE

By the time the sun was hot enough to send shimmering heat waves dancing over the blacktop, I was a hundred miles northwest of San Antonio. Interstate 10, as usual, was bumper to bumper with coast-to-coast truckers and took more attention to drive than I was prepared for on so little sleep. It was kind of like jumping in a stock car and taking a lap around the Talladega racetrack when all I wanted was to go to the grocery store for a gallon of milk. I was glad when I reached the exit for State Highway 83 at Junction and turned north on the narrower and less traveled route. It was a six-hour drive—five and a half if you pushed it—through arid, empty country that was once the sole domain of Comanche Indians following free range buffalo. With the complete demise of the herd and the tribe, there was really nothing to see.

I stopped in Ballenger for coffee and topped off my gas tank. The restroom smelled like a portable toilet at an outdoor concert, but I didn't complain. I didn't want to get the attendant in trouble. She looked like a high school kid who needed the job. The town was close to the famous Permian Basin that had made a good many Texans, including the Allison family, rich from the large oil deposits and still kept a good portion of them employed. The pipeline Grandpa was upset about originated there.

I was making the drive to find out if Danny and Marissa left any trace of their relationship in their college town. No one seemed to know they were together in San Antonio. The mother was out of the loop, and Marissa's best friend from high school wasn't talking. I had contacted Kelly Hoffman, a former Marine officer I'd been stationed with on my last deployment. She worked for the university police force and had agreed to help me out even though it was Sunday.

When the vast expanse of rolling limestone hills gave way to flat red farmland, I knew I was finally getting close. The town seemed to rise out of the dark-green cotton plants that stretched in neat rows as far as the eye could see. I followed the signs to the university and found an empty parking spot next to the new crime lab building. The one thing Lubbock had was plenty of free parking.

Kelly had the wholesome good looks of a farmer's daughter. She was born and raised in the country, five miles south of Lubbock, and had joined the Corps as an MP after getting a degree in forensic science. She still wore her blond hair cut short following the female military standard, and when she met me at the front door, she still looked like she could ace the Marine physical fitness test.

"Sarge, you scallywag. I wasn't expecting you till after lunch." She took off her lab coat and extended her hand.

I glanced at her new sergeant stripes and name badge. She had traded one uniform for another. She looked good in both. I shook her hand. She didn't have delicate, long fingers like Sylvia. She was built solid like an athlete. Her hands were calloused from lifting weights and helping her dad on weekends with the farm work. Her nails were painted red but filed down so they didn't interfere with the instruments she worked with in the lab or the bales of hay she bucked for the livestock.

"You look like you just got off the obstacle course," I said.

"Who says I didn't?"

"What're you working on?"

She showed me the unit's new Rapid DNA instruments. They could process DNA samples in two to three hours while a perp was sitting in a jail cell. A process that normally took months now could put a suspect away before he was back out on the streets or clear him before he was locked away.

I followed her to her office down the hall. She had a collection of Marine Corps paraphernalia on her wall along with a picture of us together on the base in Afghanistan. She sat behind a metal desk and watched me study other pictures of her in uniform at other bases I knew.

"Make you wish you'd stayed in?" she asked. I detected a hint of longing in her voice.

"Not me," I said. "But I was enlisted. It was a whole different Corps than you experienced."

"Don't give me that BS, Sarge. I did everything y'all did, and extra because I was female." She laughed and seemed to be waiting for me to argue her point.

I got the feeling she wanted to swap war stories. She didn't seem to be in any hurry, and I wondered if her excuse about working on Sunday morning was really true. I didn't want to hurry her and seem ungrateful, but as much as I was enjoying her company, I was hoping to get some information and hit the road. When the silence stretched for another minute, she sensed my impatience.

"Let me run Allison's name in the law enforcement database and see what pops up," she said, booting up the computer on her desk and accessing the files.

While we waited, I asked if she liked being back in Lubbock or if she preferred South Texas. She kept her eyes on the screen and didn't answer. The last time I saw her was when she was stationed in San Antonio. She had called out of the blue, and I met her for a beer. I had just started dating Sylvia at the time.

"My family's here," she finally said. "The job is what I've always wanted. This is one of the most sophisticated labs in the country. Last year we got approval for the upgrade by the FBI. We stay busy." She scrolled through a list of names, then stopped. "I got a hit on your boy."

I got up to look, but she blocked my view.

"I know you told me about this on the phone, but you are on this case, right? The mother hired you to find the killer?" She was a good MP and had transitioned into a by-the-book civilian policewoman. I gave her the details, starting with the bracelet and what Skeeter and I found on the surveillance tapes.

"She was pregnant," I said, finishing my explanation. "Everything points to Danny Allison as the father. He didn't come forward or lift a finger when she died."

Kelly's features hardened. The story definitely left Danny smelling like week-old roadkill. She studied my expression, then nodded, convinced. She turned back to the monitor and read Danny's record.

"There was a sexual harassment report filed his sophomore year. The woman was a foreign exchange student from China. She dropped the charge and has since moved back home."

"That won't help," I said.

"Here's another one the following year. The same charge."

"Another foreigner?"

"Nope, this one was a local."

"Spread the love."

"She dropped the case too."

"Is that unusual?"

"Not really. Even with the MeToo movement, if the guy's got money he can hire the best lawyers and private investigators to dig the dirt. Pretty soon the case doesn't look so good, and the victim gets cold feet or settles out of court."

"He does have money and a high-powered lawyer. But not the best private eye."

"What makes you say that?"

"I'm the best, and I don't work for him."

She smiled. I always liked that smile. Bright, clean, crisp. The kind of smile that turned heads even if it was hiding under a helmet. I turned back to the screen. If I stared at her any longer, she might think I was flirting with her. Maybe I was and wasn't willing to admit it. I didn't want to complicate my relationship with Sylvia any more than it already was.

I made notes on the details of the last complaint made against Danny, then offered to buy her lunch. Instead we went to the university cafeteria where she had a punch card. The food reminded me of military meals, which were hard to describe but stuck to your ribs. I was hungry after the long drive, so I took a plate of meatloaf with mac and cheese on the side. I'm sure the coastal universities had a more vegan-friendly menu, but Lubbock was in the heartland and had too many farmer's kids to be too politically correct. There was a long line waiting for chicken fried steak. Kelly and I met at the iced tea dispenser. I went for the unsweetened.

"What are you, a yankee?" She laughed. "No one drinks unsweetened tea in the South."

"I'm watching my weight," I said.

"Don't say that out loud," she whispered.

We filled our trays and sat at a corner table. The sound of clacking silverware and ice being dispensed provided a constant undercurrent to our conversation.

"How's your girlfriend, the Victoria Secret model?" she asked.

"She sold furniture." I laughed. I knew Sylvia and Kelly would never get along if they were ever to meet.

"Whatever, I'm surprised she lets you do this kind of work. I thought she wanted you to go back to law school."

"If I did what other people wanted, I would have stayed in the Corps."

"You'd be a gunny by now."

"Or busted back to private."

"I always wondered how a guy like you that has a problem with authority ended up in the Marine Corps."

"I had something to prove," I said.

Kelly sensed that she had strayed into territory that I wasn't ready to talk about with her. She didn't press it. We finished lunch listening to the clanking of silverware against plastic trays and the laughter of college students who didn't seem to have a care in the world.

## CHAPTER TWENTY-TWO

When I got back to my pickup, the infamous North Texas wind was sandblasting the pavement and filled my eyes and nose with red grit—a byproduct of converting the prairie to dry farmland. I took an antihistamine as a preventative measure, then drove out on Broadway Street past a half dozen Baptist churches. In ten minutes, I had crossed the state highway and the city limit sign. I was looking for the Buena Vista Mobile Home Village—the trailer park listed as the last known address for Valerie Martin. She was the coed who filed sexual harassment charges against Danny Allison last year, then changed her mind.

I found Buena Vista and stopped at the neglected plywood sign. The advertised *good view* to the south was a red haze of windblown cotton fields. To the north stretched the Texas Panhandle. It was characterized as an uncharted, inhospitable ocean of grass to the Spanish and any American settlers searching for a homestead. So flat, ranchers used to say, that if you stood on an apple crate you could see the Canadian border. I was sitting in my four-wheel-drive pickup and could only see as far as the dairy farm across the barbed-wire fence. I was raised on a ranch and didn't need to roll down my windows to know what the giant mounds behind the milking sheds were made of.

There was only one road in and one road out. No need for the GPS. I got a few curious looks from the older inhabitants who were resting in the shade of their retractable porch awnings and rocking away the hot afternoon. They were probably immune to the dairy stench. It seemed an odd place to find an acquaintance of the very affluent Allison family, but then Marissa had been a complete surprise too. I wondered if there was a pattern to Danny's pick of female companions, and if so, what he was looking for.

I found the number on the mailbox and parked my pickup in the gravel driveway. The mobile home was a single-wide with a worn wooden porch that was missing a few railing boards. The loose awning flapped in the wind. Other than that, someone mowed the small patch of grass out front and the junk in the driveway was kept to a minimum. I had lived in worse places. I waited to see if there was movement behind the windows, but there was nothing. I made my way to the door and knocked.

When no one answered, I knocked again. I could hear a medium-sized dog barking just inside the door but no sound of human activity. It was Sunday afternoon. Maybe Valerie worked weekends or was honoring the Sabbath. I had passed enough Baptist churches to easily accommodate the entire population of Lubbock. I clopped back down the wooden porch steps and spotted an older lady wearing a red apron over a flower-print dress crossing the street toward me. She looked like she'd just hurried home from church to pull a pot roast out of the oven. As she approached, I remembered to smile really big.

"Do you know Valerie Martin?" I asked.

She seemed a little nervous. "Oh, she moved out at the end of last year. November, I think. She got an apartment in town. I still have the forwarding address. She was getting monthly checks in the mail. Didn't want to miss any. I think it was financial aid."

I told her I was from the university and needed to ask Valerie a few questions. It only took a minute for her to shuffle over to her trailer and find the forwarding address. If every trailer park had a friendly neighbor, the private eye business would be a snap.

The address she gave me was in a much newer residential area. It was only a fifteen-minute drive from the dairy farm, but a world apart. I went back through town and turned north toward the country club. When I found the condos, it looked like they couldn't have been over a year old. There was a gate out front with a bored-looking guard checking the license plates on cars going in and out. I pulled up beside him and rolled down my window. He had a droopy gray mustache that obscured his lips. With a little wax he could probably enter the facial hair competition with the Germans in San Antonio, but then he would have to take a bath, and I didn't think he wanted to do that.

"Howdy, I'm Valerie Martin's brother, Tom. It's her birthday today, and I drove up from Austin to surprise her. She's in thirty-three-oh-four."

He stared at me and chuckled. "Her brother?" he asked, like he knew more about Valerie than I did. "I'll have to call." He was thin, and his breath smelled of cigarette smoke and vodka masked with peppermint candy. His once-white undershirt below his brown security guard uniform was yellow with age and frayed on the edges.

"It's a surprise, Doug." I read his name off his nametag. I took out a twenty, folded it in half, and held it between my fingers, palm up. "I'll sneak you some cold beer. What d'ya say?"

I knew I had him with the beer offer. He buzzed me through the gate, and I cruised around the corner following the signs to thirty-three-oh-four. The complex had two pools. One on each end. I counted thirty units, all with a private garage and a patio that opened toward a tree-covered center park. The units were two stories and put together with terra-cotta bricks, dark wood trim, and shake shingles. There were tennis courts between the pools and several wooden picnic tables under the trees. It was quite a step up from the trailer park across the fence from the dairy farm. If Valerie was getting financial aid, she wasn't using it to pay for school. That or she had won the lottery.

I found the number and parked behind her garage.

It was two o'clock in the afternoon on a Sunday. If she was a student, she could be home studying. This was the first week of classes. I knocked. Bare feet slapped on tile behind the door. I got out my private investigator credentials and held them up to the peephole. The door opened, and a strikingly pretty young black woman squinted against the bright sunlight. I understood why Doug hadn't believed my story.

"What's this about?" she asked. Judging by her appearance and her disheveled hair, she was not an early riser. She was petite and had on a man's oversized white T-shirt, which looked slept in.

"Valerie Martin?" I asked.

She looked at my forehead and hesitated with her hand on the door like she regretted opening it. "Yes."

"My name is Nick Fischer." I smiled and tried to sound apologetic. "I'm a private investigator hired by the university to follow up on sexual harassment cases." I had her attention.

She stood straight and focused on my ID. She was nervous and self-conscious of the thin T-shirt. "I don't have anything to say," she blurted out.

"Ms. Martin, if you'd let me come in, I just have a few questions about—"

"No." She cut me off. "There's nothing to it. I already explained. I can't talk about it."

"Please, just—"

She slammed the door in my face. It wasn't the first time someone had done that, and it wouldn't be the last. I didn't push it. If she wouldn't talk, she wouldn't talk. Walking back to my pickup, I thought about her last line. *I can't talk about it.* Did she mean she didn't want to, or was she prevented from doing so by a legal agreement? I suspected the latter.

I checked the handle on her garage door to see if it was open. It was. Why lock it when Doug the security guard was on duty? What I found was a new BMW. White with cream leather seats. I wasn't a car guy but guessed it was worth north of fifty grand. How did Ms. Martin go from a trailer park overlooking a dairy to a luxury condo and a Beemer while going to school and working at a bar?

I waved to Doug on my way out. I knew he was looking forward to a cold beer on a hot day, but I had things to do. I searched the work history Kelly had found for Valerie and drove to her last known place of employment. It was a bar near the university named the Library, as if university students needed an excuse to go to a bar. I was expecting a trendy, upscale nightspot where frat boys met sorority girls and jocks wore tight jerseys to show off their muscles. Maybe Danny stayed late one night and offered Valerie a ride home after work.

From the outside, the Library didn't look like much. It was in an older part of town across the street from a car dealership. Parts of the street were still paved with red brick. The sign on the outside said they didn't open until seven on Sunday, but the door was unlocked. I went inside and paused to let my eyes adjust to the dark and to soak up the air conditioning. The North Texas air was less humid than San Antonio, but it was hot enough in September that it didn't matter. A hundred degrees was a hundred degrees no matter where you stood on the planet.

Once my eyes adjusted, I saw a collection of used books against the back bar. The place had the feel of an old high school library but smelled like hops and orange peels. It was the kind of place I wouldn't have minded spending a few hours in, but I had work to do. For six months after I got out of the Corps, I called the VFW in San Antonio home and spent most of the time at the bar with my lips wrapped around a Jack Daniels bottle. That was before I moved back in with Grandpa and started to make the transition back to civilian life.

The bartender wore a Pink Floyd T-shirt and a manbun. He didn't look up until I tapped the little library bell on the counter. He looked young, hip, and annoyed.

"We're closed," he sneered.

"I just wanna ask you a few questions," I said.

"We're a little busy getting ready for opening. Why don't you show yourself out?"

I flashed my private eye credentials. "It's about an employee."

He glanced at my license while he pulled a tray of shot glasses out of the washer behind the bar. "You a cop?"

I wanted to say I was Rodney Dangerfield, but I knew he wouldn't get it. Nobody was impressed by a private eye anymore.

"Private investigator," I said. Manbun was getting on my nerves. It had been a long day following a short night, and I still had a six-hour drive back to San Antonio. I wanted to grab his trendy ball of hair and slam his left ear on the counter, but I figured he would shit himself and call the cops, so I flashed my best disarming smile instead. I was working on my people skills.

"I'm not asking much. Answer a few simple questions, and I promise not to slice off your topknot with my Buck knife."

He looked puzzled, trying to figure out if I was kidding or not. I stopped smiling and held his gaze. He seemed to notice my scars for the first time. He decided I was serious.

"All right, all right," he stuttered. "Fuck, dude. What d'you wanna know?" He backed off a few steps down the bar.

"Does Valerie Martin work here?" I asked as politely as I could.

A female coworker poked her head out of the back room. "Everything kosher out here?"

Manbun looked at me. I smiled again.

"Yeah, no problem," he said.

She ducked her head back inside.

He placed another tray of dirty glasses in the washer. "No, man. She left a year ago. Bitch said she didn't need the job."

"Not a happy ending?"

"She left on Thanksgiving weekend. Busy time. Home game. We had to cover for her."

"Were you friends before that?"

"I wasn't her type."

"What type is that?"

"Rich," he said. He didn't have to spell it out. I knew the type. Every university town had gold diggers. It cast doubt on her accusations, but since she dropped the charges no one would ever know the truth.

"One more question. Do you know Danny Allison?"

He shook his head. "Look, I'm sorry about being an asshole. I'm working double shifts and classes just started."

"Don't worry about it," I said. Everyone had an excuse for being a jerk when they were called on it. I laid a twenty on the bar and walked out.

I hopped back in my pickup and found the state highway leading south. I had a pretty good idea where Valerie Martin got her money. I couldn't prove it, of course, but it wouldn't take too much digging. I would put Skeeter to work on it. Paying hush money didn't make Danny Allison guilty of murder, but it established a pattern of behavior.

The last stop on my list was Lamesa, sixty miles south of Lubbock. It was where Valerie grew up and where her mother still lived and worked at the local café. I called ahead and found out the mom was working until eight.

The little town of Lamesa was on the red-dirt flatland halfway between Lubbock and Odessa. In other words, in the middle of nowhere. It looked like any of a dozen other half-abandoned towns in the flat expanse of North Texas, like a movie set for *The Last Picture Show.* I found the café on the main highway where Bunny Martin, Valerie's mother, worked. I wondered if she would be as tight-lipped as her daughter about the relationship with Danny Allison and if Mom was benefiting from the same windfall Valerie enjoyed.

The inside of the café was cozy and air conditioned. There was a highway patrolman perched on a counter stool. His girth on top of the metal pedestal resembled a mushroom with a cowboy hat. There was a group of teen girls in the corner booth snickering like teen girls do while their faces were glued to their smartphones.

I took the management's advice and sat myself at a table in the far corner of the room, away from the teens and the mushroom. A plump woman with ebony skin walked out of the back room wiping her hands on a towel. She looked to be about the right age to have a twenty-something daughter. Her hair was short and sprinkled with gray. She wore jeans with tennis shoes and a tank top. She had once been a beauty like her daughter, but it seemed that part of her life was over. When she brought me a glass of water, her eyes were blank and checked out.

She added silverware wrapped in a paper napkin to my table. Her name tag read Bunny. There was no last name. I wondered if her mother had given her the name or if she had adopted it in order to work at the café. I smiled and waited for her to make eye contact. It took her almost a minute to look up at me.

"Well?" she said. A jarhead with a few scars didn't faze her. I could have been a Hell's Angel with a bloody machete on a date with the Queen of England and she would have still tapped her foot impatiently like we were keeping her from the other customers.

"How's the pie," I said, pronouncing it *pah*, trying to sound local and friendly, but she took it the wrong way.

"We're out of *pah*," she insisted.

I looked over at the slice of key lime Mushroom was shoving in his face.

"He got the last piece," she said.

"Just coffee."

She grabbed a pot from the warmer behind the counter that had probably been going since breakfast and sloshed stale coffee into my cup.

"How's Valerie," I said. That got her attention and curiosity.

"You know my daughter?"

"Sure, Valerie Martin. She's doing well. I saw her new BMW."

"You must have the wrong girl. My Valerie drives an Escort."

"Did she show you her new condo?"

She was getting annoyed. "Look, you got the wrong girl. My daughter lives in a trailer park west of town. She's a student. Studying business marketing. She works at a bar on nights and weekends."

"When did you see her last?"

"She's busy with school. Doesn't get down here much."

The university was sixty miles away. I had just driven it in under an hour. I was starting to understand where some of Bunny's bitterness came from. I didn't ask any more questions. She didn't want to talk about her daughter.

I ordered a sandwich to go so that I wouldn't have to stop again before I got back to San Antonio. I avoided the day-old coffee and bought a bottled water from behind the counter. Valerie's mom didn't say goodbye or have a nice day. When the glass door closed, I noticed she was head to head with Mushroom. They'd have a good laugh about what I'd said. When she got off work, Bunny would be thinking about her daughter. She would try to call.

Valerie wouldn't answer.

Nobody involved with this case seemed to be willing to talk.

# CHAPTER TWENTY-THREE

SAM AND I CROSSED THE river at the Eagleland Drive trailhead behind the high school and jogged north. At that point, the river was contained in concrete banks and lined with trees and overgrown grass, but the trail was paved and well lit. Ever since the Sosa shooting, I'd been using alternate routes for my evening run. Now that the Allison name had shown up in both murder cases I hoped to solve, I would crank the precaution level up to eight which meant checking my backtrail and always packing my .38. In a few blocks, the rough grass turned into a manicured park that received more regular maintenance. The air was still and hot, as usual. I was thankful that the African dust seemed to have settled after sundown.

When Sam and I hit our six-mile-an-hour pace, I started thinking about what I'd learned so far. Danny Allison fit all the requisite criteria. He had means, motive, and opportunity. He also had a history of harassment, and unless I was way off base, he had paid off at least one woman to buy her silence. Had Marissa wanted money? Would the baby have jeopardized his inheritance?

What I needed was proof that he was the father of Marissa's child. That would require a DNA sample from Danny to match the fetal DNA from Marissa's autopsy. Kelly had agreed to run the sample though the rapid DNA test at her lab. The only problem was, how was I going to get a sample of Danny's DNA? I doubted he would give it to me voluntarily. That left me with trying to convince Peterson he had probable cause to get a court order or squeezing a sample out of him myself.

I felt a punch on my arm that spun me to the ground in midstride, followed by a muffled pop. I knew instantly what it was. My brain processed sniper fire. The whiff from another bullet flew near my head. I recognized the suppressed rifle noise. It was the same compressed-air pop that took out Sosa.

I grabbed Sam and pulled him into the shadow of a palm tree beside the trail, keeping the trunk between us and the shooter. He sniffed my bloody arm. Another round hit the tree, showering us with splinters. This time I saw the flicker of light from the muzzle blast. The shooter was in a parking garage across the river, less than a hundred yards away.

Sam sat next to me, the loose skin around his forehead curled into a question mark. He thought it was a game until he saw the .38 pistol appear in my hand.

Warm blood dripped down my bare left arm, but there was no pain yet. I still had control of my fingers and was able to move my shoulder. The bullet had missed the bone. Careful not to expose my body outside the tree, I ripped a strip from the bottom of my T-shirt and wrapped it around the wound. The loss of blood was already making me lightheaded. I needed to fight against shock. If I passed out, the shooter would simply come out of his hiding place for an easy kill shot.

Sam and I waited. He panted heavily and watched my reactions. I kept my .38 ready, but at this range it was useless. Five minutes went by. I checked my watch. Nine thirty. Climbing the retaining wall behind the tree seemed out of the question. I would be exposed for at least several seconds. Beyond that was an empty parking lot. I had no doubt the shooter had a night-vision scope and would be able to see even the slightest movement. He had picked a good location for an ambush.

I studied the parking garage. The structure provided ideal cover and an easy getaway. It also would be empty tomorrow because Monday was the Labor Day holiday. No one was coming to the rescue. It reminded me of the countless nights I'd spent huddled with my platoon brothers waiting for a dawn attack.

Sam's mouth hung open, dripping from the heat. He would last the night, but the lack of water wouldn't be good for him or me. I checked my makeshift bandage. The blood flow had stopped, but I still felt lightheaded. I needed to move my cramped muscles.

Another bullet splintered the tree trunk and hit the limestone retaining wall, spraying the grass with white pebbles. The angle was different this time. The shooter had changed positions, trying to gain a better angle. He was on the move, and I wouldn't be able to wait him out until morning. The plan I was forming was risky, but so was the alternative. If I stayed behind the tree, eventually, the shooter would find a position that gave him a clear shot.

Sam was anxious to move. He looked at me and whined, waiting for me to make a decision. I stood and examined the space beyond the ten-foot retaining wall. The dirt along the edge was removed in preparation for new landscaping. That was the first bit of luck all night. If I could get over the wall, the depression looked deep enough to provide cover. From there, I could inch my way to the bridge and out of sight. I scratched Sam behind the ears. He seemed to understand something was going on that involved him. I hoped he remembered his training.

"All right, Sam," I whispered. "Time to play Rin Tin Tin." I held up my hand, pointing to the shadow under the bridge. Sam looked into the dark. His muscles tensed, anticipating what was coming next. I didn't think the shooter had the skills to hit a sprinting Labrador or I wouldn't have put Sam at risk.

"Fetch," I yelled.

Sam took off like a bat out of hell. Two steps into his run, I heard the first pop. I couldn't look because I needed to focus on the edge of the ten-foot retaining wall and my dive over the ledge. I heard a bullet strike the limestone. I didn't hear Sam yelp. The second shot would be the real test. A good marksman will miss the first running shot but compensate for movement in the next round. I was counting on the shooter not being that good.

I cleared the ledge and squeezed my bulk behind the narrow lip of the wall, crushing my face against the dirt. I couldn't risk looking to see if I was covered. The only proof would be if I didn't get shot again.

I heard the second whoosh of compressed air. The bullet hit the rock wall twenty yards farther away. There was no painful yelp. The plan had worked. The long hours I'd worked with Sam as a puppy training him to follow my point to a downed bird had paid off. I lay still for five long minutes. Nothing. No shot. My muscles began to cramp. A colony of ants explored the sweaty hair on my forearms and discovered the sticky blood farther up. I tried to blow them way, but I could feel them cling harder to my skin. I waited a moment longer, then slowly began to inch forward.

The sweat on my legs and arms quickly turned the dirt mixed with mulch into mud that stuck to my skin. If it took more than fifteen minutes to cover the distance to the bridge, Sam would realize there was no dead duck and lead the shooter directly back to me.

I inched forward, using my toes and outstretched fingers. In boot camp, I'd been forced to crawl through mud under barbed wire spaced eighteen inches off the ground wearing a backpack and carrying an M1. Our drill instructor fired live rounds above the wire to simulate combat conditions. The training paid off. I knew how to keep my butt down and keep moving.

I stopped ten yards short of the bridge. The ever-active city crew had already planted this section with ground-cover, and tiny vines were starting to sprout. Going forward would put me in full view of the shooter. I checked my watch. It had taken fifteen minutes to get to this point. My forearms and calves ached. My bullet wound throbbed. I was dehydrated. The tiny ants continued to feast on my arm.

My plan had almost worked, but the open ten yards to the bridge might as well have been a hundred. It reminded me of a WWII movie I'd seen where the prisoners had tried to dig out of a German POW camp only to come up short of the tree line.

Then I heard a splash. Sam was in the river searching for that imaginary duck. I jumped to my feet and sprinted to the bridge, hoping the noise would provide a distraction. I heard a pop. The bullet hit behind me. I reached the bridge and safety. Sam swam to the edge, and I helped him scramble out of the river. He gave me a disappointed look because he couldn't find the bird. I scratched him behind the ears and reassured him he had done his job well.

## CHAPTER TWENTY-FOUR

I stopped in the shadow of a U-Haul truck parked across the street from Sylvia's condo and studied the surrounding area. I was already starting to second-guess my judgment. Getting shot at does that. It makes you think about mortality and the dozens of other jobs that didn't require you to risk your life. The shooter had used the same weapon to take out Sosa, which meant he was shooting at me that night. He had hung around hoping to finish me off. But why? And what had caused him to try again? The only explanation was that whoever hired him had found out about my trip to the oil rig. Other than discovering that Marcus Lopez was the new owner, I hadn't really gained any information. That transfer had taken place in July. Why would Allison or Marcus want to cover that up?

When I was certain the coast was clear, I knocked on Sylvia's door. She gasped when she saw me covered in a mixture of mud, sweat, and my own blood.

"What happened?" she said, pulling me inside. She wore a pair of my boxer underwear and a pink tank top.

Sam wasted no time rubbing his wet, muddy self against her bare legs.

"Sam, you're filthy," she said, and led him out the back door. I could hear her fill his bowl with fresh water. "Has he eaten?" she called through the door.

"Give him some food. He earned it," I said. I heard her toss a cup of dry dog food in another bowl while I grabbed a beer from her fridge.

"Out with it," she demanded.

"I played lead-ball with a spook between here and the McCullough bridge. Sam saved me from being KIA."

"What does that mean? You were attacked? Speak English," she insisted. "I'm not in the Marine Corps."

I realized that I had slipped back into military mode out of habit. The strange part was that I was sitting in my girlfriend's condo drinking a beer and talking about it, when I felt like I should have been briefing my platoon for a counterassault.

"Someone shot at me from a parking garage while I jogged down the River Walk. I didn't see who it was."

"You're hurt?" She checked the bloody bandage.

"Just a flesh wound. I should clean it out." I was calm on the outside, but angry at the shooter for trying to kill me and forcing me to crawl through the dirt. I was also angry that he had caused me to second-guess myself.

Sylvia grabbed her cell phone. "I'm calling the cops, right now," she insisted.

I put my hand over her phone. "No. Not now."

"When?" she asked. "After you get killed?"

"The shooter used the same weapon that took out Sosa."

"Why would he be trying to kill you? You're not on that case."

She watched me take a drink of beer. I pressed the cool bottle to my forehead and clenched my jaw.

"Damn it, Nick. What're you doing?"

"Calm down. I'm a private investigator. I'm doing my job."

"The police warned you specifically to stay away from the case."

"Then what? Ruin my reputation? Marcus was right. Sosa's death was not good for my business." I explained to her about the trip to the oil derrick with Grandpa and what I'd found out.

"You think Marcus is mixed up in this?"

"I'm not accusing anyone until I get more evidence. I'll go to the police when I find out who did it."

"What about the other case? What about Marissa Luna?" she asked.

I told her what I'd found out about the bracelet and about Danny's track record in Lubbock.

"Danny Allison?"

"That's right. He's a spoiled member of the privileged class. He thinks the sun rises and sets in his asshole."

"You've always had a chip on your shoulder against rich people."

"Just the ones who didn't earn it. Danny never had to work a day in his life."

"What do you think will happen when Patrick Allison finds out you're investigating his heir apparent?"

I clenched my jaw and kept silent. I knew she wouldn't like my answer.

She shook her head. "Take a shower," she commanded. "You're filthy. I'll fix you a sandwich."

I realized it had been a long time since the food to-go from Lamesa. That and the extreme exertion left me nauseous. She directed me to the shower, ordered me to strip, and watched me step under the warm running water. She took my filthy shorts and T-shirt and tossed them in the sink.

When I was done, she put a fresh bandage on my arm while I finished my roast beef sandwich and opened another beer.

"You have enough evidence for them to reopen the case," she said.

"No!" I was adamant. "The police tried once and failed. I'm not going to let that happen again."

Sylvia studied my expression. "You want me to describe your face right now? You look like the little boy who won't go to his room."

I couldn't help but smile. "Okay, you caught me being stubborn."

She pushed closer and let out a deep breath, then put her lips on mine. "You're shaking," she said.

I held out my hands and realized she was right. She stripped off her pink tank top and pressed herself against me, waiting for my heartbeat to return to normal. I held her tightly.

"At least consider getting help."

I pulled her into my lap.

"Think about it," she said. The beer mixed with her perfume, after the close encounter with the sniper, made it hard to concentrate. She ran her hands through my short hair and kissed me again.

"I'm thinking," I said, but it wasn't about getting help.

I pushed the coffee table over with my foot, and we slid to the carpet.

• • •

I woke to the sound of Sam yipping and scratching on the sliding-glass door. The concrete slab in the unshaded ten-foot-square patio did not meet with his approval, and he was letting me know it was time to go. Sometime during the night, Sylvia and I had moved from the living room carpet to her king-sized bed. I could hear her in the kitchen making coffee. My arm was sore as hell and a constant throbbing reminder that someone was trying to kill me. I didn't enjoy looking over my shoulder every second wondering if a sniper was waiting to take the next shot. I had lived that life in Afghanistan. It left me jumpy and on edge. Sylvia wanted me to quit, but that wasn't an option.

I went outside and took a garden hose to Sam. All the signs said fall was coming. The Longhorns had played and lost their first football game and hunting season had started, but it still felt like summer. Sam was happy to get a bath and some food. High cirrus clouds drifted over the city. Grandpa called them "mares' tails." They either signaled rain was on the way or more of the same weather pattern. I couldn't remember which. I popped open the patio umbrella, so Sam would have shade until I was ready to go, and went back inside to face the music with Sylvia.

She was showered and in the kitchen by the time I came back inside. She made toast and I poured coffee.

She smiled and kissed me. "How's the arm?"

"Sore, but I'll live."

"Until next time?" It was a loaded question.

"I'm not going to run and hide."

She stood still in the kitchen and watched me while I took a couple of eggs from her fridge and got out her frying pan.

"You think Danny Allison killed Marissa Luna?" She was in lawyer mode. The soft cuddly sex kitten was safely tucked away. She was switching tactics and had me on the stand, ready to grill a hostile witness. She handed me the pepper shaker.

"He was with her the night she was killed," I said, cracking the eggs into the hot pan. "He's an amateur MMA fighter, easily capable of drowning her. And he was the father of her unborn child. Something I'm sure his family wouldn't have approved of. Means, opportunity, and motive."

Sylvia shook her head like she was scolding an impudent child. "How many males in a Texas bar play amateur sports?"

I knew where she was going with this. "Ten percent." I dumped my over-easy eggs onto a paper plate and sat down.

"More like eighty percent, which was probably two hundred men with means and opportunity." She had always been better at arguing than I was.

"I'm not a numbers guy. Anyway, he had a fight with her. I've got it on video."

"Why didn't the police see it?" she asked.

"I don't know. Maybe they didn't watch all of the tapes."

"What about the motive? How do you know he's the father of Marissa's unborn child?"

"He gave her an expensive Mother's Love bracelet."

"Some men buy jewelry for women as a token of affection." She wasn't going to let me off the hook easily.

"I brought you flowers." I remembered I had bought her a bracelet at the factory store. I decided not to bring it up. She wouldn't believe me anyway.

"Dead flowers." She poured us both more coffee.

"Now you're being picky," I said. She was enjoying shredding my theory. "What about his prior history? Two women accused Danny Allison of sexual harassment. At least one of them benefited financially. You can't defend him for that, counselor. The guy's a dirtbag."

"Will those women testify in court?"

"They dropped the charges."

"Unfortunately, you have nothing that will overrule the police theory. There's still a reasonable doubt. Being a dirtbag isn't a crime."

"What about the terms of the trust fund? You work for Marcus. You must have heard something."

"I can't tell you that."

"Come on. We're trying to establish a link here. All I want to know is if there were conditions for him to inherit the money. I'm not going to take it to the DA."

She sipped her coffee and looked out the window. Her legal mind was searching for an answer. It was at the heart of our disagreement from the time I decided to drop out of law school. She was thinking of courtroom rules. I was thinking of justice. She was considering what could be proven in court. I was thinking of the truth.

"I just want to know if a pregnant girl could interfere with his inheritance."

Her lips pinched together. I didn't think she would answer.

"Yes," she said.

"That sounds like a motive. The rich bastard." My blood was starting to boil. "Silver-spoon-sucking frat boy was willing to murder his girlfriend and unborn child so he could maintain his rich and privileged lifestyle. You know in Texas that counts as killing two people. The charge is capital murder, counselor. That means a minimum life in prison."

"If convicted. You still don't know Danny Allison is the father," she said.

"All I need is a drop of his blood."

"Even people you decide are guilty are allowed a rigorous defense. It's called due process. You can't be judge, jury, and executioner."

"I'm not a vigilante."

"Then let the system work," she insisted.

"Marissa Luna is dead, and nobody was held accountable!" I saw disappointment in her eyes. I heard Sam barking and realized I was shouting.

"Don't look now, but you're showing emotion," she said.

I took her in my arms, but she felt different. There was a harder edge to her normally soft touch. She studied my face as if searching for some indication that I would reconsider, that I would walk away and let the police and the DA handle everything. They had had their chance.

"When we were in law school, we both wanted to fight for the little guy—the underdog who couldn't fend for himself," I said.

"I was young and naïve," she said. She meant I still was.

I turned to go.

"Nick," she said. "Be careful. You still don't know who's shooting at you."

She didn't need to remind me.

# CHAPTER TWENTY-FIVE

I JOINED A HANDFUL OF PEOPLE waiting at the bus stop on my street corner. I recognized them all. Sam accepted a few compliments while I studied my yard from half a block away. There wasn't much traffic because of the Labor Day holiday. The neighborhood high school was closed. Kids were sleeping till noon. A flock of white-winged doves dive-bombed a rooftop and reminded me that it was opening weekend for white-winged dove hunting. As if I needed another excuse to finish this case. The doves were always plentiful in the city because they seemed to realize it was a no-hunting zone. In the legal fields outside of town, they were harder to find.

I checked the porches and the parked cars lining the street. Four houses down sat a black Super Duty Ford pickup with dark tinted windows. It looked like the same pickup I'd seen in the restaurant parking lot across from the mission. Could have been a coincidence. Everybody drove a pickup. I memorized the license plate. If I saw it again, it wouldn't be a coincidence.

When the bus arrived, two of my neighbors got out. They worked the night shift as civilian employees at the base. Sam and I said hello. They seemed unaware of the potential danger. Like the doves on the roof calmly pecking seeds from the shingles, most people felt safe in their own neighborhood where hunting was supposed to be off-limits. The black Super Duty made a U-turn in the street and drove to the end of the block.

Rose Gustafson was backing her pickup out of her driveway, so I stopped to open her gate. She rolled down her window and looked me over like my grandmother used to do when I'd stayed out all night with the boys in high school.

"You look like a man on a mission," she said. "Are you on a case?"

"Just out for a jog," I said. I didn't want to involve her in any details.

"Humbug. Be careful," she said. "Would you keep an eye on my place? I'm going to Seguin to visit my sister."

"Happy to," I said. "Drive safely."

"I always do," she said. "Don't forget, tomorrow's trash day." She drove off, and I closed her gate. I wondered if she braved the freeway or took the back roads. I remembered her complaining about cataracts and how her sight wasn't what it used to be.

My pickup stood in the driveway beside the house. There was a scrap of white paper trapped under the wiper blade. I pulled it out. It was a torn piece of a takeout bag from Whataburger with a note scrawled in pencil.

*Stay away from Luna. Next time I don't miss.*

I glanced quickly in the direction the Super Duty had gone, but it was out of sight. I ran to the end of the block and checked the parking lot by the high school and the Mennonite church. The black pickup was gone.

Sam followed me back to my yard. I checked under my pickup's hood, looking for signs of tampering. It wasn't touched. No obvious prints on the windows. I checked the perimeter of the house. Sam made a show of sniffing the bushes and barked at one of Rose Gustafson's cats, trying to be helpful. To Sam, cats were always guilty of something. I unlocked the front door and searched the house. Everything seemed in order. The surveillance cameras were intact. Nothing was missing, and no one had done my dirty dishes or laundry.

I threw a set of gym clothes in my duffle bag along with a handful of cotton swabs, bandages, and a Ziploc baggie. My wound was sore, but the injury didn't affect my grip or arm strength. Had the bullet hit the bone, the hollow point would have shattered and torn out most of my muscle. I would have been in the hospital with a missing arm. The first aid gear was for Danny Allison. I had no intention of staying away from Luna, and Danny was my prime suspect. He had already challenged me to a fight. If he left a little blood on the canvas, there was nothing to stop me from having it analyzed.

• • •

Lucky's gym was on the west side of San Antonio. It was an older part of town not connected to the upscale north or the newer expansion to the far west. Instead of the fashionable Hill Country views of cedar trees and limestone rocks, there was a dense sea of flat green that flowed in every direction. I rolled down a street lined with two-story apartments, car repair shops, and Hispanic markets. Most of the businesses showed their age, but they were open. The area bustled with a gritty working life. Taco stands and one-room restaurants offering fresh tamales were abundant. In the last twenty years, the only new addition to the local economy seemed to be the dollar stores that sold everything except alcohol.

Lucky's gym was the anchor store for a strip mall that also housed a Mexican restaurant, a tattoo and massage parlor, and a mom-and-pop gas station. It was a big two-story building that had once been a furniture store. Caesar Hernandez, or "Lucky," bought the building and the mall with earnings from an impressive welterweight professional career. He was an aggressive,

Mexican-style boxer that I'd once seen pummel an opponent to a round-one TKO. He still trained and managed a stable of young up-and-comers.

The ground floor looked like a high school gym. It was Lucky's way of giving back to the community. He wouldn't let the kids in unless school was out, but it was the Labor Day holiday, so teen girls and boys were engaged in all aspects of training. A skinny girl not much more than thirteen was swinging for all she was worth at a punching bag twice her weight. A half dozen other kids were in the corner on the speed bags. Lucky was leaning on the center ring ropes watching two featherweights dance around each other.

"Mix it up," he shouted at them. Both seemed reluctant to throw a punch.

"Hey, champ," I called to him. "Those your new prospects?"

He turned to me and smiled. His front two teeth were missing. When he went outside the gym, he wore two gold replacements. In the gym, he kept the false teeth in his pocket.

"Why don't you get dressed and teach them a few moves, huh?" Lucky let me spar with the young guys he was training in the heavyweight division. I wasn't a natural boxer but could hold my own in the ring, and he liked that I could take a punch.

"They look like eighth graders," I said.

"High school. What you working today?" he asked, keeping an eye on the young fighters.

"I'm gonna try my luck upstairs," I said. "I wanna hang out with the cool kids."

He raised both eyebrows. He knew I never went upstairs, which explained why I had never run into Danny.

"Don't hurt those guys," he said, showing the gap in his teeth. "I need them healthy to pay rent."

I didn't say anything. There were no guarantees I wouldn't break Danny's neck.

I walked up the stairs and took a look around. There were no school kids on the second floor. Lucky didn't allow it. Four years ago, he partnered with an ex-Army Ranger who offered classes in mixed martial arts. Tough guys and wannabe tough guys who were watching MMA on TV figured they should get in on the action. Lucky was cashing in on the craze. Danny Allison was a wannabe tough guy who got a taste of MMA in Lubbock, and he and his trend-following crowd were making Lucky's gym the in place to train.

There were free weights in one corner and practice mats in the other. In the center was a sparring ring, where two women were doing their best Ronda Rousey imitation, huffing and panting and staring each other down. A handful of guys practiced Brazilian jiu-jitsu moves led by Lucky's partner, Jerry Muth. He wore black pajamas and looked like Chuck Norris with a gray ponytail. Everyone called him Sarge.

The wannabe tough guys on this floor all wore specialized, name-brand outfits and shoes that they bought on the MMA websites. Most of them decorated their exposed skin with RockTape, the popular kinesiology tape that was supposed to relieve pain and provide joint support. I was five years older than everyone on the second floor except Sarge and could use joint pain relief, but the red, green, and black strips looked more like a fashion statement than anything useful—like wearing a baseball cap backward on a sunny day. The kids downstairs were in gym shorts and T-shirts issued by their school's athletic department. Those kids came from the streets, where you didn't need money to be a tough guy.

I found Danny Allison doing barbell curls and watching himself in the mirror. He wore a string tank top that let him admire his steroid-enhanced muscles without interference. I stood and watched him while he completed a set. He was bulky but not a bodybuilder. I could tell he did aerobics. He had quick movements and a spring in his step that eluded the heavy lifters. He had an inch of height on me and about ten pounds that he probably packed on with whey protein. Strips of black-and-green RockTape covered his knees and both elbows.

Danny had a happy-go-lucky facial expression that didn't change whether he was looking at himself in the mirror or the other guys in the room. Sylvia didn't say how much he would inherit, but the Allison family was one of the richest in the state. Had he weighed the money against Marissa and his unborn child? If it was less than a million would he still have killed her? The more I thought about it, the angrier I got. Spilling Danny's blood would be a pleasure.

Danny racked his barbells and finally looked up. A rakish smile spread over his face. "Nick. Didn't think you'd show up," he said in a cocky, challenging way, as if we were comparing manhood in the high school shower room. He wasn't old enough to know that size doesn't matter.

"You said Monday," I said with a smile. I wanted him to stay cocky and at ease until after I laid him out on the canvas. "You up for this?" I pointed with my gym bag to the ring in the center of the floor.

Danny stepped toward me drying his hands on a designer gym towel. "Always," he said.

"I'll get changed." I went to the locker room and stowed my street clothes. By the time I came back out, a small crowd of Danny look-alikes had gathered around the ring. Lucky met me ringside. I set my bag down just outside the ropes, so I had easy access to the swabs and the plastic bag.

"My gym. My rules," Lucky said loud enough for Danny and the dozen or so onlookers to hear. Word had spread quickly about our challenge match. Sarge joined the crowd and nodded at me. We had traded stories over beers at the VFW a time or two. He was the real deal. Someone I wanted in my corner.

Danny sauntered over. "Sure, anything you say." He grinned,

trying his best not to look worried. He was doing a good job, but he was already standing on the balls of his feet. He had his shirt off and his shoulders and chest puffed out.

I didn't smile, transitioning into fighter mode. I stayed loose and flat-footed. "Fine," I said. "We use four-ounce gloves. I want to get a workout, but I don't wanna be here all day."

Lucky looked at Danny, then back at me. "Okay, but use headgear."

"Done," I said, effectively taking Danny out of the negotiations. I was making psychological points—playing the adult in the room.

Lucky handed us the padded headgear. I slipped in my own mouthpiece and climbed into the ring. I held the ropes apart for Danny. Another signal that I was in charge. He noticed the bandage on my upper arm where the bullet had hit me. I had traded out the bulky gauze for a square skin-tone patch, so it wouldn't draw too much attention.

"That gonna interfere?" he asked, pointing to the patch.

"I'll manage," I said and walked to the opposite corner of the ring.

Danny's cheering section barked encouragement. I stood rock-solid while Danny danced for the crowd. He put on a shadowboxing show. He stretched. He showed off a combination roundhouse and front scissor kick. All very impressive. Skeeter had said Danny won a few matches in Lubbock. I let him go through his routine. He was telling me everything I needed to know about his fighting style.

"Aren't you gonna warm up?" Danny said, still bouncing up and down on the balls of his feet.

I didn't say a word. His frenetic movements told me he was nervous, ready for the punching to start. I waited for Lucky to make his way to center ring.

"Looks like somebody's got something to prove here," Lucky

said. He gave both of us a knowing look. He'd been in the fight business too long not to know what was going on. He fixed me with a cocked eyebrow and whispered so Danny couldn't hear: "I don't want nobody hurt. Are we clear?"

I shrugged.

Danny glanced from side to side at his buddies for support. I heard one say: "Take the old man out." Times were changing. Nobody had ever called me "old man" before. To these twenty-somethings, thirty-three was over the hill.

"MMA rules. Stop if I tap you out. Got it?" Lucky barked above the noise.

"Got it," I said, keeping my focus on Danny.

"Yeah, man," Danny said. He held his gloved hands out. I bumped them hard.

The fight was on.

Danny bounced up and down and side to side. Held his arms up and flexed his muscles. I could tell he'd never been in a street fight against an equal opponent. What he did was show off.

I watched Danny's eyes. He shot a left-hand jab toward my face. I dodged and slapped his hand away. I moved just enough to keep him off balance. My hands were at the ready, but lower than my shoulders. I wanted him to build up his confidence and start into the kick combination that he'd been practicing. I was sure that he thought it was his knockout move. He was waiting for the right moment to unleash it on me.

"You don't have much style," he shouted through his mouthguard.

"I had a different teacher," I said.

He was already breathing hard. Nervous energy. He threw another left-right combination. I batted both down and hit him with a backhand just to give him a taste. The blow caught him on the chin below the headgear. His neck snapped back. He felt it.

"The Marine Corps doesn't give you points for style," I said.

Danny recovered from the blow. I gave him credit for taking a punch even though I'd only given him a taste. He tested out a roundhouse kick. It wasn't his full combination. He was practicing. I saw him targeting the bandage on my arm. His heel grazed the bullet wound. Pain shot down my arm. Danny noticed and tried to throw another kick in that direction. He smelled a weakness. His muscles tensed. He was ready to kick my ass.

"How do I measure up to your military standards?" he said. He was fishing for a compliment, still playing cocky.

"You tell me. Do you have what it takes to be a killer? Maybe you already have a taste for blood." I watched him for a reaction.

"I'm just playing around," he claimed, but I saw a slight change in his attitude. He wanted to hit me with everything he had. I started to wonder if his frat-boy shtick was just an act.

"Are you a killer?" I asked. I saw a faint hint of recognition in his eyes like he knew what I was talking about.

He swung a couple more punches, trying to get me to move into the corner so that he would have enough room for his kick-punch combination. I stepped back and let him have all the room he needed.

"You know where this came from?" I asked, holding up my bandaged arm. "Someone took a shot at me."

"Dangerous work," he said.

"You can tell whoever did it, I won't back down," I said.

"You're one crazy dude," he said. He wasn't going to give me a confession. Not then anyway. He wanted to kick my ass.

I saw his kick-punch combo coming before he executed it. His body language telegraphed his attack like a sci-fi movie prologue scrolling into outer space. I was enjoying every second of it. There would be enough blood for a dozen DNA tests.

The roundhouse came and went. I moved as little as necessary and felt the breeze on my cheek as his foot cruised through empty air. He did have strength and speed. That kick had probably taken out a dozen opponents in Lubbock. I saw the disappointment on his face when he didn't connect.

He launched the scissor kick next. I waited for it. He had good form but no imagination. He landed on the balls of his feet, ready for the punch combo. He swung his left hook like a cleanup hitter for the Astros. I took it on the shoulder and felt my arm go numb. Danny noticed my reaction. I needed to finish him off while I still had the strength.

He flashed his right jab. The move I'd been waiting for. I stepped inside of it and let go with my own right hand. The punch landed just under his nose—that space not covered by the headgear. I wanted plenty of blood.

His face caved in like a Prius hitting a freight train. I followed up with my right elbow. I felt the bone snap. Blood gushed from his broken nose and lip like water from a breached dam. Danny collapsed on the canvas. Lucky slipped through the ropes and knelt beside him. He shook his head at me.

"What?" I said innocently. "It was a fair fight. The kid challenged me."

I grabbed my bag through the ropes and pulled out the cotton swab and a baggie. I held the cotton to Danny's nose and soaked it with blood. Lucky popped an amyl nitrate in his face. Danny came around slowly.

"Take it easy. Don't get up too quickly," I told him. I was playing the adult again. His eyes weren't quite focused. He never knew what hit him.

"What happened?" Danny asked.

I didn't say anything.

Lucky waved me out of the way. "Go home," he said. "The kid learned his lesson." Lucky was the only one in the room besides Sarge who knew what I had just done. In his prime, he could have done the same to me.

I slipped the blood sample into a plastic baggie and put it in my gym bag. I didn't bother to change clothes, just walked down the stairs. The group of Danny's friends gave me a wide berth and nodded their admiration. They'd just seen their champ get beat.

Outside on the street, a bronze F-350 pickup with oversized tires and a chrome roll bar took up the first three parking spots. The license plate read *Danny One.*

# CHAPTER TWENTY-SIX

I DREADED MY NEXT MOVE, BUT there was no faster way to get Danny's blood sample to Kelly's lab in Lubbock than to drive it up there myself. I had to keep the pressure on before the shooter came after me again. I didn't really have any doubts that Danny was the father or that he was Marissa's killer. The only remaining question was, How was Marissa's death connected to Sosa? I spent the five-hour drive going over the possibilities. Sosa couldn't have been directly involved because he had been in Mexico in July. Skeeter had checked on his whereabouts. The timing of Marcus Lopez's takeover of Allison Oil seemed significant. Both Marissa's murder and the business transaction took place in July. By the time Lubbock emerged out of the late summer cotton fields, I was no closer to a viable link.

I found a parking spot and called Kelly. She told me to meet her at the back door by the air-conditioner unit. I grabbed the plastic bag I was using to transport Danny's blood sample and stepped out into the North Texas air. The Panhandle was enjoying much cooler weather than South Texas. It wasn't quite jacket weather, but it was close.

Kelly already had the fetal DNA. She had connections with the lab used by the San Antonio medical examiner's office and was waiting to run the test. There was a marked difference in the town. The university was back in session. The traffic was heavier. Red-and-black signs supporting the football team decorated every streetlamp. Tuesday marked the second week of classes. Week one was usually devoted to pledge week, which translated into drunken parties and freshman orientation. The students were busy moving into new apartments and renewing old friendships that had lapsed over the summer. Week two was when the professors began dishing out assignments and, of course, it was football season.

Kelly was waiting in the open door when I walked around the corner of the building. She was looking the other way, anticipating my approach from the street, giving me a moment of observation before she saw me. Asking her to run a DNA sample on an exclusive piece of equipment under FBI supervision was pushing the limits of an old Marine buddy favor, but I couldn't afford to wait three or four months for the results when someone was trying to kill me. I couldn't help but think she had ulterior motives for helping out, but at the moment I didn't want to guess what those were.

When she turned her face into the light, I involuntarily took a sharp breath. She wore her normally tightly wrapped hair loosely curved around her oval face, accentuating dark-red lipstick. I'd never seen her dressed as a civilian. I had only seen her in either her military or campus police uniform. Her lab coat was open exposing tight jeans and a western belt with a turquoise buckle that accented a set of black ostrich-skin boots. Her black shirt was a silky material that sparkled in the halogen light and clung to curves that I'd never seen her show off.

"Hello," I said. "You look amazing."

A shy smile spread across her made-up face. Her cheeks turned a shade redder. "You're late," she said and swatted at the moths circling the outdoor lamp.

"Traffic was a bitch. You got a hot date?"

She gave me a hug. "Yeah," she said, like I should have known. "You owe me dinner. This is gonna take three to four hours. Did you think we were gonna wait in my office?"

She smelled like lavender with a hint of perfume. When I realized her date was with me, I checked my own clothes self-consciously. I had on Wrangler jeans and boots. Not my best boots, but at least they weren't muddy. My button-down shirt was clean, but I'd been in a pickup for six hours.

She laughed and took my arm. "You look fine," she said. "If I'd told you to dress up, you'd have worn the same thing."

I was going to say I had a tux, but I remembered it was torn and bloody. We walked side by side down the hall to the lab. This area of the building was still buzzing with activity even at nine in the evening. The express lab was doing a booming business.

"You have one ahead of you," she said. "I've already loaded the fetal DNA."

I waited in her office while she prepped the sample and loaded the machine. I looked at her collection of photos and memorabilia. There was a snapshot of her father on his tractor, and one of me in Afghanistan. We were the only men in the pictures. My photo was taken before I took a face full of glass. It was hard to remember what I looked like without scars. Kelly had never mentioned it or asked me about the attack. We'd had only one contact since she resigned her commission. We had met at the historic San Antonio VFW. I remembered telling her about Sylvia. We had just started dating, and after a few beers, I probably said more than I should have about our chemistry. Shortly after that, Kelly told me she was going to take a job in Lubbock, her hometown. That was three years ago. Now, things were different. Part of me clung to the hope that Sylvia and I could work out our differences and that she would accept my chosen line of work, but I was starting to think that chemistry alone wasn't enough to hold us together.

Kelly knocked on her office door and came inside. "All we can do now is wait," she said with a smile and a raised eyebrow. She slipped off her lab coat revealing the tight-fitting outfit that stretched from her black silk T-shirt to bootcut jeans.

"Never saw you out of uniform," I remarked. It was all I could think of to say.

She spun around on her new bootheels. "You like? We never went out on a date before." She took my arm and led me out the door and down the hall. I felt her warmth and smelled the hint of lavender. I wasn't prepared for this.

We used my pickup, and she directed me to her favorite steakhouse on the west side away from the throngs of hungry students. It was a cozy place that I'd been to before. They had tablecloths and strived for upscale, but jeans and boots were always welcome in a Texas steakhouse.

I ordered a beer even though the place was proud of their wine selection. Kelly selected a Malbec. I occasionally drank wine, but it usually put me to sleep and I had six more hours on the road before I could crawl in bed.

"How's Sylvia?" she said. No beating around the bush.

"Honestly, I'm not sure." I decided to confide in her.

"What does that mean?" Our drinks came, and she took a large sip of Malbec.

"I think her new job reminds her of the lifestyle she grew up with." I was trying to break down my own thoughts into pieces I could understand.

"She likes money and everything that goes with it," she said. "Her boss has it. You don't." She had a way of cutting through the BS.

"The thing is, I don't know if she knows it. I don't know if she's aware of what she wants." I was being honest. I really didn't think Sylvia knew what kind of a life she was after.

"I never met her. She seems very high maintenance. I can't

believe you put up with her." She took another sip of wine. "How's the campaign going?"

"Marcus is ahead in the polls. Unless there's an October surprise, he's moving to Austin."

"She's going with him?"

"I don't see any way around it," I said.

Kelly took my hand under the table. Her hazel eyes didn't have the depth that Sylvia's had or the exotic passion. They were open and direct.

"I know what I want," she said.

I took a swig of beer. I wasn't expecting this from Kelly. "So, you're having the T-bone medium well?" I didn't want her to finish her thought.

She smiled and squeezed my hand. "How'd you guess? I could eat two. I'm starving."

The waiter appeared wearing black pants and a white button-down shirt. He looked like a college kid working his way through the semester. Kelly let me have my hand back, and we ordered our meal. I didn't want to shut her out. She was going out on a limb for me, but on the other hand, I didn't want to lead her on. Kelly sensed my discomfort and shifted the conversation.

"What happens when you get the results of the DNA test?" she asked.

"If it's a match, it means Danny had a motive to kill her. It would cut him out of the family fortune."

"Only if he knew about the baby," she said.

"He bought her a Mother's Love bracelet. I think he knew. I think they argued about it the night he killed her."

The college kid brought the steak. I cut into it to make sure they didn't overcook it. The meat was red and juicy and perfect. I nodded to the waiter and took a bite. There weren't many places that served steak this good. I closed my eyes and enjoyed the smoky, rich flavor.

"If it is a match, you're going to go back to San Antonio and shoot him in the head?"

"What do you take me for, a Neanderthal?"

"Yeah. Look at your steak." She pointed to the half-eaten portion on the plate. The center section still leaked red blood. "Your German palate was formed before they invented fire." She said it with a smile, but she meant it. "Am I going to have to spend my vacation time getting you out of jail?"

"I'm not going to shoot him. Not yet. I'll give him a chance to confess first."

"Danny Allison is not the kind of person you confront on your own. He's taken a shot at you twice. His family has all the money in the world. I know you don't trust the police and this Detective Peterson to do his job, but you don't have a choice on this one."

I grinned at her. "Of course," I said. I wanted to see Danny on trial. I wanted to see him sent to prison. I wanted justice.

We finished our meal and walked back to my pickup. We brushed against each other. Our hands touched. Our fingers laced together. The move felt natural, like we'd done it before. Her hand was warm. The stars were out, and the dusty wind had taken the night off.

When I walked her to the passenger-side door, Kelly put her arms around me and nestled her blond head into the curve of my neck. "It's getting late," she said. "What if the test is negative?"

"I'll stay. That would mean I have to start all over. Since Marissa was in school here until the first of June, the father was either a student or a local."

"That might take a while," she said. Her lips were close to my chest. I could feel her heart beat. "You'd need a place to stay."

"You're offering to put me up?"

She answered with a kiss. She tasted like warm honey with a hint of Malbec. She pressed harder. We held the pose for an extra minute. I couldn't help thinking how different Sylvia felt and tasted. She drank pinot gris and her lips were closer to jalapenos than honey. The two couldn't be any more different.

"I know what you're thinking," she said.

"Are you kidding? I'm a Neanderthal, remember? You're pressed against me. There's only one thing on my mind."

Kelly smiled. Even in the dark, I could see her blush.

"You're lying. You're thinking of a girl in San Antonio." Her smile faded, and her hazel eyes bore into mine. "I respect that."

"Look, Kelly—"

She cut me off with a finger on my lips. "You don't have to explain." Her cell phone buzzed. She listened, then disconnected.

"It's a match."

# CHAPTER TWENTY-SEVEN

SPLASHING THROUGH A PUDDLE IN my driveway in the early dawn light reminded me what Grandpa had said about mares' tails—they predicted rain. The moisture was the remnant of a hurricane that struck the Pacific Coast and traveled east, blocking the north wind that brought cooler, dryer air to Lubbock from reaching South Texas.

I could see by the mud on the sidewalk that someone had been to the house. The tracks weren't big enough for Skeeter. He wore a size fifteen when he could find it. Sixteen if he ordered online. I examined the tracks across the lawn. The toe of the print was deeper than the heel as if the person who made it ran.

I glanced at Rose Gustafson's empty house and remembered she had asked me to watch her place while she was gone, which meant feed her herd of cats. I went to her back porch and filled the cat bowls with food from a plastic container she left by the door and was suddenly surrounded by Rose's feline friends. I hurried back to my place before Sam could see me and think I had gone over to the other side.

When I reached for my key, I saw a two-inch gap in the doorjamb. There were splinters around both deadbolts where someone had used something large and heavy to smash through the door. The extra locks I'd added as a precaution had barely slowed him down. I pulled my .45 and waited by the door, listening for any sound of movement inside the house. The only noise came from the ever-present cicadas and white-winged doves. It was too early for morning traffic.

I eased the door open with my boot. The front room was empty. I caught a whiff of something stale and pungent. The muddy shoe tracks trekked up the stairs and into my bedroom. The room looked like a Texas tornado had touched down on my queen bed. Even a loose board I had neglected to fix had been pried up to expose the empty space beneath.

The mud was dry. Whoever left the tracks had been gone at least two hours. I took a breath and called for Sam. No answer.

I went downstairs. The same tornado had cut a path through my office. My state compliance business papers were scattered, and my books were tossed on the floor. The locked cabinet meant nothing. The padlock was cut. The contents dumped. Hopefully, the security cameras Skeeter installed had captured the intruder. The alarm should have triggered a police response. I would have to find out from Skeeter what went wrong, because I hadn't been notified. I went to the fireplace and pulled out the grate. The one place he hadn't looked. The burnt log was left over from last winter. The day I moved in was coincidently the only day cold enough to light a fire. I kept the log to cover the hidden compartment below. I lifted the layer of bricks and pulled the handle on the hidden metal safe. Inside, the surveillance tapes, the engraved bracelet, and my notes were untouched.

I called out again for Sam. Still no answer. I walked toward the kitchen. The stale smell got stronger. A swarm of flies lifted off the bar and buzzed my head. I thought I'd left venison steaks on the counter to thaw for dinner, which I sometimes did when I knew I'd be home early enough to cook for myself. There was nothing on the countertop.

I rounded the bar into the kitchen. Sam was on the floor. A half-eaten cheeseburger beside his stiff body. The deep pool of blood on the hardwood floor was still tacky to the touch. It had soaked into the green kitchen rug below the sink. I found a small entry wound behind his ear. The shooter had an easy job. Sam never met a stranger. He probably barked until he smelled the burger. He never had a chance. The hole was small, probably from a .22 pistol. One shot. At least he didn't suffer.

The killer had taken Sam's collar and nametag off and left it on the floor on top of a note. This one was scrawled on my own spiral notebook. It was a list of names. *Sam, Sylvia, Grandpa, Clarence.* Sam's name was crossed off the list. On the bottom it read: *Last warning. Stay away from Luna.*

# CHAPTER TWENTY-EIGHT

I GRABBED MY CELL PHONE AND hit speed dial. Sylvia picked up on the first ring.

"Nick?" she asked like she'd been waiting for my call.

"Are you all right?" I asked.

"I'm fine. Where have you been?" She sounded more irritated than scared.

"Never mind," I said. "You're in danger. I put you in danger. Whoever shot at me and killed Sosa, killed Sam. He left a note threatening you, Skeeter, and Grandpa."

"You took it to the police, right?" she said.

"I will, after I find Danny Allison," I said.

"Nick—"

I cut her off. "Where are you right now?"

"Driving to work."

"Stay there. I'm going to have Skeeter watch you."

"I don't like it," she said, sounding scared and pissed off at the same time.

"I don't either. It's only for a day. Maybe two. Then it will all be over. I promise. I love you."

"Nick…" she said and paused. She seemed reluctant to continue.

"What is it?" I asked, not really wanting an answer.

"When this is over. We need to talk."

"Whatever you want," I said.

She disconnected. I didn't blame her for being pissed off. She had wanted me to stay away from the case. I knew what *we need to talk* meant.

I called Grandpa next. As usual, the phone rang and rang. I let it go eight times and disconnected. I knew he wouldn't be caught dead indoors after seven a.m. I remembered seeing a sign for the neighbor's petting zoo. I wondered if I could contact him and get a message to Grandpa. I wasn't sure what I would say. *Be careful. Go to town*. He wouldn't listen. When this was over, I would insist he carry the cell phone.

I called Skeeter next and briefed him on the DNA results. Then I told him about finding Sam in the kitchen and the threatening note.

"You didn't get a call? There was no police response?" Skeeter asked.

"Nothing. The guy must have disabled your system. Check the surveillance footage to see if you caught anything on tape."

"I'm doing that now. The feed goes to my computer."

"My guess is you won't find anything. If the guy was good enough to bypass the alarm, he's not gonna show his face on camera."

"I'm looking at it now," he said. "Athletic guy, just under six feet, wearing a black windbreaker, surgical gloves, and a ski mask."

"So much for security," I said.

"At least they didn't get the evidence."

"No thanks to your security system."

"You live in a hundred-year-old house. It wasn't made for that kind of security."

"We'll talk about that later. Leave your house. Take stuff for a couple of days. Don't go home until this mess is over," I told him. "Your name was on the list."

"My name?"

"Yeah, your real name."

"Sonofabitch," he said.

The morning traffic buzzed outside my window. At some point I had walked outside, started my pickup, and put it in drive.

"Don't do something you're going to regret," he said.

"I'm calm, cool, and collected," I lied.

"I know you. You're about to go all Afghanistan. Then the police will come after me because I'm on your payroll."

"You volunteered for the job," I said. The morning traffic wasn't cooling my anger.

"'Cause I owe you. I appreciate what you did for me more than you know. But somebody shot your dog and threatened your family. And right now, your vision is cloudy. You loved that animal, and you want somebody to pay for his death."

"What the hell's wrong with that?" I slammed on the brakes to keep from rear-ending a woman in a white Honda with the visor down putting on makeup.

"Nothing," Skeeter said. "That's what I like about you. When you take a case, the guilty party gets punished."

"And it's time to dish out some punishment."

"You're not taking down a gangbanger. This guy's got connections that you or I can't access," Skeeter said.

"You wanna quit? I'll wave the two weeks' notice. I'll mail your final paycheck. Consider your debt paid in full."

Skeeter didn't reply right away. I heard him breathing. I set the cell phone on the seat and put it on speaker. I was stuck at a red light behind the Avalon.

"I'm with you," he finally said. "What do you need?"

"The number for a petting zoo in Gillespie County."

"Not what I expected..."

"I can't reach Grandpa, and the zoo is next door."

"Got it. What else?"

"I need you to watch Sylvia."

"All right," Skeeter said. "Where are you right now. I'll come to you."

I looked up and realized the light was green. Cars honked and pulled around me. A guy with a pipe rack on his pickup flipped me off. Skeeter was right. I needed to talk it out. I scanned the street signs out my window.

"I'm at the corner of North Main and Quincy," I said.

"You're two blocks from Lulu's Bakery. I love their cinnamon rolls. Go in and order two for me and coffee. Wait for me. Give me twenty minutes."

I agreed and disconnected.

Lulu's parking lot was overflowing. The place was popular with the breakfast crowd. I found a place on the street and turned the engine off. My muscles relaxed. I realized I'd been doing isometric exercises on the wheel.

I went inside the café and found a table that two cops were just leaving. I shoved their dirty plates aside and sat down. The sharp anger I felt after finding Sam was slowly turning to dull throbbing pain. I wondered at the kind of person who could take an innocent life for no other reason than to send a message or because the life interfered with the family inheritance. Had Danny led such a sheltered life that killing meant nothing more than an exclamation point? When I took a life in combat, I took comfort in knowing the evil that life represented. I had watched the enemy kill women and children and my brothers. When I went hunting, the animals I killed were part of the food chain and thinning their numbers helped control population density and preserve habitat. The hunt itself was infused with ritual and the spirit of the pioneers. Killing for sport, pleasure, or monetary gain represented evil.

The young waitress stood beside me for a full minute before I realized she was there and waiting. I looked up and forgot to smile.

She took an involuntary step back. “You okay?” She glanced at the cops in the parking lot. When I didn’t answer immediately, she pressed on. “Would you like to order, sir?” She was no doubt used to early morning customers angry for no reason other than they had to go to work.

I had a better reason, but there was nothing she could do about it. I ordered coffee for two and Skeeter’s cinnamon rolls. She rushed off to fill the order. Normally, I ordered the migas plate with scrambled eggs, tortillas, and refried beans, but I wasn’t hungry.

Skeeter texted me the petting zoo number. I called, but no answer. They only opened on weekends. I left a message explaining who I was and that I needed to contact Grandpa. Exactly twenty minutes later, Skeeter came through the door. He got the usual looks because of his size before he found my table. This time, he was probably right—they were wondering why anyone would sit next to me.

I was on my second cup of coffee. The young waitress came back and offered to heat his rolls. Skeeter gladly accepted her offer. She took the two dinner-plate-sized rolls back to the kitchen. He sat down and studied my face.

“Let me see your hands,” he said.

“What for?” I said.

“Let me see them,” he repeated.

I held my hands above the table. I couldn’t hold them still.

“When your hands shake, I know somebody’s gonna get hurt.”

“You think I’m a vigilante?”

“You ain’t no vigilante. Did you shoot the guy who set me up?”

"I meant to."

"Who you foolin'? You caught him with a gun in his hand."

"There were innocent bystanders. I couldn't get a clean shot."

"You didn't kill him because you wanted him to stand trial and prove the cops and the DA got it wrong." He was right. Killing him would have been too easy. It would have allowed the prosecutor and the police to brush Skeeter's case under the rug. Instead they had to put the real murderer on trial and expose their own malpractice.

"Fine," I said. "I'm not going to shoot Danny. When I'm finished with him, he might wish he were dead. He's gonna confess to killing Marissa and her unborn child. Capital murder. I'll let the State of Texas execute him."

"What about Sosa?"

"What about him?" I asked.

"How is Marissa's murder tied to Sosa?"

"I think Danny knew I'd take the Luna case, and he came after me. Sosa was collateral damage. I was the target from the beginning."

"How would he know that?" he asked.

"When I find him, I'll ask him."

"How you gonna get to him?"

"Through Marcus Lopez."

"What's he got to do with it?"

"He's still the family lawyer. I think those two families are closer than they would like anybody to know."

The waitress brought back the hot cinnamon rolls with a new pad of melted butter on top. He cut into one of them with a knife and fork and shoved a large slice of buttery cinnamon dough into his mouth. Pleasure spread across his face.

"What if he tells Danny to run?" he asked.

"Danny won't run."

"Why not?" Skeeter asked around the edges of the roll.

"Too arrogant," I said. "He thinks the sun rises and sets in his asshole. Think about it. He paid off a girl in Lubbock. He murdered a girl in San Antonio because she got pregnant, and he killed Sosa and Sam to get me off the case. He's not scared of me or the law. He thinks he's untouchable."

"Maybe he is," Skeeter said.

"I'm going to bring Danny in. In the meantime, stay armed. I want you to watch Sylvia."

"The note said he was coming after me? What did it say?"

I showed him the note. "Still want me to take it easy?"

He read the note and clenched his teeth. "How'd he get my real name?"

"Maybe he read it in the paper. That article about your release." I was thinking about the article that Mrs. Luna had showed me. The one that someone left in her mailbox.

"Give me a shotgun. You know I can't hit the side of a bus with that pistol you gave me." It was true, he wasn't a marksman by any stretch of the imagination.

"Got you covered," I said and finished the last of my coffee. The tables around us were empty. Most of the patrons had gone to work.

"You want me in her office?" he asked.

"No one will touch her there. Marcus has his own security in place. I want you to set up surveillance at her condo and put a tracker on her car." I grabbed the check.

Skeeter looked at me and then the second giant cinnamon roll. "Mind if I finish this first?"

"Go for it." I handed him Marcus's business card with his personal cell phone number written on the back, something I'd lifted from Sylvia's desk. "I wanna know who he calls when I leave his house," I said.

Skeeter took the card and smiled.

"I'll give you thirty minutes." I knew he loved a challenge. "Keep your phone charged," I said. For a tech guy, Skeeter had the hardest time keeping his array of gadgets charged. I paid the bill and left the waitress a twenty. She had earned it.

# CHAPTER TWENTY-NINE

Marcus lived in a newer gated community outside Loop 1604. It was one of a dozen gated communities that had appeared over the last fifteen years in the hills west of the city. There was no guard on duty, only a keypad that unlocked the gate. Sylvia brought me to the Christmas party last year and had given me the code.

I stopped at the entrance—a twelve-foot-high metal gate. To the east, San Antonio stretched out like a flat, green ocean. The modern buildings floating above the dense city trees resembled ships heading out to sea. The houses outside the Loop seemed to drift above the urban center with no more connection to the Alamo than the clouds.

I punched in the code. Nothing happened. Naturally, they had changed the number. While I was trying to come up with an alternative plan, a man in a lawn service truck pulled up and punched in the new code. I followed him in and down a row of identical limestone houses lining the back nine of the community golf course. A foursome dressed alike in white polo shirts and Panama hats rolled down the center of the street in a four-seater golf cart, lost in conversation. They didn't see my pickup and didn't seem to care if anyone else was on the road. I putted along behind them until I found Marcus's street.

His house butted up against the par-four twelfth fairway with a spectacular view of cedar-covered, limestone hills. He kept his golf cart and clubs in a shed that looked more like a guesthouse. He could call the grounds crew and start eighteen holes from his backyard anytime he wanted. At the Christmas party, he had insisted that Sylvia and I pay close attention to his version of the finer things in life. I was sure it was Sylvia he was trying to impress.

Marcus's wife and two kids had been at the party too, but would no doubt be long gone by eight o'clock on a Tuesday. His wife was on the board of directors at one of the local banks, and school was in session.

The front of his house broke with the limestone-block traditional look. It was a three-story glass and steel building that seemed more like a post office than a residence. I wondered how the structure ever got approved by the HOA committee. More than likely Marcus wrote its bylaws. I spotted a security guard standing by his front door. Marcus was running for governor, so I should have expected it. The guard wore a black uniform and was sipping coffee, looking bored but alert while he watched my pickup roll slowly past the house. I stopped a few houses down at the end of the cul-de-sac and planned my next move.

I held my hands out above the steering wheel. Rock solid. The shakes were gone. Skeeter was right. I had needed to cool down. Going up against the Allison family was going to take all my powers of focus and restraint.

I walked around the last house on the block, pretending to look for survey stakes if anybody was watching, and slipped over the chain-link fence along the fairway. Then I backtracked to Marcus's yard, betting that he wasn't too worried about home invasion. He'd grown up on the west side and probably figured he could take care of himself. The gate was open, and I found a worker cleaning the pool. He didn't seem alarmed. I imagined that neighbors came and went by the back gate all the time. I said good morning, but he was too busy with pool chemicals to look up. There was no guard, so I let myself in through the double glass doors.

The ceiling in the back room was three stories high, more like a hotel lobby than a residence. I remembered the sunken fireplace in the center surrounded by two white leather couches from the party. The only thing missing was the twenty-foot-tall Christmas tree. A wide staircase along the wall led to rooms on the second and third floors. I heard the distinct musical flourish from the NPR morning radio program.

"Pool service," I called. I didn't want Marcus to step out with a gun in his hand.

After a few moments, Marcus leaned over the railing from the second floor. He blinked, obviously groggy with sleep. He had dress pants on and a white T-shirt. I saw specks of shaving foam on his neck. After a beat, his eyes adjusted to the light streaming in through the floor-to-ceiling windows. Recognition kicked in.

"Hi, Marcus," I said. I pointed to his neck. "You missed a spot." If I'd met him at his office, I would have been talking to Marcus Lopez, high-powered lawyer and politician. I wanted Marcus the family man with something to lose. I wanted him to feel vulnerable.

"Nick? What're you doing here?" He was off-kilter. I could see the wheels turning.

"I wanted to see how the future governor lived."

"How did you get in here?"

"You mean, through security? Piece of cake. You want real protection, hire me."

"That didn't work out too well for Mr. Sosa," he said.

"Cheap shot," I said. "Turns out Sosa wasn't the target. I was." I held up the bandage on my arm. "He tried again, but he's a lousy shot."

Marcus wore leather, hard-soled slippers that clacked as he

descended the metal stairs. "Sounds like you should be talking to the police. What are you doing here?"

"The shooter is your client."

"Who are you talking about?"

I could see I had his attention. He probably had a dozen clients who would pull a trigger or hire a hitman if they felt threatened.

"Danny Allison," I said.

"You're out of your mind."

"How about a cup of coffee?" I asked. "I've had a long night, and someone shot my dog. I could use some java."

"I think you should leave."

I ignored him and followed my nose toward the coffee I'd smelled when I came in. Marcus trailed behind me, his slippers echoing down the wide hallway lined with family photos. I walked into an open kitchen with granite counters and an island with recessed ceiling lighting.

An older woman stood polishing the silver cutlery by the sink. She had dark features and wore a white apron over a blue uniform. She seemed annoyed at the interruption. Marcus dismissed her in Spanish, and she disappeared reluctantly into the back of the house. He fiddled with the settings on a French press coffee machine.

"It has to do with the death of Marissa Luna, a college student found in the San Antonio River on the fifth of July," I said.

Marcus had his back to me, listening. The machine came to steaming life. He placed a cup the size of a soup bowl near the spout.

"What's Danny Allison's connection to this?" He handed me the full bowl of coffee.

I took a sip and had to admit it was good. Better than what my drip coffee maker could produce. Not as good as Grandpa's stovetop percolator. Marcus made himself a cup, and we sat across from each other on polished, metallic barstools.

"This is really good coffee," I said. Marcus watched me and waited. "The dead girl was carrying Danny's child," I told him. I watched him closely for a reaction.

Marcus didn't blink. Didn't move. He was waiting for more explanation. That was all I was going to give him.

"You know this how?" he asked.

"Danny's DNA matched the fetal tissue."

Marcus took a sip of coffee. "How did you obtain a DNA sample from Danny Allison?"

"That's not important."

"So, Danny knew a girl who drowned in the river. Now you think he's shooting at you and killed your dog?" He seemed amused.

"I'm taking what I have to Detective Peterson as a concerned citizen. He handled the original case."

He smiled when I mentioned Peterson. It wasn't a friendly grin. It reminded me of the Grinch when he decided to steal Christmas from the children of Whoville.

"You know Detective Peterson?" I asked.

"I know *of* him. He seems competent," he said. Not a choice of words I would have used.

"Why not have Danny stop by the police station. He can save me a lot of time by confessing."

"You want me to bring Danny in, so he can confess to a murder that he didn't commit based on evidence that's inadmissible?"

"Sounds reasonable."

"Get the hell out of here," he yelled. His temper was showing, and I suspected it was only the tip of the iceberg. "If you make one move against Danny Allison, I will have you arrested." His face turned red, and his voice was climbing to a higher octave. "You can't come to my house and threaten me. I'm going to be governor of Texas. I'll bury you!" He paused to catch his breath. He didn't just have an anger management problem. He was showing signs of coming unglued. A vein popped out on his forehead forming a column from his left eyebrow to his receding hairline. "The Allison family is one of the most respected families in Texas. I will not have you impugning their reputation with ridiculous accusations." He was showing me the street fighter who had clawed his way out of the west side and would take down anyone who challenged his position. He waited for my response. Expecting me to run or apologize.

I smiled. "That's funny," I said. "Danny told me you and Patrick had a falling out."

"Patrick Allison and I have very deep ties."

"Deep enough for you to cover up a murder?" I thought the vein on his forehead would explode.

He reached for his cell phone and hit the speed dial. So far so good. I hoped Skeeter was ready to trace the call. I finished my coffee. A male voice came on the line.

"Yes, sir?" the voice responded.

"Just remember, I have the DNA," I said. "Danny can run, but he can't hide." I walked toward the back door.

Marcus said, "Never mind," and disconnected.

# CHAPTER THIRTY

I PULLED INTO A CONVENIENCE STORE off Loop 1604, topped off my gas tank, and waited to hear from Skeeter. Ten minutes later, my phone rang. Skeeter said Marcus had made four calls. He was rattled. That was my intent. Skeeter started to explain how he intercepted the calls, but I didn't want to know. The first call was to the Heights Security Company—the guard sitting on Marcus's front porch. The second was to Danny's cell phone—Danny hadn't answered. The third was to Lucky's gym, and the fourth was to the Dominion. That was a problem.

The Dominion was an exclusive neighborhood that the Allison clan moved to after the world-class golf course was built in the 1980s. It had a high concentration of very pricy real estate that was home to some of the Spurs basketball players, a few Hollywood celebrities, and at least one famous country music singer. Rumor had it that a high-ranking Gulf Cartel boss also had a house there. The security gate was manned twenty-four hours a day and looked more like an entry point on the Mexican border with really nice landscaping instead of a housing development. The residents were serious about security and willing to pay for it.

While I was wondering if Skeeter still had a connection working for the Dominion security who might help me gain access, Skeeter called back. Marcus had made another call. It was to the Allison family ranch in rural Edwards County. I asked Skeeter for GPS coordinates and hoped the security there wasn't as airtight. It was the last place Marcus had called, and the most likely place for Danny to go.

I took I-10 northwest, passed the turn to Grandpa's ranch, and got off at Kerrville. From there I followed the Guadalupe River west through a narrow, winding limestone canyon, which blocked out cell phone reception. Unlike the trip to Grandpa's ranch, which over the years showed increased cell coverage, the more isolated western edge of the Hill Country that approached the Mexican border seemed to resist civilization.

The Allison spread was a sprawling forty-thousand-acre ranch that in its own way seemed part of the resistance. From the paved two-lane state highway, I turned south on a caliche road marked only by a row of mailboxes. There were no signs marking the road, and I gathered Allison wanted it that way. The white ribbon of caliche wound through rolling limestone hills covered with oak motts and cedar brush. I passed a pair of vultures floating in circles looking for carrion, their wide black wings buoyed by the updraft from the canyon. The road then dipped into the Nueces River bottom where giant pecan trees that gave the river its name, which meant *nuts* in Spanish, mixed with gnarled oak trees covered with ball moss. A tom turkey scurried across the road, stopped to take a closer look at my pickup, then disappeared behind an outcrop of gray, weathered limestone. It wasn't hard to imagine Butch and Sundance making this trek and feeling safely hidden from anyone chasing them. There were tourist cabins farther downriver and a guest ranch along Hackberry Creek that fed into the Nueces, but nothing like the bloom of growth that threatened to overwhelm Grandpa's ranch near Fredericksburg.

After three more unmarked turns, the road emerged between two eight-foot game fences. The GPS showed I was getting close. In less than a mile, I spotted Rocky Mountain elk, tiny Asian sika deer, and a dozen giant, bluish Nilgai antelope grazing on the sparse, dry grass. All the animals stopped and stared at my pickup like they were as reluctant to be there as I was. I realized that if my meeting with Danny Allison went south, there was no one coming to my rescue. I'd only had cell phone reception twice since I'd left Kerrville.

When I finally reached the main entrance to the Allison ranch, it looked more like an entry control point to a forward operating base in Afghanistan. There was a stone arch featuring the YA cattle brand in use since before the Civil War. The gate was set back fifty yards off the road, and concrete security barriers forced drivers to zigzag on approach. The stone guardhouse featured a Texas flag and a red-and-black Texas Tech banner along with four surveillance cameras that covered the front, the back, and down the fence in both directions. Before I finished the zigzag to the gate, a security guard in his late twenties that looked like one of the MMA fighters that worked out at Lucky's gym stepped out of the guardhouse. He wore a black Heights Security uniform like the guard in front of Marcus's house and the German at the drilling rig. I was definitely starting to see a pattern. His short-sleeve shirt was a size too small—some kind of stretch material that was tight around the chest and upper arms. The mustache covering his upper lip looked like the one Burt Reynolds wore in *Smoky and the Bandit*. He held his left hand up signaling me to stop and his right hand on the butt of what looked like a Glock 17.

I got out of my pickup and held my hands at shoulder level. I didn't want any misunderstanding. Burt looked jumpy, like he was new on the job.

"Howdy," I said, trying to sound like a friendly local rancher.

"Can I help you, sir?" he asked.

"I'm lookin' for Danny Allison." I took another step forward and put my hands down by my waist.

Burt watched my move. He had some training. He kept his hand on the Glock. "Do you have an appointment, sir?"

I figured that confirmed Danny was there, otherwise he wouldn't have asked about an appointment. "No. I wanna make one, now."

"You'll have to call in at least twenty-four hours in advance."

I stepped closer. Inside his comfort zone. "I'm here now. Call him. My name's Nick Fischer. Tell him it's about Marissa Luna. He'll see me." I gave him my practiced I'm-gonna-kick-your-ass look and waited for his reaction.

Burt decided to make the call. I waited while he went back to the guardhouse. I could see him through the window using the landline mounted on the wall.

A few seconds later, he hustled out and punched in the key code for the gate. "You're clear, Mr. Fischer. Sorry for the delay," he said. He stood by the open gate while I drove up beside him. "Stay on the main road for two-point-six miles," he said. "It's paved to the house. Be careful of the animals. They're usually near the road this time of day. Feedin' time. Mr. Allison will be waiting." He said "feedin' time" like it was the highlight of his day.

I pulled my .45 pistol from the glovebox and rested it on the console beside me. Getting into the Allisons' isolated property was the easy part.

# CHAPTER THIRTY-ONE

THE PAVED ROAD THROUGH ALLISON's pasture had fewer potholes than the street in front of my house, probably because they had more money than the city of San Antonio, but the grass had turned brown in the late summer drought just like everyone else's. No amount of money or maintenance could mitigate the effects of nature. I checked my odometer when I pulled away from the gate so I would know how far I would have to run in case things got out of hand. I was starting to wish I'd eaten breakfast or at least shared one of Skeeter's plate-sized cinnamon rolls. The digital clock on the dash read five thirty. It had been a long day, and it wasn't over yet.

The exotic animals rushed my pickup looking for food as if I was on a safari. The tiny spotted antelope came first. Ten of them. They were so close I could have petted them out the window. The Rocky Mountain elk herd was next, led by a trophy six-by-six bull. He stood in the middle of the road, daring me to drive off without leaving his daily hay ration. I couldn't help him, so I honked the horn. The noise startled a kangaroo lounging near a mesquite tree. I wondered if they hunted them or raised them just for show. I also wondered if the animals missed their natural habitat or if they were like humans and just adapted to their surroundings. The tight security and exotic animals added to the strange aura that seemed to surround the Allison family.

At two-point-two miles I topped a ridge overlooking the ranch compound. I'd seen towns with fewer buildings. Seven structures were larger than my house, including a three-story newer home and a horse barn with stalls for fifty horses. On the other end of the compound, corrals stretched over a ten-acre area. Near the road, there was a garage that could hold a small airplane. An older single-story structure sat behind the newer buildings, put together with smaller limestone rocks that were darker in color and weathered with age. It was obviously the original home. The design resembled Grandpa's house. There was a massive oak tree in the yard whose limbs supported two kids' swings and shaded a white picnic table. I counted five men working near the corrals. Two were loading hay on a one-ton flatbed truck. I guessed they were the crew the bull elk was waiting for. Danny's bronze F-350 with the oversized tires and chrome roll bar was parked beside the garage.

It didn't look like an ambush, but before I drove into the yard, I pulled my Colt AR-15 from behind the seat, locked in a twenty-round magazine, and jacked a shell in the chamber. I hadn't lived through three deployments by taking unnecessary chances.

I slipped my pickup into second gear and let it idle downhill toward the open garage. Danny strolled out of the original ranch house. He was carrying an AR-15 and had a pistol strapped on his waist. He looked anxious but wasn't pointing the rifle at me. As I got closer, I noticed he had a bluish tint under both eyes and his nose was swollen from the pounding I had given him. His bottom lip was packed with snuff.

I stayed in my pickup and watched Danny approach with the AR-15 slung over his left shoulder. If he made a move to point it in my direction, I was ready. I saw movement in the open garage. An older man in a straw cowboy hat stepped out of the shadows.

He had a revolver in a leather holster on his waist and a look of concern on his weathered face.

Danny's eyes were glassy like he'd just polished off a six-pack or something stronger. The swelling made it difficult to hold the snuff in his bottom lip, and the brown tobacco juice dribbled down the peach fuzz on his chin. It was probably too painful to shave.

There were two men standing in the shadows behind the cowboy. They wore the same black security uniform as Burt and the guard in front of Marcus's house. Both carried AR-15s and wore tactical belts with pistols and extra ammo. Things were about to get western.

Danny's rifle sported a Marauder D-750 night-vision scope that probably cost more than my old pickup. The kind the shooter would have used to hit Sosa and fire at me along the river trail. The rifle also had a suppresser: an oversized tube with air vents attached to the end of the barrel to reduce the sound and recoil.

Danny held up both hands. "Come for a rematch?" He tried to smile, but his swollen face interfered. He looked like he'd just come from the dentist. I kept the cowboy and the two guards in the corner of my eye while I unrolled the window.

"Tell your boys to stand down," I said.

"It's okay," Danny said to the guards. Both hesitated. "Mr. Fischer's here for the evening hunt."

The guards reluctantly walked back inside the garage. The cowboy stayed where he was. Danny walked to my open window. He noticed the butt of my AR-15.

"I wasn't expecting you so early," he said in a loud voice. He held his hand up to the open window. I shook it. He spoke under his breath without moving his swollen lips. "I told them you were here for the evening hunt. Take your rifle out of the pickup."

I wasn't sure what he meant, but having my rifle in my hand made me feel safer. I tucked the .45 behind my belt and stepped out.

"Night hunting's the best," he said in a louder voice. "That's when the hogs come out to feed. They're out of control out here. Eating all the grazing reserved for the exotics."

We both glanced at the sky. The sun was already setting behind the rugged limestone cliff to the west, casting a shadow over the ranch compound and painting a handful of puffy clouds bright orange. It was easy to see that the first Allison had chosen this place for privacy and defense. The cliff made a wide U on the west and north side of the homestead. To the east and south, the terrain sloped downward providing a panoramic view. Comanches, outlaws, or a posse couldn't approach without being seen for at least half a mile.

"Tell me about Marissa," I said.

Danny threw me a nervous glance. "*Quédate aquí, Juan. Iremos solos*," he said, indicating we would go alone.

Juan shrugged. "*Cómo no*," he said and walked into the barn.

I was surprised that Danny was obviously fluent in Spanish. He was showing a side of himself that I hadn't seen before.

Danny waited until Juan was out of sight before turning back to me. "I'd rather talk away from the house. Do you mind?" It was a request, not a command—a tone I hadn't heard him use before. Maybe the beating had softened him up.

"Makes no difference to me," I said.

The cowboy reappeared driving a four-seater, all-terrain vehicle. He left the motor running, nodded to Danny.

"Gracias, Juan," Danny said.

Juan walked toward the men loading hay.

Danny hopped into the ATV, and I climbed into the passenger seat. He propped his rifle in the gun rack between the seats. I kept mine in my lap. I wasn't sure what was going on, but I wanted to be prepared. He took off on a caliche road that followed a creek that fed the main river.

"Hogs like to come to water just after dark. They're smart.

You rarely see them in the daytime." While he drove, he pulled a sixteen-ounce can of Lone Star beer from the ice chest on the back seat. He offered me one. I declined. He cracked his open and hung his head out the doorless side of the ATV. He used half the beer to wash the snuff from his mouth before he took a drink.

Twilight was turning into night. The shadows from the cliff and the thick brush turned the countryside into a soft gray. Danny was doing twenty miles an hour on a dirt road without headlights. Brush slapped the sides of the vehicle. I let him go for fifteen minutes, keeping my arm in front of my face to protect it from the limbs, then I reached over and turned the key off. The ATV coasted to a stop. I took the key out of the ignition.

"I don't care about hunting hogs," I said. I jammed my left leg against his AR-15. If Danny went for it, he wouldn't be able to pull it from the gun rack. "Put your hands on the wheel," I told him.

He shifted uneasily, then followed orders. I unsnapped the holster on his waist and pulled out an Infinity .40 caliber Smith & Wesson pistol. Not a sidearm the average Joe could afford. Every Infinity weapon was made from each customer's specifications. His was a beautiful collector's piece. The stainless-steel barrel was hand engraved with what looked like a medieval knight doing battle with a fire-breathing dragon. It wasn't hard to believe that Danny thought of himself as royalty.

"Nice pistol," I said.

"Graduation present from Grandpa." Danny talked fast. He was nervous.

I eased my own pistol out of my pants so that I could sit back further in the seat. I pointed it in Danny's general direction. The AR-15 was too bulky to maneuver in the small cab of the ATV, and I wanted to be ready when I told Danny I knew what he'd done.

"How come security's so tight? What're y'all afraid of?"

"We get all kinds of crazies up here. Animal rights activist groups and that kind," he said. "We take precautions, but the anti-hunting crowd is persistent. The Allison name is a high-profile target. Sometimes they try to sneak on the ranch. Disrupt our hunts. That kind of thing."

"You know why I'm here?" I asked.

"Yeah, Marissa Luna," he said.

"She was murdered. You killed her, so she wouldn't keep you from your inheritance."

His eyes got wide. He polished off the last of his beer. "You got that wrong."

"She was pregnant when she died. You're the father. That's capital murder."

Danny shifted in his seat. The crickets chirped a warning that darkness was coming. A frog on the creek bank joined them. A mourning dove cooed, searching for a mate. There was no wind. The air was dry and started to cool as soon as the sun went behind the cliff. I waited for Danny to speak. A minute stretched into two.

Finally, he said: "That's why you came to the gym… you got a blood sample?"

"That's right. I matched it to the fetal DNA from Marissa's autopsy."

Danny packed his bottom lip with snuff. He seemed to need it to think clearly. "How'd you get the results so fast? Don't that take months?"

"You thought you had more time? Is that why you're still here?"

"I wasn't gonna run. I didn't kill her." He spit out the door. "You saw the police report. It was an accident."

"Bullshit."

"I swear to god," he whispered.

"Then why are you trying to kill me? Why did you shoot my dog and threaten my family?" I grabbed his shirt collar and squeezed it tight around his neck.

"I didn't do any of that."

I loosened my grip before he could black out. "I saw the video surveillance from the dance club. You had a fight. You bought her a four-thousand-dollar bracelet. You told her to have an abortion. She wouldn't do it."

"That's not what happened. I wanted the baby," he said. "That's why we fought. She wanted to have an abortion."

"You're lying."

"She promised to wait until we talked about it again. We were going to meet the next day, but she never made it to the meeting."

I shoved him back across the seat. "Where did you go that night?"

"Home. The Dominion. I was there by one. You can check with security."

"Why didn't you come forward?"

He didn't answer. He stared into the dark, like the answer was out there somewhere if he could just find it. We were so far from any lights that the Milky Way formed a banner over the night sky.

"Detective Peterson came to my house. He asked a few questions. He checked my alibi. That was the end of it," he said. Tomahawk had failed to mention this to me.

"I know about the girls in Lubbock," I said. "I tracked down your ex, Valerie Martin. She moved out of her trailer park and bought a BMW. There was another the year before. She moved back to China. How much did you pay *her*?"

Danny spit out the door. "That's one of the problems with being an Allison. Everybody knows the name and knows you're rich. I tried to date girls that didn't know or didn't care. Valerie found out. She wanted money. She wanted everything. No one believes the guy. You're guilty if you open your mouth. Marissa was different. She didn't know who I was from Adam. She'd never heard of my family, and she didn't want anything to do with them. She was refreshing. When she got pregnant, I was the one who wanted to make a family with her. She wanted a career. She wasn't ready to be a mother. I would have taken care of her. That's all the other girls wanted—my name and my family's money. Marissa wanted to make it on her own." There was just enough light to reflect off the tears forming in Danny's eyes. If he was acting, he was good.

I pulled his AR-15 out of the rack and popped a round into the chamber.

"I didn't shoot your dog. I didn't threaten you. I swear to god," he said and wiped his lip with the back of his hand.

".308?" I asked him.

"Yeah," he said. His muscles tensed, ready to jump if I leveled the rifle at him.

"Why the suppressor?" I asked. I knew what it was for. I wanted to hear Danny justify using one on the ranch.

"The noise doesn't scare the game as much. I can shoot two or three hogs out of a herd before they run. Helps with the recoil, too. It's easier to keep it steady on the second shot."

I stepped out of the vehicle and brought the weapon to my shoulder. I searched the brush through the scope. The view was amazing. The Marauder scope was better than what I'd used in the Marines Corps. There were no hogs in the area. I swept the scope over the side of the cliff to the west. Found a mesquite tree about four inches in diameter clinging to a rock. The range finder in the scope read one hundred and seventy-five yards.

I handed the rifle to Danny. He stepped out of the ATV and pointed at the dark cliff. "Hit that mesquite tree halfway up at a hundred and seventy-five yards."

He swept the cliffside with a smooth, practiced motion. "I see it," he said. He pulled the trigger three times in quick succession. The sound was quiet, but not the soft compressed air sound I'd heard on the street. The empty brass flipped in an arc and landed in the dirt. This wasn't the rifle that had shot at me. If it was, he had done something else to modify the sound. I picked up the brass. Still warm. Danny watched me tuck them into my jeans pocket. He held the rifle pointed in my direction. I knew what he was thinking. One shot would end this conversation. I wondered if he had the guts to do it. I didn't give him a chance to decide.

"Look at me," I said. When his eyes shifted to my face, I grabbed the rifle and put the scope on the tree. There were three neat holes in the center of the trunk less than a half inch apart. I pulled the magazine, ejected the live round, and tossed them on the floorboard.

"If you didn't kill her, who did? Who threatened me? Who's shooting at me?"

Danny shuffled his boots in the dirt. His face twisted as if he expected me to smash it in.

"Who are you protecting?" I asked him. "Did your Grandpa find out about the baby and have Marissa killed?" I was losing patience. If he wasn't the one who killed Sosa and shot at me, he knew who did. He cleared his throat. Miles away from Patrick and Marcus, I hoped he was finally ready to come clean.

Suddenly, the small clearing lit up like a sports arena. A dozen spotlights converged on the cab of the ATV.

"Drop the weapon!" a voice shouted from behind the wall of lights. I heard metallic clicks and recognized the sound of weapons being prepared to fire.

"Better do what he says," Danny said.

I put my pistol on the ATV seat and raised my hands. Four bodies appeared in silhouette. The closest one held a Glock pointed at my head. The three others held AR-15s aimed at my waist.

"Step forward," Glock said.

I couldn't see their faces because of the glare from the bright lights.

"It's okay, Ricky," Danny said. Ricky was holding the Glock. "It was just target practice." Danny's voice was high and thin. He was scared. Whatever was happening, I got the feeling Danny wasn't in charge.

One of the guards grabbed my rifle and .45 from the ATV. Ricky frisked me. He didn't find the .38 in my ankle holster. Not that it mattered. He took my pickup keys and put them in his pocket. I was outnumbered and outgunned. I wasn't going to try to shoot it out with a five-shot revolver.

"Change of plan," Ricky said. "We'll take him from here."

"Why?" Danny said.

"Orders," Ricky said.

Two of the men grabbed my arms. My eyes adjusted, and I could see Ricky and his team all wore the same black uniform. Heights Security Company. I did a quick scan of the perimeter. I counted eight men altogether. They had walked up on us in the dark while I argued with Danny. I should have guessed they would have followed.

We walked fifty yards back down the trail to where four ATVs and a pickup were waiting.

"Put him in the truck," Ricky ordered. He holstered his Glock. He didn't think I was a threat any longer. We were on an isolated ranch. I didn't like my odds. My mind was racing for a plan. Anything. If I disappeared out here, no one would ever find me.

The two guards tightened their grip on my arms and shoved me toward a four-door Toyota pickup.

"What the hell are you doing?" I yelled. "Danny, tell these goons you're coming with me."

Ricky had his Glock out and aimed at my head again. There was silence. A coyote yipped, followed by another, and another. They were starting their night hunt.

Finally, Danny said: "Sorry, Nick."

"Sorry, Nick?" I didn't like the sound of that. "What does that mean?" I jerked my arms free of the guards and took a step toward Danny. "Do you run this place, or do they?"

The guard on my left grabbed my arm again. I slipped his grip and kicked his knee. His partner swung the butt of his rifle at my head. I ducked under the rifle and shot a flat hand to his throat. He dropped to the ground. I grabbed his rifle and leveled off on Ricky.

"Back off!" I shouted.

Something hard hit the back of my head. My knees buckled.

Everything went black.

# CHAPTER THIRTY-TWO

When my head cleared, I was in the back seat of the Toyota pickup between two black uniforms, my hands zip-tied behind my back, and my head and wounded arm throbbing. The dome light showed their faces. They were the same two I'd seen in the garage when I arrived. They both held their AR-15s muzzle-down. They weren't worried about me grabbing their rifles because the guy in the front passenger seat had me covered. He sat with his back against the dashboard and his AR pointed at my chest. Ricky drove the pickup. I'd been in worse situations, but it had been a while.

"Everybody knows where I am, Ricky. My answering service, my employees, even my girlfriend. If I don't show up by midnight, they'll sound the alarm," I lied. No one was coming to my rescue.

Ricky chuckled under his breath but didn't say anything. His three companions played dumb. The guard pointing the rifle didn't smile, but he was clearly enjoying himself. I didn't have any doubt that if I made a move to escape, he would enjoy shooting me.

"Where's big Patrick, Ricky?" I asked. "Is he on the ranch? Let's go talk to him."

"You know Mr. Allison?" Ricky said.

"Hell yes. We're old pals. Our families go way back. Before the Civil War."

Ricky didn't respond. He drove with the dome light on, so it was difficult to see where we were until the road began to descend into the family compound. He stopped beside my pickup.

"We'll escort you back to the main gate," Ricky said. The two men in the back waited until the front seat rifleman was standing outside. He opened the passenger door of my pickup and pointed his AR at my waist. I got behind the wheel, and the rifleman climbed in beside me, his AR still pointed at my midsection.

Ricky handed back my keys. "Follow me," he said.

I started my pickup and backed up slowly. When I pulled in behind Ricky, the two ATVs with the spotlights followed me. I glanced at my companion and his AR.

"How long have you worked here?" I said casually, as if I'd just picked up a hitchhiker.

He didn't speak. I gathered the Heights Security Company trained them not to talk or hired them because they couldn't. It was a good policy. I liked the fact that they did have some training. I hated to think some gun-happy cowboy traded his spurs for tactical boots and took the night shift. I goosed the engine just a tiny bit to see what he'd do. My pickup jumped forward quickly, closing the distance between my bumper and Ricky's Toyota. The rifleman jerked his head forward. I let off the gas and fell back ten yards.

"Sorry," I said. "My foot slipped."

The rifleman did what most people would do. He looked forward to see what we were going to hit. What he should have done was kept his eyes on his prisoner. Maybe he hadn't gotten that far in his training. It was information I would use if they planned on leading me out into the brush somewhere and leaving my dead body in my pickup.

When I could see the lights from the main gate, I began to relax. They weren't taking me into the brush. Ricky stayed on the paved road. He turned away at the last moment, and I stopped in front of the gate. Burt hustled over to the keypad. Ricky walked up to my open window.

"Thank you for visiting the Allison ranch," he said, almost sounding sincere. "I hope you had a good hunt." The smoke from the engine exhaust created a white cloud under the gate lights.

"I'd like to come back. I didn't get the trophy I was after," I said.

"I'm sorry," Ricky said. Any pretense of sincerity was gone. "You wore out your welcome."

"Where's my pistol and my AR?" I asked. "I want my weapons back."

"We'll arrange to have you reimbursed."

"Who do you work for? Allison or Marcus Lopez?"

"Have a nice night," Ricky said.

"Fuck you very much," I said, feeling a knot forming on the back of my head.

Ricky smiled and walked back to his pickup. The rifleman got out and slammed the door. In my rearview mirror, I watched the four guards from the ATVs form a semicircle around the rear of my pickup.

I drove through the gate, and Burt shut and locked it behind me. I had a two-hour drive back to San Antonio. I had enough adrenaline pumping through my veins to keep me awake for an hour, if not for most of the night. As I drove back toward civilization, I thought about the strange encounter. The pieces of the puzzle seemed to be falling together. The picture of Marissa's murderer was looking more like Patrick Allison than Danny. He didn't want the family name tarnished or the bloodline diluted, so he staged the murder to look like an accident.

As soon as I had cell phone service, I called Skeeter and briefed him on my visit to the outback. I told him what Danny had said about being home by one and asked him to check with his contact at the Dominion. I knew it was a waste of time to question his family and the staff. They would do and say whatever Patrick wanted them to. It would be much harder to fake the security video.

He filled me in on his surveillance. He had followed Sylvia to the grocery store and to the gym after work. She had gone home after that. He was watching her condo from the street. He set up intruder cameras on her front and back doors. If anyone tried to get in, an alarm would go off on his laptop. He was fifty feet away. I was satisfied she was safe, for now.

I knew one thing from my meeting with Danny—he knew what happened to Marissa that night. If I hadn't been thrown off the property, I had the feeling he would have finally told the truth. There was only one play left, one that would take all my powers of persuasion and a lot of luck.

I parked on the street a few houses down from my fixer-upper. I thought of spending the night in a motel, but I had left Sam on the kitchen floor and the lock was broken. I spent five minutes watching my house for signs of movement. I checked the other cars on the block. I could see Rose Gustafson watching television in her front room, her favorite white cat perched on her shoulder. I was glad to see she had made it home safely.

I jumped when my phone rang. It was Skeeter. He had called his contact at the Dominion security gate. They had Danny on video checking in at 12:57 a.m. on July fifth. That part of Danny's story checked out.

When I went inside, the mess was cleaned up, and Sam was out of sight. Skeeter had come over and taken care of everything. I was grateful for that. He put Sam in the freezer to keep him from decomposing in the heat and to give me a chance to decide what to do with him. I didn't have time for a pet funeral. It was a strange thing to keep in the freezer, but it would have to do until I could take Patrick Allison down.

I had gotten very little sleep in forty-eight hours. I wanted a shower and a nap. My limbs felt heavy on the staircase. My wounded arm was throbbing, and the knot on my head was tender. I'd lost round one to Allison's thugs.

I stripped out of my musty clothes and spent fifteen minutes in a hot shower. I opened the window and let the steam billow out. In the military, anything over five minutes we called a "Hollywood shower." I was pampering myself after a hard day. I stumbled into the bedroom and called Sylvia.

"Where have you been?" she asked.

I felt guilty for not calling sooner. "On a safari." I tried to sound upbeat.

"Don't you dare make a joke," she insisted.

"I've got everything under control." I tried to sound convincing, but I didn't believe it myself. I didn't want to give her any more details, and I didn't want her advice.

"I know that voice, Nick. You're holding out. Tell me what's going on," she insisted. "Marcus told me you went to his house. What were you trying to do?"

I let the uncomfortable silence stretch while I stood and paced my small bedroom. "What did you tell Marcus?"

"I didn't tell him anything he didn't already know from you."

"Did you tell him about my investigation before?"

This time she went silent. I waited for her to speak, listening to her shallow breathing. I saw my own reflection in the bedroom window. I suddenly got the feeling that she had told Marcus everything. That my investigation had been the topic of lunchtime conversation or maybe he had called her into his office and asked her questions. I hated to think she shared our conversations willingly.

"Did he threaten you?"

"What're you talking about? Allison is his client. Of course he'd wanna know."

"Did it ever occur to you that he might be involved?"

"In what? In murder? You're talking nonsense. Marcus would never do anything like that."

"I've gotta go," I said. Her response left a bad taste in my mouth.

"What're you going to do?"

"Take what I have to Detective Peterson and ask him to re-open the investigation."

"You know he won't. What happens when he says no?" she asked.

"I'll keep going," I said. I didn't have any intention of contacting Tomahawk again, but apparently Sylvia played fast and loose with the details I shared with her. I wasn't going to tell her my real plan. For all I knew, Marcus was sitting beside her on the bed.

"Because your gut tells you he's guilty? What about logic? Keep going and get killed?" There was an edge to her voice she hadn't used before.

"How's that logical?" I asked. "What about keep going and get the truth?"

"Danny has an alibi. The police said it was an accident. You haven't got anything beyond a reasonable doubt. What are you trying to prove, that Danny Allison is a spoiled rich kid and his grandfather is a powerful man? Everybody already knows that, Nick. Drop it. Drop the case."

"You know I can't do that," I said.

More silence on the line. She disconnected.

I checked the front door and noticed Skeeter had fixed the latch and added a new deadbolt. He also set up additional security cameras by the doors and in the hallway. Cameras gave me the feeling that I was on a reality TV show. I was pretty sure Skeeter was watching me on his laptop, wandering around the house in my birthday suit. I waved to one of the cameras just to amuse him. I dug out my spare pistol—a Springfield XD .45—loaded it and put it on the nightstand. I wasn't as comfortable with it as the Para-Ordnance, but it had a thirteen-round magazine and would get the job done. The worst thing about the night's activities, other than being betrayed by my girlfriend, was that Allison's peckerwood guard had taken my favorite pistol.

# CHAPTER THIRTY-THREE

I TOSSED AND TURNED FOR A few hours. This time, fractured pieces of my final deployment mixed with my dad's murder, Sam's bloody corpse in the freezer, Sylvia in bed with Marcus Lopez, and Grandpa sending smoke signals from his hayfield. I woke drenched in sweat and needing another Hollywood shower. My subconscious was dumping every unpleasant thought into a horror movie marathon.

I called Skeeter to check on his surveillance. He answered on the second ring. No one had gone in or out of Sylvia's apartment, and he was hungry. I told him to follow Sylvia to her office and wait for me. I called Grandpa next and listened to his phone ring. I tried the petting zoo number and got the answering machine again. I left another message.

My next call was to Detective Ochoa. Meeting with Peterson was a waste of time. Ochoa seemed more reasonable. She said Peterson had taken the day off and agreed to give me some time if I could get to the station before eight o'clock.

I put Sam's food dish on the back porch and started the coffeepot. Then I realized Sam was in the freezer. Life without him was going to take some getting used to. I got dressed and took the .308 casing from my dirty jeans pocket, put it in a proper evidence bag, and dropped it into an accordion folder. I gathered my notes, the bracelet, and the surveillance tapes, and dumped them in with the casing.

I made copies of the DNA analysis Kelly had given me, added the warning note the shooter had left beside Sam's body, and I wrote Marissa Luna on the side of the folder with a black marker to make it look official. Nothing got a lawyer or detective's attention like a folder with a label. I put the file in the leather briefcase Grandpa had given me for Christmas while I was still in law school. I rarely used it anymore, but I was making every effort to look professional for Detective Ochoa's sake. My sheriff department Kevlar vest filled out my list of morning accessories. When I quit the department to go to law school, the county was in the process of upgrading their equipment using a federal grant. I got to keep the used but still serviceable bulletproof vest as a separation gift. I wasn't looking forward to spending a hot September day with another layer of clothing, but it gave me an extra layer of security.

I usually made breakfast for myself, but I didn't feel like cooking. Homemade sausage and eggs was one of my favorite meals. Once a year, after deer hunting season, Grandpa and a few of the local ranchers got together near Willow City for a weekend of sausage making. A German tradition. The men would bring game from the season's hunt, and we would join forces grinding, stuffing, and packaging the meat. I usually ended up with fifty pounds of breakfast patties and at least that much in link sausage.

On the way to the downtown police station, I stopped at Las Tapatias for taquitos, again. Cops always liked free stuff. Maybe the breakfast would soften the blow. I was going to tell Ochoa that the case she and her partner closed as an accident was really a murder case involving one of the richest families in the state, and that Sosa was collateral damage. Not something a detective wants to hear on an empty stomach.

It took several turns around the parking garage to find an empty spot. When I did, it was next to a Mercedes with its driver's-side tires on the line. I pulled into the space making sure to get as close as possible to the door. There were three- and four-story buildings in the area, including the police station. I paused at the entrance to the parking garage, holding my leather briefcase and bag of breakfast, and scanned the surrounding windows and rooftops. The move brought back memories that I was still trying to repress. Rooftop snipers were a common hazard in a war zone, not something I ever thought I'd encounter in San Antonio.

I felt a presence beside me and jumped back, drawing my Springfield .45. A cross-dressing prostitute in black stilettos and a leather skirt took a few steps back and smiled. She'd been out all night, and black facial hair was starting to show through her heavy makeup.

"Late for work, officer?" she said, exposing large yellow teeth.

I holstered my pistol and mumbled an apology. She didn't seem spooked or surprised. My nerves were strung a little too tight. If I didn't relax, I was going to hurt somebody.

"Aren't you in enemy territory?" I asked.

"Jail's air conditioned," she said. She smelled the taquitos in the greasy paper bag. "Come on, suga. Do mama a favor and feed me a big taco."

I just shrugged. I'd worked downtown Austin with the sheriff's department and knew what she wanted.

"What's the matter, honey? Never seen a black man in heels?" She seemed offended that I wasn't going to arrest her.

"I'm not a cop," I said.

Before I could say she looked good in heels, she abruptly

stepped into the street. A police cruiser swerved to miss her and slammed on its brakes. I wondered what time they served breakfast in jail.

The inside of the building was cool, and I paused to let my temperature return to normal before announcing myself to Sergeant Vera. He studied the restaurant bag and my Kevlar vest, then he sighed and shook his head.

"Just like your father," he said. "Stubborn as a barn-sour mule."

I shrugged. "What can I say?" No one had ever compared me to my father. I took it as a compliment. I told him I was there to see Detective Ochoa. She was expecting me.

I waited with my briefcase and my bag of breakfast while Vega called upstairs. I watched a dozen plainclothes and uniform officers hustling to work. The usual police station collection of hookers, gangbangers, and drunks were housed in the detention center a couple blocks west. I should have felt safer surrounded by law and order. Instead, I was jumpy. I felt like I was missing something, and if I didn't figure it out, I might not make it through the day.

Five minutes later Sergeant Vera motioned me toward the stairs and buzzed me through the security door.

Ochoa was at her desk when I walked in. I opened the bag of breakfast and set the coffee on her desk. She smiled and seemed much more relaxed without Peterson around. The attitude was much more attractive. She wore a stylish white blouse with gray slacks, and her dark hair was pulled into a tight ponytail.

"Thought you could use some breakfast," I said.

She held vending-machine coffee in a paper cup with playing cards printed on the side.

Ochoa reached for a cup of coffee. "Beats the shit out of the stuff we got here. What's with the vest? You pretending to be a detective today?" She dived into the breakfast bag and took out a chorizo and egg taquito.

"Someone took a shot at me. I think I know who." I opened

my briefcase and took out the file. Ochoa suddenly seemed interested. My briefcase and the file with Marissa's name on it had the intended effect. That and the bulletproof vest got her attention.

I finished opening my briefcase and set out what I had. The .308 casings, the warning note, and the DNA results.

"More shell casings?" she asked. She caught a large dribble of orange chorizo grease a second before it landed on her white blouse.

"These are from Danny Allison's rifle. He has a fancy night-vision scope for hunting hogs," I said. "And a suppressor."

"Danny Allison? Patrick Allison's grandson? You think he killed Marissa Luna?"

"Danny killed her because she was pregnant. It would have jeopardized his inheritance. Or Patrick killed her when he found out Marissa was pregnant because he didn't want an illegitimate heir. Take your pick. Maybe they were in it together. They also tried to kill me because I know the truth." I pushed the DNA report in front of her.

She wiped her mouth and read it over. "Who authorized this?"

"Doesn't matter. Danny knew he was the father."

"You talked to him?"

"That's right. I visited his ranch. Nice spread. Heavy guard. And I wanna report my stolen weapons. A Para-Ordnance .45 and a Colt AR-15, in case they decide to use them to shoot somebody else."

"He ratted on his grandfather?"

"You know he wouldn't do that."

"You know what Peterson's gonna say," she said.

"That's why I came to you."

She stood and glanced around the empty office. It was early and none of the other cubicles were occupied. "Between you and me, I didn't like what he did with the Luna case."

"What do you mean?"

"I mean, he shut me out. It was my first case, and he said it was open and shut. I got the feeling he didn't want me involved."

"Did you look at the surveillance tapes from the dance club?"

"We saw them. We did see Danny. Peterson checked his alibi."

"That's not in the report," I said.

"Because he's Patrick Allison's grandson. Peterson didn't want to involve him in a media frenzy when he was innocent."

I pulled out the bracelet and showed her the engraving. "Danny bought this and had it engraved with Marissa's initials. That and the fight the night she was killed should give you probable cause to get a warrant for his DNA."

"We already cleared the case. My advice is to drop it, or Peterson will come after your license. The DA is a close personal friend of Patrick Allison."

"I can't do that."

"I thought you'd say that." She took a sip of coffee. "I've got a dozen other cases waiting for my attention. A gangbanger shot up a Walmart 'cause he didn't get last week's fifty-percent discount on a flat screen TV. Three murders last weekend were linked to a cartel turf war."

"Patrick Allison gets a pass because you can't handle the workload?"

"I understand how you feel. But Peterson's been around a long time. He has a lot of connections and a lot of clout. If I do anything with this, I'm going to have to do it quietly. You understand?"

"I don't have time for that. Somebody took a shot at me and left a warning note." I showed her the note. "He used the same weapon that shot Sosa."

"You're sure?"

"Unmistakable. There can't be two shooters on the loose in San Antonio using the same ghost-quiet suppressor." The glass doors opened at the end of the hall. Two detectives wearing white shirts and dark ties came in carrying playing card coffee cups.

"Like I said, I can't help you," she said loud enough for the two detectives to hear. Then she pulled a business card from her top drawer and wrote her phone number on the back. Both suits looked my way before sitting down at their desks. "This is my cell," she said in a low voice. "I'll do some digging."

I took the card and handed her one of mine. "I appreciate this. My opinion of the SAPD just went up a notch."

"We're not all assholes," she said. "In the meantime, do me a favor and stay off the grid. I don't wanna add your name to my lists of murder investigations."

# CHAPTER THIRTY-FOUR

I TOOK COMMERCE STREET WEST TOWARD Marcus's law office and called Sylvia's number. When she didn't pick up, I let it go to her voice mail. "Hey, babe," I said. "Call me when you get this." I hung up. After last night's phone call, I knew she was still pissed off. But I had reached the "what if" part of our conversation. I couldn't wait for Detective Ochoa to do some digging, and I was not going to stop until I had the truth. Whatever impasse we had reached in our relationship didn't matter. Her life was in danger. So far, the only plan I could come up with involved Skeeter and me storming the Allison ranch to get to Danny.

I wondered what my dad was thinking before he served the warrant on the drug house in rural Gillespie County. He had gotten a tip about a little girl being held inside the trailer, but he hadn't gone in right away. He waited for the judge to issue a warrant, which took twenty-four hours. He had followed the rules as he always did. When he got to the trailer house, the little girl was already dead, and the occupants were waiting for him. The Texas Rangers sorted out what happened next. The report they gave Grandpa said Dad's pistol was empty. He'd used two seven-round M1911 magazines and six blasts from his Mossberg pump shotgun.

In the end, it wasn't enough, which was why I always carried an extra large-capacity magazine and a backup on my ankle. The volatile chemicals the drug gang used to cook meth went up in smoke. Everything, including my dad, burned to a crisp. The official story was that the perps burned with their drugs, but there was a rumor that they staged the fire and had gotten away. Dad had gone in alone with a seven-shot pistol and a shotgun. Fearless. But he was dead and so was the little girl he wanted to save.

It was midmorning and the traffic was light. When I got to Marcus's building, I drove to the back of the parking lot. The good thing about doing surveillance work in Texas was that nearly everybody drove a pickup. My F-150 never looked out of place. The only two vehicles not pickups or SUVs in the parking lot were Sylvia's Toyota Camry and Marcus's Lexus LS 500.

I smiled for the first time in a week when I saw Skeeter. I smiled because he was on the job and because he drove a pristine four-wheel-drive pickup. Grandpa ranted about people in the city buying four-wheel-drive pickups just to drive to the grocery store. He drove an ancient two-wheel-drive Dodge with a standard transmission over some of the roughest roads in the state. Said if he couldn't get there in his two-wheel drive, he'd saddle his horse.

Skeeter was sitting under the only shade tree. I backed in beside him.

"You bring my shotgun?"

For a guy who didn't really like guns, I was glad he understood the danger of the situation.

"I think you're gonna like it," I said. A woman in a red skirt and high heels left the building and walked to her Silverado. I waited until she was out of the parking lot, and then handed Skeeter a Remington 870 Express shotgun through the window. It had a short barrel and a pistol grip. It was the kind of weapon you didn't want pointed at you.

Skeeter smiled. "This is more my style."

It looked like a toy in his huge hands. He tested the trigger guard to see if it was big enough to fit his finger. It fit, but there was no room to spare. I handed him a box of double-aught buckshot. He looked at them both, then back at me. My backup in the assault plan didn't know how to load a shotgun.

He handed me a GPS tracking device. "You wanna do the honors?" he asked.

"My pleasure," I said.

The tracker was the size of my thumbnail and attached to the car with a magnet. I walked over to Sylvia's Toyota. I pretended to examine the tire while I attached the GPS under the rear bumper. I didn't want to answer questions if Marcus had security covering the parking lot.

Skeeter watched me get back in my pickup. "You should be an actor."

"I saw that move in a movie once," I said.

"They're having auditions at the Community Play House for *A Christmas Carol*. You'd make a good Scrooge," he said.

I looked at him to see if he was serious. "Thanks," I said. "I've got plans for Christmas."

"I do lights and sound for the productions. Been doin' it since high school."

I'd known Skeeter three years and never knew he was involved with community theater. I guess it never occurred to me to ask him.

"Call me if anything unusual happens."

"Like what?"

"Like somebody with a .308 rifle takes a shot at you."

"How do I know if it's a .308?" he asked with a smirk.

Any thought of storming the Allison ranch with Skeeter went out the window. He wouldn't be any help in a firefight or know how to reload and cover my back in an ambush. Taking him would just get him hurt or worse. I was going to have to come up with another plan. I watched him chew his bottom lip. He had something to say but was afraid to say it.

"Spit it out," I said.

"You sure she needs protection?" Skeeter asked. His face was neutral.

"What the hell are you talking about?" I asked. "You saw the note."

He shrugged his huge shoulders. I wondered what he really had on is mind.

"Where you goin'?"

"To talk to Danny."

"You go out to his ranch again, you ain't comin' back."

"I'll think of something." As I drove away, he was Googling the manual for the shotgun.

# CHAPTER THIRTY-FIVE

I FOUND LUCKY WORKING WITH A lightweight southpaw in the center ring downstairs. The local school wasn't out yet, so the gym wasn't full of teenagers.

"Come by to beat up more of my paying customers?" Lucky sounded pissed off, but he always did. After you got to know him, you realized that was just the way he talked. He had learned English from watching American cartoons on TV in the sixties. He reminded me of the way Japanese soldiers sounded in all the old WWII movies. The subtitle would read, *Have a nice day*, but the character looked and sounded like he was saying, *I'm gonna cut your balls off!* I was counting on that voice to motivate Danny.

"I came to pay my monthly dues," I said.

His smile showed off his missing teeth. Offering him money brought out his softer side.

"Get some cardio," Lucky said to his lightweight. "Let's go into my office."

His office was small and cluttered with boxing trophies and paraphernalia from fifty years of Lucky's career both inside and outside the ring. He had signed photos of all the greats, from Cesar

Chavez to Tommy Hearns, along with his own championship belt. He also had a signed picture of Tony Ayala, a local fighter who was the last great contender from San Antonio who took a turn to the dark side and never quite reached his potential. Lucky said his lifestyle killed him, but he sure had a beautiful knockout punch.

"What's up, Nick?" he said, sounding suspicious.

"I came to pay my rent." I put two hundreds on his desk, the last of my tip from Sosa.

"The rent's twenty-five a month," he said. "Ten for veterans. That's two years in advance. You're already paid up till Christmas. So what's this about, huh?"

I explained to him what was going on and filled him in on Danny Allison. I told him my plan to lure Danny off the ranch and into town. I also let him know that it could be dangerous. If Danny came, he would likely bring backup. I told him how the ranch was crawling with guards and they had stepped in when I tried to take Danny last night. Lucky smiled again, showing his missing teeth. The two things that made him smile were money and the prospect of a fight.

He picked up the money and handed it back to me. "Keep this. Buy me lunch sometime. I think a couple of old guys can handle a little trouble," he said. He was talking about himself and his partner. I knew they had both been tough guys, but both were pushing seventy.

Lucky took a clipboard off the bulletin board and consulted the list of names neatly printed on it. "Check this," he said. "Danny's on the schedule tomorrow for a tune-up fight with Sarge's light heavyweight division contender. I'll tell him the fight's moved up to today."

"You think he'll come?" I asked.

"He'll come. He's been talking trash about it for two weeks."

Lucky made the call. I listened in on his side of the conversation.

He was very convincing. If Lucky told me I needed to drop everything and come to the gym, I wouldn't hesitate.

Lucky went back to training the lightweight, and I took advantage of the time it would take Danny to drive in from the ranch by slipping in a workout. The job was interfering with my regular routine. I should have been grateful, but I missed having all that free time.

I'd just finished a third set on the speed bag when I heard Lucky whistle from the top of the stairs. That was our pre-agreed signal that Danny had arrived. I grabbed my towel and duffle bag and headed for the upstairs locker room. I caught a glimpse of Danny at the front entrance followed by Ricky and the crazy-eyed rifleman. I had no doubt that they were both armed.

Lucky was waiting for me on the upstairs landing. He and Sarge were side by side on the top step. I nodded and kept walking into the locker room. I saw Lucky motion Danny up the steps. Lucky and Sarge stood with their arms at their sides. I couldn't hear what was said, but I saw Danny put up his hand and motion Ricky to stop. So far, my plan was working.

I leaned against the wall of the locker room so that when Danny walked in I would be between him and the only exit.

"Hi, Danny," I said when he strolled through the door.

He didn't look surprised to see me. He wore his square-toed cowboy boots and jeans, topped with an untucked Lone Star Beer T-shirt and a camo cap sporting one of those dark-colored American flags.

"Hey, Nick," he said. He bounced from boot to boot with nervous energy. His eyes were glassy like he'd popped a few cold ones on his drive in from the ranch. I was starting to wonder if he was ever sober. "I guess there's no fight today. You put Lucky up to this?"

"We need to talk. We got cut off last night. Don't blame Lucky for anything. I told him what's going on."

"I'm sorry about what happened last night," he said. He shifted his weight again and took off his cap.

I took two quick steps toward him. Pinned him in the corner. "Marissa Luna was murdered. You know who did it."

He squeezed his hands into fists and tensed his shoulders as if he was going to take a swing at me.

"Relax your hands," I said. "I know you didn't kill her. It was your grandpa, Patrick. He's the one who had everything to lose. Who'd he hire?"

"No. You got it wrong. You don't know what you're dealing with." Danny's face showed pain and fear as if he felt his fingers slipping from a ledge ten stories above a parking lot.

"Why don't you fill me in?" I said.

"He'll get to you. It doesn't matter what you do. He won't stop," Danny said.

"I don't care about your grandpa's money or connections. He's going down for Marissa's murder."

Danny hesitated.

I slapped him. Not hard, but enough to pop his head back. "Talk, goddamnit," I said, not wanting to give him time to make up another story.

"It's Marcus Lopez."

"Don't start this again." I was getting tired of his BS.

"That's the truth," he insisted.

"Tell me what you know. We'll go to the police."

"Marcus has the police in his pocket," he said. His goofy grin fluttered across his face.

I couldn't tell if he was telling the truth. Every time I questioned him, he had a different look and a different story.

"Ricky and Joe work for Marcus. There're two more outside. All the guards at the ranch work for him, except Juan. He's been there since I was born. The others Marcus hired to keep an eye on the family. That's why I couldn't say anything."

"What about Patrick? What about your grandfather?"

"He's dying," Danny said. "Stage-four cancer. He doesn't have long." Danny looked at his boots. He chewed on his bottom lip.

I didn't know how much of his story I could swallow. There had to be something more to it. There had to be one big piece of the puzzle that Danny wasn't telling me.

"How did Marcus get control of Allison Oil?" I asked.

Before he could answer, my cell phone rang. It was Skeeter. He whispered so fast and low I could barely hear him.

"Skeeter, I can't hear you. Slow down. Speak up," I said.

"Marcus is on the move. Sylvia's with him."

I put the cell phone on speaker and tossed it on the bench. "Talk to me, Skeeter. What's happening?" I pulled my street clothes from my bag and stripped out of my gym shorts.

"Marcus and Sylvia got into her Toyota," he whispered.

"Why are you whispering? They can't hear you." I slipped on my jeans and boots. Danny stood watching me and listening to Skeeter.

"They're headed for the freeway," he said in a normal voice.

"Monitor the GPS. Don't get too close."

"What's going on?" Danny asked.

I checked my watch. It was twelve ten. "Marcus is with Sylvia." I slammed Danny back against the metal lockers. "What's he gonna do?"

Danny's eyes went wide. I pushed my arm into his windpipe. Danny clutched at his throat. I let him choke for a moment, then backed off and let him breathe.

"I don't know," he gasped.

"Go back to the ranch. I'll take care of the guys outside," I said.

Danny nodded while he massaged his sore neck.

"What's going on?" Skeeter said. I'd forgotten he was still on speaker.

"Follow Marcus. Keep me up to date." I disconnected the call and stuffed the phone in my back pocket.

Danny sat down on the bench and put his head in his hands. "What are you gonna do?"

"I'm going after him."

Danny chewed his bottom lip. Stayed silent.

I left him on the bench and walked to the steps, where two extra guards had joined Ricky and the rifleman. Lucky and Sarge hadn't moved an inch. The four guards were spread out four steps below them. Ricky had a pistol in a shoulder holster. They would all be armed. It was me and two old-timers against four armed guards.

I stopped on the top step between Lucky and Sarge.

"Danny tells me you're looking for me," I said to Ricky.

"The boss wants to talk to you," he said through a grin. His pistol gave him confidence.

"You mean Marcus Lopez? Is that your boss?"

Ricky didn't say anything. He didn't move.

I turned to Lucky. "Are these guys about the dumbest bunch of thugs you ever saw, or what?"

Lucky smiled, showing off his missing teeth.

"What do you think, Sarge?"

Sarge didn't say a word. Every fiber of his five-foot-ten, sixty-nine-year-old frame was focused into a razor-sharp weapon of destruction. He had total concentration on the four guards. I was starting to feel better about the odds.

"They work for Marcus Lopez," I continued. "The lawyer running for governor."

Lucky hated lawyers as much as he did politicians. He hated Marcus Lopez in particular because he said Marcus was going to raise taxes for small business owners. Lucky was against higher taxes.

"You can walk out of here and tell your boss you couldn't find me," I said to Ricky.

He shook his head. "No can do, partner." All four guards balanced on the balls of their feet. They waited for Ricky to make the first move. "Nothing personal. Just business." He pointed at Lucky and Sarge. "If you come with us, we don't hurt the old dudes."

Lucky and Sarge stood up a little straighter when he said *old dudes*.

"I'm glad you said that," I said.

My phone rang. I used the old-fashioned ringer. Ricky and his thugs flinched. I slowly reached for my phone. The call was from Skeeter. I hit accept.

Skeeter said: "So far so good. He's on the interstate heading west. We're past Boerne."

"Okay," I said, not wanting to tip Ricky off that Skeeter was following his boss. "I'll catch up to you." I disconnected and put the phone back in my pocket.

"It's been real, Ricky, but I gotta go." I took a step down the stairs.

Ricky reached for my left arm. I drove my elbow into his throat. He fell back against the railing.

The rifleman and his partner were on my right just below Sarge. The rifleman made his move toward me. He never knew what hit him. Sarge brought his right foot up and kicked him in the left ear. The rifleman tumbled down the steps. His partner dove for Sarge and caught a knee to the face and a right-hand chop to the back of the neck. He dropped like a sack of shrimp. If he woke up, he'd have a mean headache. The only one left standing reached for his pistol. Lucky hit him with a stiff right that broke his jaw. It was the same punch that won him the championship belt. The whole fight lasted less than fifteen seconds. Lucky and Sarge grinned, like it was the most fun they'd had in a decade.

"Thanks for your help," I said. "I've gotta run."

"What should we do with Danny?" Lucky asked.

"Let him go," I said. "I know where to find him when I need him."

I took the stairs two at a time. A half dozen guys were lined up at the bottom of the steps to watch the show. They nodded their approval when I jogged past them and out the front door. I started my pickup and tried to think of the fastest way out of town. My phone rang.

"He's getting off at Welfare," Skeeter said.

"What the hell?" I waited for him to confirm. The call went dead.

I checked my watch. Twelve thirty. I tried Grandpa's phone on the unlikely chance he was having lunch inside. I hung up on the fifth ring. No such luck.

I hit redial for Skeeter. Heard: *The number you have dialed is not available.*

Either his phone was dead, or Marcus's thugs had gotten to him.

# CHAPTER THIRTY-SIX

THE RAIN THAT HIT SAN Antonio had missed the Hill Country, leaving very little for livestock to eat. Some ranchers were already feeding hay shipped in from greener pastures toward the coast or from irrigated fields to the north. I made the turn at Welfare and followed a rancher pulling a flatbed trailer full of green Bermuda hay. The stretch of road was a wide two-lane but about as straight as a dog's hind leg, and there was just enough traffic to keep me from passing. I turned off the radio and the noisy air conditioning and opened the windows. The blast of warm, dry air helped calm my nerves. I would have honked, but it wouldn't have done any good. There was no place for the rancher to pull over.

I was doing forty miles per hour and thinking about the worst-case scenario. Skeeter was MIA. Had Marcus's thugs reached his name on the list? I had given him a shotgun, but it wasn't much good unless he knew how to use it. I tried Grandpa's useless phone again and left another message at the petting zoo. He wouldn't be expecting trouble. There was no one for him to worry about these days except for pushy realtors and stray llamas. He had no reason to be suspicious of Marcus showing up at his gate if Sylvia was with him.

I was moving over into the left lane to look for a place to pass when my cell phone rang. The caller ID said Sylvia. I grabbed the phone.

"Where are you?" I said, cautiously. I didn't know if she was free to talk.

"Hi, sweetheart. I just got your message. You're on speaker. You'll never guess where I am." Sylvia never called me sweetheart. I could hear the tension in her voice.

"You took off early and went shopping?" I tried to sound casual. I assumed Marcus was listening.

"No, silly. I came to see your grandpa. It's such a pretty day. I was thinking about him. I wanted to bring him lunch." She liked Grandpa but would never drive out there by herself in the middle of the day.

"That's wonderful, honey-bunny."

She hated when I called her that. If she was free to talk, she would instantly chew me out. The line was blank for several seconds. Another sign that Sylvia was not herself.

Finally, she said: "Why don't you come out and join us. I picked up barbecue at Two Brothers." She knew I loved Two Brothers' brisket.

"That sounds great!" I tried to sound enthusiastic. "How's Grandpa?"

She hesitated again. I heard a muffled sound in the background. She was talking to someone. Her hand was over the cell phone speaker.

"Oh, he's good. He's anxious to see you. It will do you good to take a break," she said.

"Okay, I'll finish up in town and head out there. Give me two hours." I looked at my watch. It was two o'clock. "I'll be there at four," I lied. I would be there as fast as I could drive.

"Hurry. We'll be waiting." She emphasized the word *hurry*.

"Bye, sweetie-pie." I let her disconnect first. If "sweetie-pie" didn't get a response from her, I didn't need any other clues to her state of mind. Marcus was going after Grandpa and Sylvia at the same time.

I hit my horn twice to warn the rancher I was coming around him and floored the accelerator. There was always a chance of traffic or an animal on a rural road, but I didn't have time to wait. The rancher's hand emerged from his open window and waved me on.

Ten minutes later, I slowed to make the turn onto Grandpa's road. There was no exit. Because the terrain was steeper to the south, the road simply stopped. Anyone driving on it lived there or was lost.

I moved the seat back as far as it would go so that most of my face would be behind the doorjamb and slowed to just under thirty miles an hour, the normal speed for the local ranchers. As a kid, I remember asking Grandpa why he drove so slowly. He would always respond in his half-irritated and half-joking way: *If I wanted to get there sooner, I'd have left yesterday.*

I studied the familiar stone fence and the clearing beyond. There was no sign of a vehicle or a person near Grandpa's cedar-post gate. I slowed even more to look up the gravel road that led to the house. Nothing. It didn't mean there was no one there. The live oaks and cedar brush beside the road provided enough cover for a platoon of men.

I made a U-turn and cruised back by the gate. Still nothing. I passed the friendly llama sign for the neighbor's petting zoo, then drove to the gas station on State Highway 290 a few miles out of Fredericksburg. I needed to collect my thoughts and get a cup of coffee to sharpen my senses. The recon had told me nothing. I knew something waited for me at Grandpa's ranch, and I had a feeling it wasn't a friendly barbecue lunch. The investigation was spinning out of control. Ochoa had promised help, but I was out of time.

As soon as I cut the engine, I heard a tap on my window. I

turned and came face-to-face with a white button over a very large man's sternum.

I unrolled the window. Skeeter leaned his bulk on the door. The F-150 tilted with him. He was breathing hard and looked anxious.

"Where the hell have you been?" I said, relieved and angry at the same time.

He took a deep breath and raised both hands as if to absolve himself of any wrongdoing. "I backed off a couple of miles like you said. They turned at your grandpa's road. I didn't want to follow them into a dead end, so I kept going."

"What happened to your phone?"

He looked down at his hands. A sheepish grin came over his face. "It died."

"How does that happen?" I asked.

"I overloaded the data card on my—"

I cut him off. "You forgot to plug it in."

He nodded. "Yep."

I realized it wasn't his fault. I took a deep breath to steady my nerves. "Shit's hitting the fan," I said. "Sylvia called. She sounded weird, like she was forced to talk. She said she took Grandpa lunch. Wanted me to meet her there."

"What's wrong with that?" he asked.

"She's never done that before, and she didn't mention she was with Marcus." I told Skeeter what Danny said about Marcus.

He looked skeptical. "You believe Danny's telling the truth?"

"I believe he's scared shitless of Marcus Lopez."

"He could be the next governor." Skeeter's voice sounded hard and angry.

I grabbed my weapons, and we hopped into his pickup. It was better to keep moving. Skeeter showed me the GPS location on his laptop. Sylvia's Toyota was parked behind Grandpa's house. If this were a military operation, I could send in a drone to get eyes on the property or link with a satellite image. This was one of the few times I missed being in the Corps with access to every high-tech gizmo known to man at my fingertips.

"Now would be a good time to tell me the plan," Skeeter said. He was driving past the turn to Luckenbach, which would have taken us to the bar and dance hall. Any other day, that's where I'd have taken him.

I could feel Skeeter waiting for an answer. I studied his size triple-X features. His good hand was shaking, and his shirt was soaked through with sweat. He didn't have the training or the skills for what we were about to do, but he was willing and the only help I had. So, I filled him in on my plan.

"You want out, I'll understand," I said when I finished.

His eyes stayed fixed on the road. "No. Your grandpa and Sylvia are in danger. Let's do this."

"Did you figure out how to load this thing?" I grabbed the shotgun off the back seat.

"It has a seven-shot capacity." He was reciting from the manual. "The receiver is milled from a solid billet of steel for maximum strength and reliability. The silky-smooth twin action bars prevent binding and make it a very efficient weapon. This workhorse features—"

"Okay." I smiled. "You did your homework. Just remember to pull the trigger."

# CHAPTER THIRTY-SEVEN

I CLEARED THE NEIGHBOR'S FENCE, PASSED the friendly petting zoo sign, and jogged into the pasture that was adjacent to Grandpa's driveway. The neighbor had cleared much of the land and left huge piles of brush every twenty or thirty yards. When I lived there, the thicket was home to a flock of wild turkey. The new residents were llamas, donkeys, and a half dozen miniature horses, who all seemed to be waiting for a handout. When I didn't offer anything, one of the llamas tried to take a bite out of my Wranglers. I hoped there was a friendlier group of animals for the kids.

I covered the hundred yards in under two minutes, the last fifty of it escaping the hungry llama. There was a line of cedar and live oak trees along the fence that blocked my view of Grandpa's ranch house. I checked my watch. Three o'clock. Sylvia's call had come at two. I was still an hour ahead of schedule. If Marcus believed me about being in town, I had the element of surprise. I found the barbed-wire fence that marked Grandpa's property line.

The fence was older than I was, but the wire was still as tight as a guitar's strings. Too tight to crawl through. I gingerly climbed the wires and jumped down on the other side. A stick snapped when I landed. I stopped dead still to listen. The house was still fifty yards away, but I wasn't taking any chances on being seen or heard. When I detected no sound or movement, I inched forward. Thirty yards closer, the brush thinned out. I had to finish the approach on my hands and knees. Leave it to Grandpa to keep the area around the house clear. He was worried about fires these days and not Comanches, but the effect was the same. Neither one could get near the house without being seen.

I dropped to my belly and crept closer. Nothing moved in the house or in the barn. Sylvia's Toyota was the only vehicle in sight. Grandpa's pickup must have been in the barn. If someone was watching from the windows, I would be an easy target approaching the house. It was time to put the Skeeter diversion in motion.

I put my phone on silent and texted the word *go*. Skeeter sent a thumbs-up emoticon almost before my fingers were off the screen. He was anxious.

Moments later I heard the front gate rattle. There was a metal latch, and it sounded like Skeeter was putting all of his three hundred pounds into shaking it back and forth. So far, he was following my instructions to the letter. I heard his pickup engine rev and tires crunching over gravel. More rattling. I hoped he wasn't overdoing it. Everybody within a five-mile radius could hear the sound.

I studied the house and the barn. Still no movement. I caught sight of Skeeter's pickup when it came around the oak mott near the pond. He was driving slowly. Barely above an idle. He wasn't in any hurry to reach the house. Apparently, no one in the house was in any hurry to come out and greet him. Had Grandpa been there alone, he would have showed himself at the front door, especially if he didn't recognize the pickup. My plan was to distract Marcus long enough for me to get the drop on him.

Skeeter parked in front of the house. I could see his face clearly. He was searching the barn from his point of view. Nothing was registering on his face. He looked down at his hands. A message appeared on my cell phone. "Nobody home."

I saw movement out of the corner of my eye coming from the barn. I drew my pistol.

I texted back: "Don't move," but he was already out the door.

His head and shoulders were above the cab of his four-wheel drive. His hands were empty. He had left the efficient Remington 870 on the seat. I saw the barrel of a rifle with a suppresser mounted on the end protruding from the second-story hayloft. I fired toward it. The rifle barrel jumped, followed a millisecond later by a compressed air blast and a sickening thud.

Skeeter hit the ground. I was close enough to see blood on his shirt. He never saw it coming. I saw his big hand move. He was alive, for now. Memorizing the specs on the weapon hadn't done him any good.

I had to get to him fast or it was all over. The vision of my Marine platoon brothers flashed through my head. They stood guard while I was pinned down inside the Humvee. I swallowed that trapped, helpless feeling and forced myself to focus on the barn and the danger inside. I had to keep moving. My mission to save Sylvia now included Skeeter and Grandpa, and I wasn't going to let them down.

The rifle barrel poked from the hayloft again, pointed down at Skeeter.

I fired. My shot hit the wooden window frame. I dove forward, running flat out for the edge of the house. I heard the air blast and felt a bullet zip past my head. I recognized the sound. It was the same shooter. This time I wasn't running away.

I flattened out against the worn limestone blocks, then slid around the corner of the house. I had a better angle on the barn. I could see a quarter of the loft opening. The rifle barrel reappeared. I squeezed off two more shots. The barrel dropped from sight.

Skeeter pulled himself to his knees. He was alive. He crawled to the far side of the pickup. I put two more rounds through the hayloft to provide cover fire. When Skeeter was safely behind his pickup, I peered inside the house. The kitchen was clear. The back porch was empty. I looked through the French doors to the living room. Empty. I checked the back bedroom where Grandpa slept. The bed was made. No sign of him or Sylvia anywhere.

I swapped out my half-empty magazine for a full one and sprinted for the back door of the barn. The ancient door opened without a sound. Grandpa hated rusty hinges. No shots. No movement. It smelled of dust and horse manure mixed with the pungent odor of fresh meat, as if Grandpa had hung a deer carcass from the rafters to cool overnight. The sun was already behind the western hills that towered over the ranch buildings. Deep shadows made it hard to see into the corners of the barn. I squatted on my heels to give my eyes a chance to adjust. Grandpa's green John Deere tractor took shape. It still had the hay baler attached and a front-end loader. His pickup was missing. The workbench was scattered with tools. Something was wrong. There was never anything out of place in Grandpa's barn. The steps leading to the loft slowly came into focus.

I studied what I could see of the loft opening. There were bales of hay. This time of year, Grandpa had the loft full of hay to prepare for winter. He had another barn near the airplane hangar on the hayfield, but he always filled this one first. It was itchy, back-breaking work to get the bales of hay into the loft. That was my job until I joined the Marine Corps.

A faint noise came from the support beam in the center of the barn. I inched closer, keeping an eye on the loft. It was Grandpa. He was sitting with his arms tied to the post behind him, facing the front of the barn. I could only see his shoulders and arms, but there was no mistaking his khaki work shirt.

I didn't dare call out or get closer, because I didn't know where the man with the rifle was. I had put six rounds through the hayloft, but I doubted very much that any had hit their mark. More likely, the shooter was waiting for me to show myself in front of Grandpa so he could finish me off. I opened my mouth to breath and waited a full minute.

With Skeeter wounded and no sign of Sylvia, I couldn't afford to wait him out. I could only see Grandpa's arms behind the post and didn't know if he was wounded. I doubted whether Grandpa would have sat down voluntarily.

I pointed my pistol up the wide loft stairs and took the first step.

Nothing. The pungent odor of fresh meat was getting stronger. I extended to my full height, trying to see into the opening. Nothing but hay.

I heard a metallic click.

"Nick Fischer," a familiar voice said.

I started to turn.

"Drop the pistol first." The familiar voice was insistent.

I placed the pistol on the step, hoping for a chance to dive for it later.

"Clever. Now, kick it off the step," the voice demanded.

He didn't go for it. I nudged my pistol off the step and heard it hit the wooden floor.

"Now, face me," he said.

I slowly turned around. Detective Peterson stood by the workbench, wearing Grandpa's khaki shirt and holding a .308 M24 sniper rifle pointed at my chest. It was standard issue for most SWAT teams, Peterson's former job. His tomahawk features were red from exertion, and a fresh cut marked his sharp cheekbone.

"Where's my grandfather, Detective?"

"That old man's a tough nut. I'll give him that." Peterson wasn't smiling. He kept the rifle aimed at my belt buckle. I warned you, but you just couldn't let it go."

"Where is he?"

"Pull up your pants leg. Show me the .38," he said.

I had hoped he wouldn't remember my backup weapon. "Grandpa give you that cut?" Grandpa wouldn't have given up without a fight.

"Lucky punch," he said.

I showed him the hammerless .38.

"Take your left hand and pull off the holster."

I did what he asked.

"Now, toss it to me," he said.

I calculated the possibility of palming the .38 and firing. The odds were a hundred to one in his favor. At this range he wouldn't miss. The .308 bullet would explode into my midsection. It wouldn't be an instant death. I would bleed out for half an hour. I'd watched stronger guys than me die from gutshot wounds before the evac chopper could get them to the field hospital.

I studied Peterson's trigger finger. It was tight against the metal. He wasn't taking any chances. I decided to wait for a better opportunity. I tossed the .38 at his feet. He kicked it toward the back door.

"You're pretty good. Never saw that coming," I said. I needed to buy some time. "How'd you get that sound reduction?" Maybe he would drop his guard if he talked shop.

"I used subsonic ammo," he said, exposing small sharp teeth. "The bullet travels slower. Doesn't break the sound barrier. I'm surprised you didn't figure that out." He sneered, enjoying being in control.

"That explains it," I said. I was trying my best to make calm chitchat while thinking about Sam's dead body slumped on the kitchen floor and Skeeter wounded outside. I waited for my chance. "You got the drop on me fair and square," I said, shaking my head like I'd been defeated. "Where's your partner, Ochoa? She in on this?"

"No, she's dumb as a door handle. Nice tits, though." He took a step closer.

"Yeah, I could tell you were the smarter one of the team. How'd you do it? Did you fake the investigation? How'd you get the ME to rule accidental death?"

Peterson's nostrils flared, and his smile vanished. "Why do you give a shit, Fischer?" he asked. "One less knocked-up spic for the government to take care of. Probably saved the tax payers a couple hundred thousand."

"Actually, she was the first in her family to go to college."

"Big fucking deal."

"It was to her mother."

"You *are* a bleeding heart. You'd have never made it as a real detective. You'd have ended up like your daddy, burnt up in a meth trailer."

"What the hell do you know about it?" It was the second time someone had compared me to my father. This time it wasn't meant as a compliment.

"Everybody knows he waited for a warrant. He should have kicked in the front door and opened fire."

"He was trying to save a little girl," I said.

"Like I said, you're a bleeding heart. He let the perps get away."

"You don't know that," I said. "Nobody knows."

"Everybody knew it was an ambush. The little girl was bait. You and your father are suckers for sweet little girls."

"What the fuck is that supposed to mean?"

"Think about it," he sneered.

I knew he was talking about Sylvia. I wondered if she knew she was being used. He looked at his watch. He was on a deadline. Somewhere, Marcus must have been waiting for him. I needed to think of a distraction. He lifted the rifle to his shoulder.

"You check that scope?"

"For what?"

"You missed me three times. Either you're a piss-poor shot or the scope is off. Which is it?"

His face turned red. I waited for my chance.

"I don't miss," he said. "Those shots were just to scare you."

"What was Sosa, collateral damage?" I asked.

"You never figured it out, did you?"

Suddenly, the pieces of the puzzle started to fall into place.

"Danny did kill Marissa," I said. "He called Marcus, and Marcus called you to cover it up. He was blackmailing Patrick Allison. That's how he got control of Allison Oil."

"You're not as dumb as you look," he said. "But you're too late."

"Why kill Sosa?" I asked.

"Sosa figured out what was going on. He got greedy."

Peterson put his eye to the scope lens. That was the chance I'd been waiting for. It would take a second for his eyes to adjust so that he could focus on me. He had been shooting out the hayloft into daylight from fifty yards away. When he looked into the scope inside the barn, he would see nothing but a blur.

I saw his hesitation. His eyes blinked. I took my chance. My legs uncoiled like a rattlesnake from a burning bush. I tackled him at the knees. The suppressed .308 bullet whooshed over my head.

Peterson fell back to the ground. The M24 rifle clattered to the hard plank floor. He grabbed my neck.

I forced my hands inside his arms and broke his hold. I went for his throat. Both my hands closed around his windpipe. I brought my weight down on his chest.

"Where's Grandpa and Sylvia?"

He didn't respond. I squeezed harder. His face turned red, then blue.

"Talk," I said.

He gasped for breath and looked like he wanted to say something. I eased my grip and let him have a lungful of air.

"At the airstrip," he whispered through his crushed throat.

I popped his head once against the wooden planks. His eyes closed, but he was still breathing. I stripped Grandpa's shirt off him. It was the last thing I wanted him to wear on his way to jail.

I noticed blood on the shirt. There was one hole over the left breast pocket. Dried blood caked the back of the shirt. At least four hours old. The hole was made long before Marcus and Sylvia had arrived. I didn't like what that meant. A knot formed in the pit of my stomach.

I searched the bottom floor of the barn and followed the sickening smell to the last horse stall. Grandpa was leaning against the limestone wall wearing a white T-shirt covered in blood. His head was slumped forward. There was a raw hole in his chest. His hands rested in his lap. Both knuckles were scraped. Otto Fischer didn't go down without a fight. I pulled the string on the bare hundred-watt lightbulb that swung from the rafter.

Grandpa's skin was pale, and the creases around his eyes and mouth looked carved in stone. I pulled his body away from the wall and tried to lay him flat. He was already stiff and surprisingly light. I felt a wave of emotion. Tears filled my eyes. I touched his face. He had been my father and my grandfather for many years. The first thought that came to mind was that I had never recorded his stories. What do you say once they are gone?

"I'm sorry, Grandpa," was all I could think of. There was no time to mourn. Skeeter was wounded, and Sylvia was still out there. I covered him with his favorite khaki shirt.

My hands were shaking. I wanted to think his spirit would stick around and keep giving me advice, but I was pretty sure it was already on its way to heaven.

I heard a sound from the front of the barn. Peterson.

I ran out of the horse stall and found him on his knees holding my Springfield pistol. When he saw me, he fired. The bullet hit the floor. I tackled him with a full-force body slam. I grabbed the pistol, and we both toppled backward. I sat on his chest and forced the muzzle of the weapon away from my body. He fired four more times, the noise deafening in the small space. The bullets pounded the roof. Finally, I pulled the pistol from his grip. He went for my throat. I grabbed his. Whoever passed out first was going to win. My wounded arm was on fire. My head throbbed and spots flickered in front of my eyes. His face was red.

"Why? Why'd you kill him?" I asked.

"You killed him when you took him to the oil rig," he said.

I worked my knee up and pressed it down on his chest. I heard a rib snap. Peterson groaned and dug his bootheels into the wooden floor. Then I saw the look of realization come over him—the realization that he was going to die. I was fine with that. I slammed his head against the wooden planks. His face turned blue. Finally, his eyes rolled back in his head. When I let go, he didn't move.

I slowly got to my feet and rested my hands on my knees, waiting for the blood to flow back to my head. Peterson's cell phone chimed. I dug it out of his pocket. The caller ID showed Marcus Lopez.

"Hello?" I said. There was a long pause. I could hear him breathing. Thinking.

"Nick?" he asked, trying to cover his surprise.

"Where's Sylvia?" I asked.

"Put Detective Peterson on the phone," he demanded.

"Your boy's dead."

"You killed a San Antonio police detective."

"He shot Skeeter and killed my grandfather."

"He was protecting me."

"From what?"

"Misguided vigilantes."

"No one will believe that. Let Sylvia go," I said.

"I already alerted SAPD." His voice was cold and calculating. "They have no reason to doubt me. I'm the future governor."

I understood Danny's fear of him. He had no limits. He didn't see himself as governor. He saw himself as king.

"Where's Sylvia?" I shouted.

He laughed and disconnected.

## CHAPTER THIRTY-EIGHT

I FOUND SKEETER UNDER HIS FRONT fender propped on his elbows and pointing the Remington 870 at the barn. He left a blood-soaked trail in the gravel.

"Is he dead?" he asked, his voice a hoarse whisper.

"Yeah," I said. "Peterson." I helped him roll over onto his side.

"Detective Peterson?"

"The one and only," I said. "I guess those Saturday church meetings didn't do any good."

"That, and he's evil."

"You need a doctor," I said. I reached for the shotgun he still held pointed at the open barn door, but Skeeter held it tight. He wasn't going to give it up. It was the last time he'd ever step out empty-handed.

"Go," Skeeter said. "Marcus is somewhere. You have to stop him." Skeeter was ready to collapse. "Find Sylvia."

I ripped open his shirt and found a hole through his shoulder. "You sprang a leak." He had lost a lot of blood. I could see the exit wound on his back. As far as I could tell, the bullet had hit soft tissue. It didn't mean he would live. It did mean he had a better chance than I had given him before. He could move, and he was conscious. It took a lot to kill a three-hundred-pound man.

"Go," he said again. "I'll manage."

"We have to stop the bleeding." I found a roll of paper towels in his pickup and pressed it against the wound. There was no way I was going to carry him into the barn. The sun was down behind the western hills. At least the temperature was getting cooler. I sprinted into the house and found a gallon jug of water in Grandpa's fridge and brought it out to him.

"Drink some water," I told him. I opened the lid and held it to his lips.

He drank half in one gulp, then took a deep breath. "I'll be fine," he said.

I was skeptical. I dialed 911. A female dispatcher from Fredericksburg picked up, and I explained the situation. I didn't want the highway patrol or the local sheriff just yet, so I told her Skeeter had a puncture wound from falling off a hay baler.

Skeeter rolled his eyes when he heard my explanation. He didn't even know what a hay baler was, and he wasn't likely to ever get near enough to one to find out. I explained that I couldn't move him because he weighed three hundred pounds. She said the county rescue helicopter was four hours away taking a burn victim to San Antonio and asked for directions.

I explained the complicated route to her. It was less than fifteen miles, but the narrow road at night would take an hour or more when they didn't know where they were going. She wanted me to stay on the line to guide them to the ranch. I had things to do.

"The ambulance is coming. Anybody else shows up, start shooting."

Skeeter nodded, holding up the shotgun.

"If I don't get to Marcus, he'll come after you."

"I'll be ready this time," he said. He had learned his lesson.

I secured Peterson's M24 rifle around my shoulder and took off running to find Sylvia. It would be full dark in twenty minutes. The sky had turned from pale-pink to fire-orange. By the time I made it to where the road crossed the creek, there were deep shadows under the willow trees. The frogs had started their evening song. The water was only an inch deep, but the rocks were covered with moss and made the roughly ten-yard crossing tricky on foot. I jumped in without hesitation and slipped and slid my way to the opposite bank.

I could see a light in Grandpa's hangar. All my life that light meant that Grandpa was there working on his airplane. The light had always been a comfort. At night, I could see it from almost anywhere on the property. It was in the center of the ranch. If I was out late hunting or riding my horse, I always knew that light would be there to guide me. More than one night out on patrol in Afghanistan, I would see a light in the distance and imagine it being Grandpa's hangar light guiding me home. That night it was guiding me to the bastard responsible for his death.

I crept within fifty yards of the hangar, then slipped into the hayfield to increase my cover. I could hear muffled voices but couldn't make out what they were saying. I lay flat between the rows of hay stubble and used the night-vision scope to scan the Quonset hut.

I could see Marcus and Sylvia through the office window. She was sitting at the small table that Grandpa used as a desk. Marcus was standing by the window. He was watching the sky as if he were expecting a plane to land. She was watching him. I didn't move. It was too dark for him to see me, but movement always caught a person's attention at night. There was only a thin glass pane and a metal window screen between us. The fifty-yard shot would have been easy. I checked the round in the chamber and put my finger on the trigger. Using Peterson's subsonic ammo, Marcus would never hear the shot.

I flipped the safety off and pulled the slack out of the trigger. I steadied the crosshairs on his pompous face. The would-be king of Texas was about to take a bullet to the head.

Sylvia got up and stood behind him. I eased the pressure off the trigger. I couldn't risk it. One shot would kill them both. Then I heard the thump, thump, thump of a helicopter. At the same time, I heard sirens. At first, I thought it was the ambulance arriving for Skeeter. Then I realized there were too many of them. It sounded like every law enforcement vehicle within the county was on its way to Grandpa's ranch. The helicopter would be SAPD.

I kept the scope on the window. Sylvia put her hand on Marcus's shoulder. She wasn't tied to the chair. She wasn't handcuffed. She was free to move around. I used the powerful scope to zoom in on her face. She didn't look scared. She looked relieved. Marcus put his arm around her. She buried her face in his chest. I couldn't believe what I was seeing.

I adjusted the scope to make sure I was getting a clear picture. I searched for a gun or a knife in his hand—something that was forcing Sylvia to act. I had risked my life to rescue her. Skeeter was lying on the driveway with a bullet hole in his chest, and Grandpa was dead, yet there she was, clear as day in the night-vision scope, clinging to that evil son of a bitch.

I forced myself to breathe and relax. The chopper sounds were getting louder. I needed to slow my heart rate and stop the scope crosshairs from jumping across their bodies. They were tight together. One shot would end the string of lies that led to this point. The truth was written on their contented faces.

I let my breath out slowly and tightened my finger on the trigger. They were a breath away from death. Then I hesitated. Pulling the trigger would make me just like Marcus Lopez. I wasn't ready to cross that line. I wasn't a vigilante. I wanted Marcus to get his day in court so everyone could see who and what he was.

The chopper noise burst over the hayfield. Running lights cleared the trees. Two spotlights speared Grandpa's runway, then crisscrossed the field. One light crossed my back, then stopped and settled on me.

An electronic microphone buzzed to life over the thumping chopper blades.

A voice shouted: "SAPD. Drop your weapon!"

If I was going to survive, I would have to run.

I got my feet under me and slowly stood. Three men watched from the chopper: the pilot, the man with the bullhorn, and a sniper hanging halfway out the open rear door. His rifle was trained on me.

"Drop the weapon," Bullhorn shouted. The downward thrust of the chopper blades kicked dust and hay stubble into a cloud. The pilot was too close to the ground, cutting visibility for his sniper.

My muscles contracted. I knew the sniper was adjusting his scope and steadying his crosshairs on the top of my head. The dust cloud would be reaching him, and he would be shouting at the pilot to pull up. A hovering helicopter was one of the most difficult places for a shooter to hit anything, especially one as small as the top of my head at night. There were sharpshooters who could hit a target at a thousand yards nine out of ten times, but never hit anything from a moving chopper. The odds were in my favor.

I dived head first cradling the M24 to my chest. When I hit the hayfield stubble, I rolled to my feet and took off like Seabiscuit at the Santa Anita Handicap. I heard a shot over the chopper noise and expected the sudden burning punch from a bullet to knock me to the dirt, but nothing came. I kept running.

The spotlight from the chopper waved across my path. I zigzagged each time the light hit me. Several more shots kicked up puffs of dirt near my feet. When I made it to the edge of the field, I plunged into the thick cedar brush. I knew what it looked like from above. I'd seen it many times from Grandpa's plane. At noon on a sunny day, brush obscured the ground.

I ran to the edge of the limestone cliff that surrounded three-quarters of the hayfield. The narrow notch I'd climbed down so many times as a kid, ironically pretending I was escaping bandits or Indians, was right where I remembered it should be. Halfway down the steep incline, my boot slipped and sent gravel raining down the cliff. It was narrower than I remembered, or was worn by time. I caught my balance and climbed the rest of the way with my side firmly pressed against the rough limestone rocks.

It was only a matter of time before they found my trail. They would know I was armed. Marcus would tell them I was dangerous. They would remember Peterson as a fine upstanding member of the fraternity now that he was dead, instead of the asshole he really was. The SAPD chief would call Detective Ochoa and give her the bad news. She would vow to bring me in. Everyone in law enforcement would want a piece of me. Exactly what Marcus had planned. He had set a trap, used Sylvia for bait, and I had walked right into it. I was at the top of the Texas most-wanted list.

I found the path at the base of the limestone cliff. It was a horse and game trail older than the ranch itself, and the only connection between the Fischer ranch and our neighbor, Mr. Hoeffner, to the south. Deer and wild hogs had been the only recent users. Brush hung low over the path in several places, forcing me to run with my hand outstretched to catch limbs slashing my face.

I heard the thump of the chopper linger at the edge of the field. They were searching the brush line, looking for my tracks. The law enforcement lights formed a pulsing dome over Grandpa's ranch. I hoped the ambulance had gotten there first and taken Skeeter to the Fredericksburg hospital, and that I could get to him before Marcus's thugs did. My next concern was for Kelly. Marcus knew I'd used her lab to match the DNA. I checked the bars on my cell phone. Zero. Warning her would have to wait. I wondered if the patron saint of lost causes was keeping watch over me. Maybe Marissa's Our Lady of Guadalupe candle was still burning.

# CHAPTER THIRTY-NINE

After twenty minutes at a fast jog, I reach Grandpa's boundary fence. The tough hog wire was in as good a shape as the last time I'd seen it, ten years ago. I grabbed a cedar post, swung myself over, and kept going. From there to the Hoeffner ranch house was downhill.

I skirted a spring-fed pond and followed the creek for the next two miles. I slowed to a walk when I spotted the dark outline of Hoeffner's barn. There were no lights. The place looked deserted. I stopped in the deep shadow of an oak tree and looked at the glow of my digital watch. Ten thirty p.m. I'd been running for an hour and forty-five minutes. When I caught my breath, I scanned the area with the night-vision scope. I didn't expect to find anyone. Senior had been dead for six years, and his son Billy lived in Houston.

I shouldered the M24 and jogged to the barn. Hoeffner Sr. always kept a surplus WWII Jeep for running around the ranch. I found the barn key where it always had been, stuck in a crack in the limestone block over the door.

When I saw the Jeep, a flood of memories washed over me. Billy and I had pushed, pulled, and dragged that vehicle over every road in the county. I was asking it to make one more trip to town. I fumbled my way in the dark to the driver's seat. The key was welded to the ignition so that when Hoeffner Sr. got drunk he wouldn't lose it. When I turned the key, nothing happened.

The next ranch house was another four miles south. I knew I could make it in a little over half an hour. I didn't know the new owners and wasn't sure there would be a vehicle. I was worried about Skeeter. He would be at the hospital very soon. If Marcus's thugs got to Fredericksburg before I did, Skeeter would never wake up.

I risked turning on the barn lights, then I pulled back the side-opening hood on the old Army Jeep. The battery was gone. I searched the workbench and found it plugged into a charger. I hoped that was the only problem. Vehicles left unattended for any length of time in the Hill Country were havens for mice and squirrels that loved to chew on electrical wires.

I attached the battery, turned the key, and held my breath. The seventy-five-year-old Army Jeep cranked to life as if it was headed to the Battle of the Bulge. I cut the lights, closed the barn door, and put the key back in the crack. So far, it seemed, Saint Jude or Our Lady of Guadalupe was looking down on me.

The wind in my face from the open top felt good. I sat up straight and let my sweat-soaked shirt air dry. I shifted into third gear. The road was curvy, but the Jeep's top speed was fifty miles per hour downhill, so negotiating the turns wasn't a problem. The problem was the gas gauge. It had been broken since I was in high school. Chewed to shreds by a family of field mice. I had no way of knowing how close to the hospital I could get.

When I saw I had cell phone reception, I called Kelly. Her phone went directly to voicemail. I explained as briefly as I could that Marcus Lopez was behind Marissa's killing and that she was in danger. I also told her I had killed an SAPD officer who was on Lopez's payroll. If she was at work, she would hear my name on an all-points bulletin before she got this message. I only hoped she trusted me enough to believe I wouldn't shoot without a reason.

In seven miles, the road from Hoeffner's place met State Highway 87, a major two-lane artery into Fredericksburg. I slowed and cut the lights on approach. An old Jeep might not arouse much attention in this part of the country, but the missing top didn't give me much room to hide, and the inspection sticker had been out of date since my high school graduation. I decided to avoid the main roads as much as possible. When I didn't see any lights, I coasted through the intersection and gunned the old engine across the highway.

By the time I reached the hospital, it was five past midnight. I parked on the hill above the emergency room. I spotted a local police cruiser making its rounds. I ducked under the dashboard and hoped he wasn't looking for an old Jeep. I watched the headlights through the rusted hole in the front passenger door. The cruiser turned left and went out of sight.

The hospital grounds and parking lot were bright as day. I didn't see any SAPD vehicles. There were two younger women smoking cigarettes and leaning against a blue minivan. From the butts on the ground, they'd been there awhile. I knew what they felt like. Grandpa and I had spent several weeks in this same parking lot while Grandma slowly wasted away. I jumped out and hustled toward the entrance.

An older man in a silver cowboy hat locked his Dodge Ram near the entrance and turned toward the door. We nodded at each other. My clothes were torn and filthy from the ordeal. He looked me up and down when we reached the door. I recognized him instantly as one of Grandpa's Texas-German rancher pals. It had been at least ten years since I'd seen him, and he seemed too wrapped up in his own thoughts to recognize me.

"Trouble?" he asked. His raspy accent reminded me of Grandpa.

"Accident on the ranch," I said, keeping my voice calm. "Buddy shot himself cleaning his rifle."

His expression didn't change. "That's a bad one," he said. "Name's Helmut Geisler. My wife had a heart attack. The doctors try to get her stabilized." I could tell he still didn't recognize me.

"I'm Nick Fischer," I said, shaking the old man's bony hand.

"Otto's *Enkel*?" he asked.

I nodded. He used the German word for grandson. His face lit up briefly. I didn't tell him Otto was dead. I didn't have time to get into it, and he seemed to have trouble enough of his own. When I had Grandpa's funeral, I knew he would be there along with most of the old-timers in the county.

I followed Helmut to the nurse on duty at the reception desk. She looked about nineteen, with ginger hair and a peaches-and-cream complexion under a sprinkling of orange freckles.

"Mr. Geisler, Dr. John just called," she whispered. "He's on his way. Stay as long as you want." Her cheeks turned a shade darker as she made a note on a clipboard. I guessed this was her first week working the night desk. The experienced nurses dealt with ER tragedy too often to let it affect them personally.

I stood a foot behind Helmut, close enough for her to think we were together. I gave her a knowing smile and nodded when he did. The young nurse waved us into the back rooms.

"Y'all can go on back now," she said.

Helmut took his hat off, like any cowboy from his generation would. I followed him to the elevator, and we road in silence to the second floor ICU. He didn't look at me. He was caught up in his own thoughts and anxious to see his wife. I saw the deep tan line a half inch above his ears. What hair he had was a shade lighter than his Stetson Rancher hat.

"I hope she's all right," I said when we stepped out of the elevator.

He looked at me with his hat in his hand and a certain resignation on his face. "This is the fourth one for her. The pastor comes tonight, I think. Give my regards to your grandpa. *Halt dich munter.*"

"*Halt dich munter*," I repeated.

Helmut found his wife's room and went in and shut the door. I paused for a moment to watch through the window as he took his wife's hand when he stepped to her bedside. I wondered if I would have anyone to call the pastor on my final night. I thought about Grandpa lying in the barn with no one to take care of him. He told me once that he wanted to be buried next to Grandma. I would honor his wishes.

I continued down the hall, not sure where or if I'd find Skeeter. I saw a doctor in one room. She had straight blond hair and reminded me of Kelly. I wondered if Marcus had the resources to reach inside the Lubbock police force. I guessed he would. I hoped Kelly got my message and got the hell out of town. I checked my phone. Nothing.

The next room was occupied. I took an anxious look. The patient was not a three-hundred-pound black man. I wondered why there were no police outside the hospital or in the ICU. There were only two explanations: Skeeter was already dead, or Marcus didn't want local police watching him.

I stepped to the last room. I had already lost a member of my family that day and did not want to lose Skeeter. Until that moment in the ICU, I hadn't thought of him as my friend. He was a client at first. Today, on Grandpa's ranch, he went as a volunteer. He could have walked away, but he had my back and took a bullet because of it. If we made it through the night, I would forgive whatever debt he owed me. He had paid in full.

When I looked through the window, Skeeter was there. He was hooked to a heart monitor, two IVs, and an oxygen mask. I slipped into the room and breathed a sigh of relief. His systems looked stable. I had beaten Marcus's thugs to the room, but I knew they wouldn't be far behind. I stepped to the side of the bed. Skeeter's eyes were closed and his breathing steady. Getting him out of here was not going to be easy. I pulled the oxygen mask down and waited to see if the action would trigger any alarm. Skeeter opened his eyes.

"Don't say anything," I told him. "Marcus's thugs are going to show up and try to finish the job."

Skeeter tried to smile. He was hurting. "I figured you'd show up," he whispered.

"We gotta go," I said.

He nodded, and I found his pants and shoes in a plastic bag in the closet. I helped him sit up and put them on. There was no shirt. It was probably too bloody to keep, so I had him use the hospital gown for a shirt and tucked the long end into his pants. He put a gigantic hand on my shoulder. I felt at least two of his three hundred pounds pressed down on me. We wouldn't get very far like this. I kicked open the door, and we headed for the exit.

The trip down the stairs reminded me of taking Sylvia's oversized couch out of her second story apartment. I had to stand it on end and take it one step at a time. Like the couch, Skeeter seemed ready to topple headfirst into the concrete with each step. At the bottom, there were two doors—one to the ER and the other to the parking lot. I slipped my .45 out of my waist and reached for the emergency exit.

"Don't open that door. The alarm will go off," an ER nurse shouted from behind me.

I kept going. If I raised the .45, she would scream even louder. I gave the door a shove. There was no sound. No alarm. The system must have been offline.

"Where are you going?" the nurse shouted.

But we were through the door and walking toward the Jeep.

I didn't look back. The door slammed in her face. Skeeter tried to move faster.

"Take it easy," I whispered. "Breathe. You're gonna start bleeding again."

He gritted his teeth and tried to smile. I knew he was in pain.

When I got him into the Jeep, a black Ford Super Duty with dark tinted windows slammed on the brakes near the entrance. Two men jumped out. I recognized them as the short-hairs guarding Patrick Allison at the convention center. That pickup had been following me all over San Antonio.

I sped south across the highway toward the high school. Suddenly, the engine sputtered. I knew that sound all too well. The Jeep was out of gas. The engine ran for another thirty yards, then cut out. We coasted into the parking lot of the Battlin' Billies football stadium, then I jumped out and pushed it between two pickups and out of sight of the street.

Skeeter looked at me.

I shrugged. "Wanna play some football?"

He looked at the sign on the stadium. "Battlin' Billies?"

It made sense to the local kids who had grown up around goats and knew how tough a full-grown male could be. For everybody else, including most of our rival teams, it was a source of constant amusement.

"You ever been in a pen with a billy goat?" I'd been out of high school a long time, but being teased about the mascot still touched a nerve.

"As in, 'Three Billy Goats Gruff'?"

"I don't have time to explain it to you," I said.

"Trip, trap, trip, trap." Skeeter laughed, then winced in pain.

I felt like I was back in high school. It annoyed the hell out of me. But it was a good sign he was feeling better. I jumped out of the Jeep and checked the doors of the four pickups parked in the lot. I had left my keys in my pickup a dozen times during high school. One of the many benefits and drawbacks to growing up in rural Texas was that everybody knew what you drove and where you were. No one I knew ever got his vehicle stolen.

"Who's that tripping over my bridge?" Skeeter was still at it, laughing to himself.

I found a set of keys in that last place I looked—a Volkswagen Jetta with pink seat covers. I wondered if it was one of the football players'. A red-and-white graduation tassel hung from the rearview mirror along with an overpowering Christmas tree air freshener.

"Will you shut the hell up about the Billy goats?" I shouted in a harsh whisper. I heard the roar of the Ford Super Duty. "Put your head down."

Skeeter tried to duck, but the bulk of his right shoulder stuck out of the Jeep like a camel's hump. The pickup flashed by without stopping. I opened the Jeep door and guided Skeeter to the Jetta. When he plopped down in the seat, the weak suspension protested. The whole car tilted to the right. I climbed in the other side and scooped the owner's pile of fast food wrappers into the back seat. My hundred and ninety pounds pushed us closer to the ground. The Jetta wasn't going far on the rough gravel roads without bottoming out.

# CHAPTER FORTY

I PEGGED THE LITTLE JETTA'S CRUISE control on seventy miles per hour and filled Skeeter in on what happened when I found Marcus and Sylvia in Grandpa's airplane hangar. He listened without comment. I knew his opinion of Sylvia and expected him to say "I told you so," but he didn't. We drove south in silence for several miles.

"I wish you'd have told me," I said.

"First of all, you're too hard-headed to ever take advice from anyone. And you were head-over-heels in love with her."

He was right. I was guilty of both.

"She picked you out at St. Mary's because you were the alpha dog."

"What do you mean?" I asked.

"She was on her own for the first time. Estranged from daddy." Hearing him say it out loud reminded me that I had known what she was doing all along.

"You think she knows what Marcus did?" I asked.

"I don't think it went that far. I think Marcus used her to get information," he said.

"I can see that. She probably thought she was doing the right thing. That I was outside the law." I found my cell phone and started to call Kelly.

"SAPD will be tracing your phone calls," Skeeter reminded me.

"I have to call Kelly," I said.

Skeeter brought out his cell phone and found the teen owner of the car's charger cord. It wasn't hard to believe it fit his phone. Skeeter always had the latest and best new tech gadgets and so, it seemed, did rural teen girls. I didn't get my first cell phone until after I got out of the Marine Corps. I found Kelly's number and showed it to Skeeter. He dialed and handed me his phone. It was one a.m. I hoped she'd gotten my message. If she hadn't, I hoped Marcus's thugs hadn't found her.

The phone rang five times. It didn't immediately go to voicemail. I imagined she would be looking at the caller ID and see it was an unknown number. I was counting on her seeing the San Antonio area code and making the connection. Her voice message came on.

"Kelly, this is Nick. Call this number as soon as you get this message." I handed the phone back to Skeeter.

"Do you trust her?"

"She helped me out with the DNA test."

"That's not what I asked. You don't have a real good track record when it comes to women. What did you say to her?" he asked.

"What are you talking about?"

"When you left her in Lubbock. You must have said something stupid. You usually do."

"Thanks a lot."

"Well?" Skeeter was watching me and waiting for an answer.

"All right. She wanted me to spend the night."

"And you said what?"

"I couldn't. I was seeing someone else."

"Sylvia?"

"Yeah, Sylvia. Who else?"

"Even if she wasn't a black widow spider, which she is, you was in Lubbock and she was in San Antonio. That's three hundred miles away. She offered her bed, and you turned her down. Don't sound like a Billy goat to me." He laughed.

"Don't start with that."

"That's why you're the only white guy I trust. You're old school. I've known Sylvia was scamming you since I met her. Those big brown eyes had you under a spell, or you'd have known it too. You think you need a fashion model with big boobs and a thousand-watt smile, but what you really need is a woman who packs heat and dips snuff."

"If me saying no to Kelly because I was loyal to another woman pisses her off, I don't want any kind of relationship with her."

"Man, you are old school. You sure you didn't time travel from a different century?"

"Your mother would beat you silly if you did any different," I said.

"That's why she likes you. You two think alike."

"Send Kelly a text. Say it's from me. Tell her it's life or death."

Skeeter nodded. He started tapping out the message. We'd been lucky on the main highway so far. No highway patrol road blocks. There were several hogs and a handful of deer, but no other cars. The ranch houses along Highway 16 were tucked behind hills or groves of trees, leaving us feeling even more isolated.

I thought we'd made a clean getaway, until I looked in the rear-view mirror and saw the Ford Super Duty top over a hill behind us. It was several miles back but coming on faster than the Jetta would go with its current cargo. The profile of the Super Duty was unmistakable. It had a bar of lights centered under the front bumper that lit up the highway like running lights on a commercial airliner.

Skeeter finished typing. Before he could hit send, the phone rang. "Here's your ex-Marine," he said and handed me the phone.

"I just got your message," Kelly said. I could hear the concern in her voice. "I was in the lab working the late shift. You're all over the wire. They say you killed an SAPD officer. Every agency in the state is looking for you. What happened?"

"You have to trust me. The guy I killed was a dirty cop. He killed Grandpa and wounded Skeeter. He worked for Marcus Lopez." I waited for her to ask questions. When she didn't say anything, I went on. "Where are you now? Right now?" I tried to sound urgent without scaring her.

"I'm in my pickup in the lab parking lot," she said.

"Start driving. Get off campus. Don't go home," I insisted. I heard her engine roar to life. "Drive normally. They might already be watching you. Make sure you're not being followed." I didn't know what connections Marcus had in Lubbock, but I was sure that he would go after her. I explained Skeeter's condition, and that we were being followed.

While I talked, I checked the rearview every few seconds. The Super Duty was gaining on us. Each curve brought the powerful lights closer. A half mile behind us and closing. They would have a clear line of sight into the windows of the tiny Jetta when they pulled beside us.

"I'm gonna hang up. I'll call you later." I rounded a sharp curve. The lights of Kerrville suddenly spread out before us like a tiny patch of stars on a cloudy night.

"Wait," she said.

I put the phone on speaker and tossed it on the dash, then cut the lights on the Jetta. Skeeter sat up, alarmed. The road disappearing at seventy miles an hour is not something that happens every day.

"Can you see in the dark?" he asked.

I couldn't, of course, but the road was straight for the next quarter mile. I forced my focus on the parallel fence so that I was looking at the road with my peripheral vision.

"I'm coming to you," Kelly said. Her voice was clear and devoid of any emotion, like she was giving me an order.

"That's not safe," I said. We shot past the cemetery on the right. I was looking for a turn to get us off the main road.

"Skeeter's hurt and you need backup. Give me your location," she said. Her voice was more insistent.

I knew that tone. She wasn't going to take no for an answer. I found a road just past an automotive shop and made the turn an instant before the headlights popped back into view. I coasted to a stop behind a row of dumpsters fifty yards from the blacktop. If they saw us and made the turn, we couldn't outrun them.

"Did you hear me?" Kelly asked.

"One moment," I said.

Skeeter saw the pickup lights and held his breath. I reached for the M24. The Super Duty slowed for the turn, then kept going. It wouldn't take them long to realize I wasn't in front of them anymore. We had managed to get away twice. The next time wouldn't be so easy.

"Nick? Hello?" Kelly was waiting for my answer.

I looked at Skeeter and remembered what he'd said about my track record with women. Kelly was a by-the-book officer. She could hang up and call the highway patrol. My gut told me I could trust her, but so much had happened over the past week that I was starting to second-guess even that.

"Meet us at Stonehenge." I picked the one place Marcus's thugs probably wouldn't look. They would check the motels and the gas stations, but not a replica British landmark.

"Give me four hours," she said. "Stay safe and try to get some rest." She disconnected.

I handed the phone back to Skeeter.

"Does she dip snuff?" he asked.

I didn't bother to answer him.

He smiled. "We going to Stonehenge? *The* Stonehenge?"

"The closest one to Central Texas," I said. I started the Jetta and continued west on the back road that I knew eventually turned south toward Kerrville.

"That's gonna take us a while." He leaned back in the passenger seat and closed his eyes. "Wake me when we get there. Always wanted to sample English tea."

The Stonehenge I was going to was located in Ingram, a small town on the Guadalupe River which, because of growth, was continuous with Kerrville. Their version was a smaller-scale reproduction called Stonehenge II that wasn't quite as impressive as the real thing but gave you a taste of the Salisbury Plain. Locals gathered at the park during the summer solstice for a festive recreation of someone's idea of a druid ceremony. When I went one year, the key players dressed like they were going to Woodstock for the 1969 music festival. When the sun rose over the eastern horizon, they all broke out in a chant that I didn't understand. The air smelled like burning grass, the kind Willie Nelson wanted legalized, and by eight o'clock I left to get breakfast. It was very spiritual, but I was hungry. The waitress at Denny's didn't know about the replica Stonehenge even though it was less than two miles down the road. She was a university student and lived near campus. I told her she missed a real nice ceremony. She said she'd be sure to check it out next year, if only to sample the grass.

The park was dark and quiet, and the replica stones cast deep shadows on the mowed grass. There was enough parking to accommodate visitors to the replica and the open-air theater that looked out over the Guadalupe River.

I stopped the Jetta facing a full-size reproduction of an Easter Island head. Why it sat next to Stonehenge, I didn't know. The blank elongated face reminded me of a law professor I had at St.

Mary's. Same big nose and sunken eye sockets. Both heads were made of stone.

Skeeter was sleeping. If he snored any louder, the moai statue was going to come to life and finally give up the secret to his existence. I could feel the fatigue catching up to me. The adrenaline rush was finally dissipating. The run from the helicopter and the rush to get Skeeter out of the hospital had sapped my energy. I was hungry, thirsty, and completely spent. Safe for the moment. It was only a matter of time before Marcus's thugs, SAPD, or the highway patrol found us. None of them were going to let us live. Marcus couldn't afford to, and as far as law enforcement was concerned, I had murdered one of their own. I pulled the Christmas tree air refresher off the rearview and tossed it out the window. I didn't like to litter, but I needed sleep, and the festive evergreen smell was making me nauseous. I opened the window, put my pistol in my lap, and let the mysterious moai take the first watch.

# CHAPTER FORTY-ONE

A *WHITE FLASH OBSCURED THE ROAD. The windshield exploded into my face. The ground traded places with the sky. Rushing water filled my ears. My legs burned. I willed my body to move. Nothing. Mangled steel pinned my thighs. My vision faded red then black. A thousand tiny needlepoints stabbed my face. I opened my mouth to scream. Nothing came out.*

*I forced myself to breathe. My fingers wiped blood from my eyes and shards of glass from my forehead. My vision cleared. I looked left. Corporal Lorenzo was bleeding from his mouth. The steering wheel crushed his chest. Ghost figures appeared outside the vehicle. Six of them. Weapons up. I saw flashes but heard no sound. Bullets punched holes in the Humvee. I pressed all my weight against the damaged dashboard. My legs wouldn't move. I wiggled my toes. I was trapped. I saw the faces of the men surrounding me. I knew them all. All members of my platoon, except one. Skeeter joined them, holding his shotgun. They were protecting me. I screamed for them to take cover. The words stuck in my throat. The movement shifted to ultra-slow motion, like a bloody action movie. I saw bullets leaving wind tunnels in the dusty air, passing through the men, and exiting their bodies leaving comet tails of blood. One by one they fell to the dirt. Their lifeless faces all turned toward me. Live, I heard them scream, but their lips didn't move.*

*The last two men stood with their backs to me. Bullets riddled their bodies. I tried with all my strength to move. Nothing. They turned. I saw my father and grandfather, their stern expressions chiseled in stone. Grandpa reached through the window. I felt him touch my shoulder.*

I jumped awake and lifted the .45 in my hand, finger tight on the trigger. Sound returned. I heard a voice.

"Reveille."

My vision cleared. I saw Kelly's smiling face. I was unsure where the dream stopped and reality began. The vehicle was right side up. The dust was gone along with the roar of battle. The sky was clear, but the pain lingered.

"Take it easy," she said, placing her hand over my pistol. "I'm friendly."

I slowly made the adjustment from Afghanistan to Central Texas. My clothes were drenched with sweat, my muscles felt raw, and the wound on my arm throbbed. The dream was so vivid and so real that I could smell the blood and the dust. I looked down at my clothes and realized I was covered with real dust and Skeeter's dried blood. A flash of red caught my eye. A cardinal landed on the moai monolith and chirped his morning song. I suddenly remembered where I was.

"Are you hurt or just getting some rack time?" she said and opened the Jetta door.

I sucked in the fresh, dry air and got out of the car. My hands instinctively went to my face. No blood. Only sweat.

"Bad dream," I said.

"Anything to do with this?" She touched the scars on my forehead.

"Everything," I said.

It was the first time she'd mentioned them. She waited for more explanation. I'd shared the experience with very few people.

Grandpa was one. Skeeter knew part of it. And Sylvia. More than anyone, Kelly would probably understand the guilt I felt.

"I brought coffee and breakfast," she said when I remained silent.

Someday I might tell her, but today wasn't the time or the place.

Skeeter stirred. "What's up?"

"The Marines have arrived," I said, finally managing a smile.

Kelly handed me a cup of coffee. She was wearing Wrangler jeans, black tactical boots, and a green fatigue T-shirt. Her straight blond hair was pulled into a short ponytail and tucked into a red-and-black Texas Tech baseball cap.

"I know you're hungry," she said.

I opened the bag and found a dozen fat, warm taquitos wrapped in foil.

"You are definitely on my Christmas list," I said.

"We in England?" Skeeter asked.

"England? Y'all must have had a hell of a night," Kelly said. She opened the passenger door of her dark-red 4x4 Dodge Ram pickup. The grill was plastered with bugs she'd picked up on the quick drive down from Lubbock.

"I'm just glad the sun came up," I said and stood to stretch. A pink tint lined the cotton ball clouds on the eastern horizon.

"Drink the coffee. Eat breakfast. Then we'll talk. We can't stay here." She grabbed a Walgreens bag from the seat. "We're not going anywhere in a Jetta. Where did you get that thing?"

"From 'Billy Goats Gruff,'" Skeeter said and smiled at me.

"Where?" she asked, puzzled.

"We appropriated a vehicle to elude capture," I said, for Skeeter's benefit. She seemed satisfied with the explanation. Skeeter rolled his eyes.

"We'll leave it. Let's go. Get in my pickup," she said. "We're too exposed here."

I knew she wasn't completely sure what was going on. She had told me on the phone about the state-wide bulletin. I had given her my side of the story. She must have believed me, because she was here alone with a bag of taquitos and a cup of coffee. Had she any doubt, the hand that woke me from my nightmare would have been attached to a highway patrolman.

"Hi, I'm Skeeter."

She opened his door and helped him shuffle to the rear seat of her pickup.

"Nice to meet you. Pull off your gown."

Skeeter chuckled. "I like her already."

"Where'd you get the name Skeeter?" she said, helping him struggle with the hospital gown. The material was stuck to the dried blood on his chest.

"I was scrawny as a kid. My cousin gave me the nickname."

"I guess you had a growth spurt." She pulled out a pair of surgical scissors from the Walgreens bag and cut the garment from his neck to his waist. She helped him sit up straight and pull the gown free.

"Sixth grade. Put on fifty pounds and grew seven inches," he said.

More dried blood caked the patch on his chest. Kelly pulled a roll of gauze, hospital tape, and rubbing alcohol from the sack. She opened a bottled water and soaked the bandage until it pulled free. She kept him talking to keep his mind off his pain.

"So, why do they still call you Skeeter?" she asked. Her hands worked constantly, pulling off the old bandage and inspecting the wound. It was clean but raw. The night's activity had broken the scab.

"They thought it was funny after that."

"What's your real name?"

I looked at Skeeter. He hated his real name and never told anybody what it was. I only knew because it appeared on his police record.

"Clarence," he said without hesitation. She had won him over.

"And you're the computer whiz?" She looked skeptical.

"You sound surprised," he said and chuckled to himself. He loved the reaction he got from people when they found out he wasn't an NFL player.

She took a black four-X T-shirt from the Walgreens's bag and handed it to Skeeter.

"I figured you needed a shirt. It was the biggest they had." She helped him slide it over his head. It fit like an extra layer of skin.

"How do I look?" he asked.

"Like a gorilla in a bikini," I said.

"Man, you racist," Skeeter said.

Kelly wasn't sure what to think until she saw him smile.

"I always tell the truth," I said.

The coffee and the taquitos were producing the desired effect. My head was clear, and my muscles were starting to recover. I glanced around the park. The puffy clouds had shed their pink tint and were ready to take on the day. I realized that the Jetta wasn't concealed in the daylight, and we were plainly visible to the main road. It was Thursday. All the locals who lived on the outskirts of town were headed to work. Marcus's thugs would be on the prowl. I'm sure he chewed their ass or worse for letting me slip through their fingers. They wouldn't let it happen again.

"Leave the vehicle," she said, taking charge. "They'll be looking for it. We'll use mine to relocate to a secure location."

"Here we go. She talks like you when you go all Marine Corps," Skeeter said.

"That should make you feel safe," I said.

"What's he talking about?" Kelly asked. She hadn't been out as long as I had, and she worked in law enforcement, so she hadn't completely made the adjustment to civilian life.

"First things first," I said. "Head call." The coffee and taquitos were making my guts churn.

Kelly reached in the console of the Ram and came out with a roll of toilet paper. "There's a tree," she said. "Go commando."

"Yes, ma'am." I grinned and took the paper. "What color would you like it, ma'am?"

"When I say 'shit,' you squat down and ask what color," she barked, doing her best sing-song drill instructor voice. We both laughed.

Skeeter was disgusted. "Great, now I gotta put up with two jarheads."

"Oorah," Kelly and I shouted in unison.

We had a shared background, but this wasn't a military mission. I didn't want to put Kelly in harm's way or take responsibility for getting her hurt or worse. The question was, Would she listen to me? She was, after all, an officer.

The outdoor theater on the river was undergoing renovations, and I found a portable outhouse set up for the construction crew beside the building. I glanced around the park, checking for any sign of the Super Duty pickup. The coast was clear. Kelly and Skeeter had their heads together and seemed to be lost in conversation. He seemed to like her much more than he ever liked Sylvia.

When I headed back to her pickup, the two of them stopped talking. Skeeter fussed with his prosthetic hand, and Kelly bit into a breakfast taquito. I figured the best way would be to tell her directly.

"Kelly, we're going on alone. Thanks for the coffee and the breakfast."

She swallowed a mouthful of tortilla and egg, washed it down with coffee, and wiped her mouth with a paper napkin. Skeeter looked at her, then at me like I had just sprouted a pair of horns. Maybe I had. We both waited for her to speak.

"No," she said. Her voice was clear and matter-of-fact.

It caught me off guard. Skeeter started to smile, then changed his mind. His face remained neutral, as if he were waiting for the punch line. She stepped out of the pickup and faced me.

"This is my fight. We're not in the Marine Corps. You don't owe me anything. You came here and brought supplies. I'm grateful for that. I'll take it from here. I'm on the job. I'm getting paid to find Marissa's killer." Despite my confidence, I could feel my face flush slightly.

"Bullshit," Kelly said. "Your grandfather's dead. You just found out your girlfriend is a lying bitch. And they killed your dog." She nodded toward Skeeter.

I shot a look at Skeeter for betraying my confidence.

He just shrugged. "I didn't know it was a secret."

She stood facing me with her shoulders square and her feet planted. Her hands were on her hips. She looked every bit the lieutenant she once was. "You can't lie to me. You're not in this for the money. You're in deep shit, and you need my help. I'm breaking the military's golden rule—I'm volunteering."

"You're an active member of law enforcement. You have to walk away or put me in custody right now. That's your duty. You know I'm a fugitive. I shot a police officer."

"A dirty cop trying to kill you. Working for a corrupt politician. He got what he deserved. You asked me for help last night. I'm here. What happens to me from here on out is not your fault."

I couldn't think of anything else to say, so I crossed my arms and stood my ground. Skeeter took that as the punch line and launched into his low baritone chuckle.

I turned to Skeeter. "You think this is funny?"

"I think she's right, and you're too stubborn to admit it," he said.

# CHAPTER FORTY-TWO

We heard the crack of the AR-15 rifle I had left with Skeeter. The wind had picked up, and my nose was running. Kelly handed me a tissue from her glovebox, along with an antihistamine.

"This wind does it to me too," she said.

We heard another shot and listened for the explosion that didn't come.

I checked the rounds in my pistol and tucked it behind my back. Kelly clipped her Glock to her canvas belt. I lifted the M24 from the back seat and snapped in a full five-round magazine. Kelly grabbed her police-issue 12-gauge pump-action shotgun and loaded extra rounds in a black tactical backpack along with wire cutters and two bottles of water.

We heard a third shot. Nothing. Another ten seconds ticked by. No explosion. I shared a questioning look with Kelly. We were less than a mile from Skeeter. If he hit the transformer, we would hear it. She chewed her bottom lip. It was the only clue I had that she was nervous.

We were waiting by the side gate to the Allison ranch, which was guarded by two surveillance cameras. I had left Skeeter under a small cedar tree growing from the base of the fence near the front entrance and below the main transformer supplying power to the ranch. The tree provided some cover and a natural place to rest the rifle. I showed him the basics of AR-15 operation—take the safety off and pull the trigger. I had left him a twenty-round magazine. If he hit his mark, one was all he needed to cut power to the compound and the surveillance cameras.

We heard the fourth shot. It should have been followed by an explosion or electrical pop. Again, we heard nothing. I was beginning to think this was a bad idea. I should have left Kelly and gone through the side gate on my own. We heard another shot and another miss. He was fifty feet from a three-by-two-foot target. He had a scope on a rifle resting on a tree limb. I knew his shoulder was wounded, but goddamn. He could throw a rock and hit it.

We heard the sixth shot. Nothing.

I counted two more shots. Both misses. I could see Kelly counting too. There was a pause. I wondered if Skeeter was saying a prayer. I hoped whatever he was doing worked. I held up my crossed fingers. Kelly did the same. If the saints weren't listening, we could use a little luck.

Shot number nine returned a loud ping and the sound of a ricochet. Skeeter had finally hit something, but there was no explosion.

We both held our breath.

I looked through my rifle scope at the surveillance cameras over the back gate. I could see the little green lights still on. We heard another pop. Round ten. That shot was followed by a ping and then an electronic zap and a string of firecracker explosions. After ten tries, Skeeter had finally hit the target.

I checked the cameras. The lights were off. I grabbed the bolt cutters, and we sprinted to the back gate. The cutters sliced through the chain, and we were through the gate in less than a minute. We pulled the gate closed, and I propped the chain back in place.

Sometime in the past ten years, a bulldozer had scraped a

fifty-yard easement around the inside of the perimeter fence. Because of the drought, instead of grass there was mostly prickly pear which made the going rough. We ran in single file to make traveling through the thorny jungle easier. A roadrunner jumped in front of me and kept pace with us for twenty yards before disappearing into a brush pile.

Once past the easement, we plunged into thicker mesquite and huisache brush, both equally full of thorns and both fully capable of ripping clothes and skin. After a mile, we found the power line that led to the house. The ground underneath had been cleared more recently, which made running much easier. We paused in the shade of a mesquite tree to catch our breath and drink some water. Both our forearms were covered with blood and scratches. The wind was keeping the temperature down in the lower eighties but was also picking up dust that filled our eyes with a fine grit.

We drank and rested for two minutes in silence. I wasn't sure how far we were from the house, and I didn't want to take any chances on them hearing us. Kelly secured the water bottle and shouldered her backpack. We took off at a slow jog. Ten minutes later we saw the house.

The compound was teaming with activity. A pickup parked sideways in the road. Two security guards in black uniforms leaned against the bed, pointing AR-15 rifles toward the main entrance. I counted two more in the barn loft. Three on the porch of the old house.

Marcus was nowhere in sight. That meant we were one step ahead of him. If we could slip in and take Danny off the property, Marcus would be forced to deal with me.

Kelly whispered in my ear. "I count nine."

I held up seven fingers. She pointed to two more in a pickup parked beside the cattle pens that I'd missed. I pointed out the old house where I'd seen Danny emerge from on my last trip and motioned for her to follow.

# CHAPTER FORTY-THREE

THE FIRST ALLISON HAD BUILT the original house and barn for defense against Comanches and banditos, but the younger generation had lost its connection to the past in more ways than one. The newer buildings blocked the southern view. The new barn and the garage faced inward, toward the cliff, instead of toward the sloping landscape. I took advantage of the blind spots and led Kelly around the corrals to the old house.

We emerged behind a portion of the original rock wall that probably had once circled the house. They had only maintained a thirty-yard section that served no function but landscaping. Inside the wall, rose bushes were stationed at five-foot intervals. I scanned the back windows for movement. Nothing.

A Heights Security guard with a black uniform appeared on the back porch. I ducked down and put my hand on Kelly's shoulder. I pointed toward the house and held up one finger. She nodded.

We both heard a commotion in the yard. Tires crunched on gravel. The guard turned abruptly and hustled toward the noise. I motioned for Kelly to cover me. She checked her shotgun and nodded she was ready. The only other sound was the coo of a mourning dove.

I vaulted the four-foot wall and thankfully landed between rose bushes. The short sprint to the porch took less than five seconds. I flattened my back against the cool limestone blocks and saw Kelly sweep both right and left with her shotgun. I slid along the wall to the back door and tried the handle. Locked. I inched back to the window and peeked inside. The kitchen was laid out similar to Grandpa's house. It was a small room with bare countertops and a round table that contained napkins, a honey jar, and four empty beer cans. I listened for footsteps. Nothing but the muffled voices from the front yard.

One building at a time. Clear and secure. I was in military mode. I could see Kelly was too. She was on the alert, weapon in position, and ready for anything. I motioned her forward and brought my own weapon up to cover her advance. There was no hesitation. She vaulted the wall with ease, despite her shorter legs, and ran to the opposite side of the door.

I pointed at my boot, showing Kelly I was going to kick the door in to gain access. The wooden doorjamb looked to be as old as the limestone blocks, and I didn't expect it would take much to splinter. Kelly held up her hand for me to wait. She reached behind her belt and produced a Marine Corps issue Ka-Bar knife—a deadly combat fighting tool with a fixed seven-inch blade that could do damage to anything in your way. I nodded approval. She sliced the blade in the jamb and quickly popped the door open.

We stepped inside and paused to listen. Wind rustled the oak limbs in the yard. The dove was silent. The kitchen smelled like stale beer and snuff spit. Kelly glanced at the empty beer cans and crinkled her nose. I shouldered the M24 and drew my pistol. It was a better weapon for close-quarter fighting.

I heard footsteps on the upstairs floor. We froze. The footsteps moved quickly down a hall and descended the stairs that were just behind the kitchen door. I pressed against the wall. Kelly behind me. We both held our weapons ready.

The footsteps paused on the ground floor, as if deciding which way to go. The next step came toward the kitchen.

I held my breath.

Danny Allison walked past me. I immediately jammed my Springfield into the side of his neck.

"Long time, no see, Danny," I said.

He took a sharp breath. "Why are you here?"

Kelly pulled out a pair of flex cuffs and slipped them on Danny's wrists. I shoved him into a kitchen chair.

"I told you I would come for you," I said.

"You were supposed to kill Marcus Lopez at your grandfather's ranch. He was with your girlfriend. He killed your granddad. Why did you let him go?"

"You better start making sense," I said.

"Grandpa said you would kill him. You were supposed to end it. Now, Marcus is coming here."

"You're saying Patrick Allison set me up?" I jammed the .45 barrel against his forehead.

"No… I mean, yeah. Don't kill me." His chest heaved.

"Talk, Danny," I said.

"He didn't set you up. He said all you needed was a little encouragement."

"He sent Araceli Luna to me?"

"And paid your fee. It was the only way to get Marcus to stop the blackmail."

"Tell me what happened," I said.

The color drained from his cheeks. His eyes darted toward the window. "Marcus is on his way. He knows you're here," he whispered.

"Make it quick and don't lie to me again."

"We met on the River Walk that night," Danny said, barely above a whisper. "I tried to convince her to have the baby. She wouldn't do it. I reached for her hand. She pulled away from me and fell back into the water."

"The water's a foot deep. What did you do?" I asked.

"I jumped in after her, but she must have hit her head. She wasn't breathing. I panicked."

"Did you call 911?" Kelly asked.

"No. I called Marcus. She was dead. There was nothing I could do for her."

"What did Marcus do?" I asked.

"He said to leave the body and go home. He would take care of it."

"Then he decided he wanted money."

"That's right. As long as Grandpa kept paying, I would stay out of prison. Marcus was going to bleed our family for everything we had. He already has Allison Oil."

"I was supposed to kill Marcus and get him off your back," I said.

"Why didn't you?" He was angry. "It'd all be over."

"You didn't think I'd figure it out?"

He chewed his bottom lip and stared at me.

The front door rattled followed by a hard, insistent knock.

"It's him. It's Marcus. What're you gonna do?" Danny asked. He looked like a boy who'd lost his mom in the supermarket. He didn't seem to have any remorse for killing Marissa.

"I'm taking you and Marcus in," I said.

"It... It was an accident," he stuttered. "I... I didn't do anything."

"That's right. You did nothing. You should have called 911. You could have tried CPR. You could have screamed for help. Instead, you called your lawyer. You let Marissa and your unborn child die without trying to save them."

Danny gave me that lost look that he had probably used to get him out of tough situations his whole life. It wouldn't work this time. I had zero sympathy for him.

The door rattled again. Another knock. Then we heard Marcus's voice.

"Danny? Open the door." His voice was calm and conversational.

"It's too late," Danny whispered.

"I found your friend on the road, Nick," Marcus continued. "Biggest man I've ever seen in person. He's going to need a doctor. He lost a lot of blood. He didn't want to tell me about you at first." Marcus's voice was cocky like he knew he held the high hand.

"That son of a bitch," I said under my breath.

"I have Sylvia too, Nick," Marcus taunted. "Too bad she's mixed up in this."

I caught my breath and rested my free hand on the table. Despite having seen her with Marcus, I still had feelings for her.

"It would be a shame if anything were to happen to her."

I stayed quiet and listened to running footsteps in the gravel. The guards were circling the house.

"I knew you'd go after Danny, Nick. You're smart. Danny will do whatever you tell him to do. I can't let that happen. When I'm finished, the Allison fortune will belong to me." I heard him take a step back from the door. "Let Danny come out," he said. "He and I have some business to attend to. Drop your weapons at the door and follow him. I'll give you one minute. Otherwise, I can't guarantee Skeeter or Sylvia will survive."

"Nick, do what he says," came Sylvia's desperate voice from outside.

I moved to the edge of the window and peeked through the ancient red-and-white checkered curtains. She wore form-fitting jeans and a white button-down shirt that was open to the middle of her chest. Her hair was curled and fell to her shoulders. She looked like she had every time I ever saw her. Flawless. Her radiant beauty turned the scene into a movie set. A movie that ended with the impossibly beautiful damsel in distress being rescued by the hero. I studied her face. There was tension in her eyes. Was it fear? From thirty yards away, I couldn't tell. Did she think I was her hero, or did she know she was bait?

"Nick," Kelly whispered. "Be careful."

I glanced at the faces of the security guards. All eyes were on Sylvia. The look was very familiar. I'd seen it everywhere Sylvia and I went together. It was the way I'd looked at her when the door at the rear of the law school classroom opened and Sylvia appeared on the top step. Every eye was on her and she knew it.

"We're coming out," I yelled to Marcus. I took Kelly's Ka-Bar from the sheath on her belt and cut the flex cuffs from Danny's wrists.

"What are you doing?" Kelly asked with concern on her face.

I didn't have time to explain. "Stay here. Wait for the commotion to start. Go out the back. Marcus doesn't know you're here. Thank Skeeter for that. Retrace our steps back to your pickup." I didn't wait for her response. I turned back to Danny. "Get up." He seemed relieved to be taking orders. "We're going to walk outside."

"Time's up," Marcus yelled.

"Then what?" Kelly asked. She hadn't budged.

"If I don't make it, haul ass. You have the DNA report. Give it to the FBI. They'll review the Luna case and find Marcus and Danny at the center of it."

"No," she said. Her voice was strong and clear. "We can both go out the back."

"We'd never make it."

She held my gaze but didn't say anything.

I knew she understood what needed to be done. "Give me your Glock," I said.

Kelly didn't hesitate. She slipped her 9mm from her holster and handed it to me. I jacked a round into the chamber.

"You've got fifteen rounds," I said to Danny and jammed it behind his belt. "This is your chance to man up." I tucked my pistol behind my back and hopefully out of sight. My gut instinct told me he had been waiting his whole life for someone to hand him a weapon and tell him to man up. I pointed the M24 at Danny. "You're going to get me close to Marcus. When I grab him, pull your pistol and hold it on the guards to the left," I told him. "You're going to stand up to Marcus and make up for not standing up for Marissa and your unborn child."

He was scared, but he was going to do it. He stuffed his lip with tobacco courage and nodded.

I opened the door, and we stepped out on the porch together.

"Tell them to drop their weapons, Marcus," I said.

"You're not gonna shoot Danny," he said, smiling from behind Sylvia.

"Why not?" I said. "I'm already wanted for killing Detective Peterson. What have I got to lose?" I stayed on the porch, using Danny as a shield. The guards kept their weapons up and ready. I counted thirteen. There were three behind the Lexus and five on each side of Marcus and Sylvia. "Danny's your golden goose. I kill him, no more money."

"You won't kill him because you want him to stand trial. Sylvia told me about you. You know she likes to gossip. You hate to see a rich kid get away with murder. We're a lot alike. I wanted to see him pay," Marcus said.

"It was an accident," Danny yelled, his voice stronger than I expected. "I trusted you."

"Shut up, Danny," Marcus shot back. He was full of himself and confident he held all the cards.

The thugs who chased us out of Fredericksburg were sitting in the back seat of the Super Duty with Skeeter between them. Skeeter's eyes were open. His lip was swollen and bleeding.

"I'm taking you both in," I said.

"I admire your tenacity," Marcus said. "But I don't like to lose. Turn Danny over or I'll shoot Sylvia right here in front of you." He drew a short-barrel pistol from his coat.

I didn't expect him to be armed, not with fifteen guards surrounding him. It changed everything. I tried to catch Danny's eye, but he was focused on the guards.

"Nick, please do what he says," Sylvia begged. A tear rolled down her cheek, glistening in the morning sun. I wondered how many men had fallen for that.

"Okay," I said quickly. "Don't hurt her." I touched Danny's shoulder. "Stay left," I whispered under my breath. "Change of plan." I pushed him off the porch toward the five guards on the left and hoped he understood.

The two nearest guards stepped toward me. I handed over my rifle. I was counting on their lack of training. I raised my hands, palm out, level with my waist. They didn't bother to frisk me.

Marcus lowered his snub-nosed pistol. Sylvia's huge brown eyes seemed calm and confident as ever. Skeeter was right. She had picked Marcus because he was the new alpha male in the pack. He was going to be governor. I had been the bodyguard to the lady in waiting, keeping annoying law school students and horny professors from bothering her for dates. I watched her walk toward me. There wasn't a mark on her. No sign of a horrible kidnapping ordeal. Her clothes were fresh and clean, and I caught a whiff of her favorite Chanel perfume. I was a dusty, sweaty mess from running through the brush and getting four hours of sleep in a Volkswagen Jetta. She was ready for her closeup, from her designer jeans to her gleaming white teeth and loosely curled raven hair. Her white button-down shirt was open just enough to keep Marcus's thugs hoping it would reveal even more of her olive skin. They relaxed their weapons. For once her beauty worked in my favor.

On my left, I saw Danny reach for the Glock behind his back. I took another step forward and positioned myself at least four steps from Marcus. I was counting on his snub-nosed pistol not being accurate outside of ten yards. Sylvia stopped in front of me and put a slender hand on my shoulder. She arched her neck, extending her ripe lips toward mine.

"I'm sorry, Nick," she said, as if she were dismissing a longtime employee whose services were no longer required. I let her pull my neck down to her level and kiss me one last time.

"It was a pleasure," I said.

"Did you really think she was in your league?" Marcus said and raised the short-barrel pistol.

Sylvia stepped to the side, giving Marcus a clear shot.

I dropped into a crouch, pulled my pistol, and fired. Marcus fired too, a fraction of second later. My .45 slug found Marcus's Botox-enhanced brow. The back of his head disappeared. Blood sprayed the Lexus. Sylvia screamed as if she'd been hit. I felt a pinch on my shoulder. I looked down and saw blood expanding into my sweat-soaked T-shirt.

Kelly burst through the front door and leveled her shotgun at the guards.

"Drop your weapons. Do it now." Kelly's voice was clear and commanding. She got their attention.

Two thumps came from the pickup. Then I heard Skeeter's low rumbling voice.

"You heard her," he said. He was leaning against the passenger door of the Super Duty, holding two pistols. The two that had been guarding him were on the ground. Out Cold.

Sylvia was still screaming. She had rushed to Marcus's side and touched his dead body in disbelief. His blood covered her hands and white shirt and soaked into her designer jeans.

Danny had the Glock out. He backed toward me with the pistol pointed at the five guards to the left. They seemed to recover and realize they had us outnumbered.

The one nearest to me swung the tip of his rifle in my direction.

I fired. My shot hit him in the chest. I was shooting for body mass. No time to aim. A volley of shots passed my head, close enough to feel the displacement of air.

I kept firing, each bullet knocking another guard to the ground. Kelly's shotgun exploded three times in rapid succession. I turned on my knee and focused on the next target.

I saw Danny out of the corner of my eye level off with the Glock on a guard to my left and pull the trigger. Blood sprayed my face and arms. Another black uniform raised his rifle. I saw the barrel spit fire. I pulled the trigger again and again until the magazine was empty.

I yanked the .38 from my ankle holster. A black uniform sprinted from behind the house. His AR-15 swung toward me. Kelly's shotgun exploded. Another guard appeared behind her on the porch. I fired.

The gunfire abruptly stopped. Sylvia's screams turned to ragged sobs. It was all over in less than thirty seconds.

I took an uneasy step. My legs turned to jelly. Stars swam in my vision. I saw more movement. I brought the .38 up. It was Kelly. Her face splattered with blood.

"Nick," she said. "Are you all right?"

I couldn't answer. The .38 slipped from my fingers and hit the ground. I tumbled forward. Kelly caught my arm. My vision went black.

I saw Grandpa's hangar light and stepped toward it.

# CHAPTER FORTY-FOUR

I WOKE TO A RHYTHMIC MECHANICAL beeping. My arms and legs felt heavy, as if tied down. They wouldn't obey my commands. My chest throbbed. A hot poker jammed into my left breast. Slowly, I realized the beeping coincided with my own heartbeat. My first thought was of the military hospital in Germany. Then Sylvia flashed through my memory, and fragments of the last forty-eight hours played out in my head. Could Grandpa really be dead? Had I imagined running cross-country to escape an SAPD helicopter?

My head was caught in a vise. I tried to fast forward to my final memory. Marcus had a snub-nosed pistol. That was a surprise. Had I shot him, or had I imagined that too? Sylvia had kissed me and stepped aside to give him a clear shot. I remember dropping to a crouch and firing, the taste of her still on my lips. I had pulled the .38, my weapon of last resort. I fell to the ground, and Kelly was beside me. Was she a figment of my imagination as well? I remembered another name. Marissa Luna. She was a young woman found floating in the San Antonio River. I was after her killer. Had I found him?

• • •

The next thing I smelled was the faint hint of lavender soap mixed with fresh flowers. I felt another presence in the room. The steady beep continued behind me. My heart was still beating. I tried my arms and legs. This time they worked. The hot poker in my chest had cooled. The events of the last week flashed through my head. From the moment I met Patrick Allison in the convention center, I had been working for him. He had used me to take out his political opponent and save his family fortune. *There is more than one way to support a candidate*, he had said. Now, I knew what he meant. He was supporting Marcus while he set me up to be an October surprise, to rid him of the blackmail threat and save his grandson from prison.

"Nick? Nick, can you hear me?" It was a female voice.

I opened my eyes. Kelly stood holding my hand, squeezing it gently. Her eyes were red and puffy. Her shirt was different. It was short-sleeved, button-down, and clean. Red scratches covered her forearms as proof of our run through the brush. It hadn't been a dream.

"How do you feel?" she asked.

My mouth was dry, and my lips were stuck together. I glanced at the nightstand, saw a cup with a straw. Kelly held it to my lips. The cool liquid tasted better than I remembered water ever tasting.

"What happened?" I croaked out the words.

Kelly pressed the power switch on the mechanical bed and raised my head. Skeeter was there with his arm wrapped in a sling. He had a cut over his eye that was healing, and his smile was crooked from a swollen lip.

"We're twins," he said, pointing to his bandage.

Kelly said I had come in and out over the last three days. She said I'd yelled about being trapped. It wasn't pleasant. She only knew the half of it. Maybe someday I would tell her the full story. She explained that Danny had called his family's helicopter to take me to San Antonio.

"Sylvia told the police Marcus kidnapped her," Kelly said. "She told them he threatened to kill her, and that she was terrified you would be harmed."

"She insisted on seein' you," Skeeter said. "But Kelly told her to, ah... take a hike."

"Thank you," I whispered. "And Danny?"

"I made sure Danny told his story to Detective Ochoa," Kelly explained. "I worked with her to piece together all the documents and evidence. The DA charged him with involuntary manslaughter. Danny lawyered up. He's already out on bail."

"Peterson?" I asked.

"After your visit, Ochoa started digging. He had tampered with the ME's findings. She knew he was cutting her out of the investigation. She traced that .308 shell you found in the parking lot to Peterson's personal weapon," she said.

"Am I under arrest?"

Kelly smiled. "The DA won't press charges against you. Your PI license is safe."

"They should give you a medal for killing that bastard," Skeeter said. "He was going to be governor."

"Danny's here. He came with his grandpa. They'd like to see you."

I could hear traffic outside the hospital window and see heat waves dancing over the city. I thought about Grandpa telling me to stay away from the Allison family. He was right.

There was a knock on the door.

"Should I let them in?"

I nodded, and Kelly opened the door. Danny walked in leading his grandpa by the elbow. Patrick was bent over a cane, and his skin seemed barely able to cover his bones. He was a shell of what he once had been. The ravages of cancer had taken their toll. He took off his signature hat.

"Grandpa insisted on coming in person," Danny said.

Patrick steadied himself on his grandson's arm. "Mr. Fischer," Patrick Allison said in a raspy whisper. "I apologize for what happened. Marcus Lopez backed me into a corner. Detective Peterson stacked the deck against us. Danny would have been charged with first degree murder. With Marissa being pregnant, he would have gotten the death penalty."

I cleared my throat. Kelly held the straw up to my lips, and I sucked more water.

"You don't have to say a damn thing," Patrick said, his voice rising. "I've instructed my grandson to pay all the expenses you incurred during the Luna investigation, including paying for your services to my family. You earned it." The arrogant son of a bitch was trying to pay me off, I thought. He pulled a bank envelope from his coat pocket. Danny took it from him and set it on the side of the bed.

"Pat," I said, but he cut me off again with a weak wave of his hand.

"It's already been done. I've also instructed Danny to arrange for your grandfather's funeral, when you're healthy, of course. That was a terrible thing. You may not know this, but the Fischer family and the Allison family have ties going back to before the Civil War."

I nodded. "I know."

"It was a rough history," he went on. "Lots of bad blood. I'd like our families to bury the hatchet."

The old man stood catching his breath. Danny held him up. He seemed to be waiting for an answer from me, some kind of absolution for his sins before he died.

I stared at him for a long time. He was a weak old man barely able to stand on his own feet. Maybe the statute of limitations was passed for wrongs committed during the Civil War and its aftermath. Maybe it was time to honor the dead and move on. It didn't excuse him from what he did—setting me up to kill Marcus Lopez. I cleared my dry throat again. Kelly gave me another sip of water.

"Get out," I whispered. "I don't want your money or your friendship."

He looked disappointed, but I didn't care. Danny started to protest. Patrick cut him off with a wave of his frail hand. An awkward silence settled over the hospital room. I handed the bank envelope back to Danny. He took it and led his Grandpa out of the room.

"I'm ready to go home," I said and swung my feet off the bed. I didn't like hospitals. I had things to do, like tell Mrs. Luna she was right. Her daughter was murdered. And take care of Sam and Grandpa. I was ready to get back to work.

"Now, you need rest," Kelly declared. She put a gentle hand on my shoulder, and I let her guide me back into bed.

Skeeter's baritone chuckle erupted in the small room. "That's a first," he said. "Never seen anyone tell Nick what to do."

It hurt to laugh, but I couldn't help it. Kelly leaned over and kissed me on the lips.

THE END

If you enjoyed this Nick Fischer adventure, please stop by Amazon and Goodreads and write a quick review. Your support will be much appreciated.

Stay in touch with George for future free book deals, updates on new releases, and bonus offers.

GeorgeLeeMiller.com
Facebook.com/George.Lee.Miller
Twitter.com/GeorgeLeeMiller
Instagram.com/GeorgeLeeMiller

Two more exciting Nick Fischer novels are on the way.

## *Second Chances* (Spring 2020)

Nick Fischer takes on the seedy underworld of sex trafficking when the estranged granddaughter of a crusty local rancher turns up missing. He tracks her from rural Central Texas to the back alleys of San Antonio. When Nick finally finds her, she doesn't want to go back. Saving her life means breaking the law but walking away is not an option.

## *Last Rodeo* (Fall 2020)

A rodeo cowboy turns up dead at the San Antonio arena clutching an empty snuff can inscribed with Nick Fischer's name and a pocket full of painkillers. Was it a cry for help—the young cowboy was a veteran—or was it an accusation? Nick finds himself on the wrong side of the law, again, as he tries to find the answers that will clear his name and catch a killer before it's too late.

# ACKNOWLEDGEMENTS

I would like to thank my daughter Ruby and sister MaryAlice, who chided and encouraged me through the process, and my friend Gus, who introduced me to the great Alamo City and taught me about suppressors. Also, I would like to thank my editors, Edmund Pickett and Lisa Gilliam, for their patience and guidance. Prost!

Because the incident on the Nueces River during the Civil War is controversial, the author would like to acknowledge two main sources of historical research. The first comes from an article in *The Southwestern Historical Quarterly* written by the historian Stanley S. McGowen, and the second comes from two eyewitness, R.H. Williams and John W. Sansom, whose self-recorded versions of the event are available on *The Portal to Texas History* website.

## ABOUT THE AUTHOR

George Lee Miller is a former cowboy, Navy corpsman, and theater director who splits his time between teaching at a local college and writing the next Nick Fischer adventure. He currently lives with his Labrador retriever in Central Texas.

www.ingramcontent.com/pod-product-compliance
Lightning Source LLC
Chambersburg PA
CBHW030818310726
48980CB00006B/545/J

* 9 7 8 1 7 3 4 1 5 6 4 2 3 *